HIGHLAND DESTROYER

A Scottish Medieval Romance
Part of the Highland Legion Series

By Kathryn Le Veque

© Copyright 2024 by Kathryn Le Veque Novels, Inc.
Trade Paperback Edition

Text by Kathryn Le Veque
Cover by Kim Killion
Drawing by Kathryn Le Veque

Reproduction of any kind except where it pertains to short quotes in relation to advertising or promotion is strictly prohibited.

All Rights Reserved.

The characters and events portrayed in this book are fictitious. Any similarity to real persons, living or dead, is purely coincidental and not intended by the author.

KATHRYN LE VEQUE
NOVELS

WWW.KATHRYNLEVEQUE.COM

ARE YOU SIGNED UP FOR KATHRYN'S BLOG?

You'll get the latest news and information on exclusive giveaways, exclusive excerpts, coming releases, sales, free books, cover reveals and more.

Kathryn's blog followers get it all first. No spam, no junk.

Get the latest info from the reigning Queen of English Medieval Romance!

Sign Up Here

kathrynleveque.com

Every family has legends behind it, but no family more so than the dun Tarh clan.

Tucked deep in the Highlands of Scotland and relatives to the MacKenzie clan, the family is said to have been spawned from the lost Roman legion, the elite Ninth Hispania. For generations, the family was known for their dark men, quick to temper, fierce fighters with comely looks. They were greatly respected in the Highlands until Lares Rayan dun Tarh, a former priest who had fallen from grace, became the head of the family.

Lucifer, they called him.

And his sons were known as Lucifer's Highland Legion.

Welcome to Book 2 in the Highland Legion series.

When a betrothal is broken by a wayward bride, Darien dun Tarh finds himself in an awkward—and unknowingly dangerous—position.

Lies, secrets, and betrayal abound in Scotland in this passionate tale of true love!

Darien, the second son of Lares dun Tarh, finds himself betrothed to a wealthy lass from a good Scottish family. He's not particularly eager to marry, but he's not particularly opposed to it, either. His new bride, a high-strung and vain woman, is insulted by his apathy, leaving a crack in the relationship between her family and his. Emelia Moriston is a troublemaker and always has been, but not as much as she is when she realizes Darien isn't falling at her feet.

Not that it matters, but she doesn't want him anyway.

She wants her sister's betrothed.

On the eve of Emelia and Darien's wedding, the bride and her sister's intended elope, leaving devastation in their wake. Darien is truthfully relieved that he doesn't have to marry the demanding Emelia, but he doesn't expect to find himself in the position of comforting her sister.

The fair and sweet Eventide.

Evie Moriston couldn't be any more different from her sister. A kind and beautiful lass, she was betrothed to a son from the powerful Cannich family. But he's left her, and although Evie wasn't in love with him, the humiliation is more than she can bear until Darien gives her what comfort he can. Then she begins to realize why she wasn't so keen on her Cannich husband.

It was because he lacked everything that Darien has.

And so, the love story—and the heartache—begin.

Join Darien and Evie in a rip-roaring tale that sees the wayward bride return with tales of a dead lover and lies that she uses to try to tear two families apart. In the Highlands, where blood is often the strongest bond men hold, Darien and Evie find that passion, and love, is stronger still. Stronger than the lies that try to break it.

Airson a h-uile àm.

For all time.

House of dun Tarh motto

Numquam vici, semper timui
Never conquered, always feared

Author's Note

And we're off with another sexy Lucifer's Legion Highlander tale!

Unlike the first book, *Highland Born*, this book actually takes place in the Highlands. Not Northern England, but the actual Highlands of Scotland. That's a new location for me. Something else that is new—not writing about a knight! Our hero, Darien dun Tarh, has not been knighted because he's, well, a Highlander. He's highly trained and politically savvy, but we're in Scotland now, gentle readers, and the Scottish politics are different—but no less interesting or deadly.

A little background on the dun Tarh family, which is important to note. Hopefully you've read *Highland Born*, but if not, let me bring you up to speed.

My fascination with the Highlands of Scotland seems to be different from many—it mostly stems from my fascination with the legendary lost legions, and there are a few, but none so famous as the Ninth Hispania. I've incorporated their mascot, the bull, into the dun Tarh's family shield. In fact, *"tarbh"* is "bull" in Gaelic and the family took that name back in the Dark Ages, but over the centuries, the spelling changed to Tarh—pronounced "Tar."

A reminder of the family's legendary origins.

Something else that is a reminder of their origins is the fact that all of the men in the family tend to have Roman names. Some have Spanish names, but most tend to be Roman as a tribute to their origins. The lost Ninth Hispania legion has been an endless source of fascination for historians through the ages because no one is really sure what happened to it. It was a big, prestigious legion that went over the Antonine Wall and then… nothing. Most historians agree that they simply assimilated into the local populations, which is probably what happened.

The story of "Lucifer's Legion," the moniker referring to the collective dun Tarh brothers, was explained in the first three chapters of *Highland Born*, so that nickname is explained in the pages of this book during certain scenes rather than my making it obvious and spelling it out like I did in the first book by taking the reader back to the moment in time when it all came about. Since that has already been done, the only thing I did do, for continuity's sake, was include the meeting scene of Lares dun Tarh, a.k.a. Lucifer, and his English wife, Mabel. Those two are quite a pair, and even if this book revolves around their second-eldest son, they are still a part of the tale.

Part of this story mentions one of the only Highlanders I've ever used as a hero, Jamison Munro. His story is told in *The Red Lion*, so if you've never read that book, you should. It was a fun one to write. Jamison was a Highlander who served the House of de Lohr, so the action takes place on the Welsh Marches—not in Scotland. Jamison and his wife, Havilland, have a secondary tale told in "Deep into Darkness," which was a novella I wrote for a Halloween collection long ago. Creepy Edgar Allan Poe stuff. *The Red Lion* was meant to be the first in a Highlander quartet of books, but I haven't gotten around to it yet, so I'm tying him into this series.

This book is going to be a little different from the vast majority of my books because it doesn't take place in England. At all! This one takes place completely in the Highlands of Scotland. I've taken a little historical liberty with the advent of Scotch whisky—history tells us the first recorded use of it was about a hundred years after this story, but that's not to say people (mostly priests) weren't distilling beverages before that. Liquor has been around for thousands of years, in various forms, but whisky was actually called *aqua vitae* back in the day.

This book is going to be a wild ride from start to finish, so buckle up. We've got a VERY naughty girl who causes a lot of trouble, and she kicks the whole thing off, so get ready. We're off to a fast start!

The usual pronunciation guide:

> Athole: this is actually a very *old* name. It's basically pronounced like "Ethel" because it's a version of that name, only it's pronounced more like ATH-el.

As I always say—Happy Reading!

Kathryn

Dun Tarh Family Tree

*Children of Lares dun Tarh and Mabel Coleby de Waverton**

Aurelius
Darien
Estevan "Stevan"
Lilliana
Caelus
Kaladin "Kal"
Lucan
Leandro
Cruz
Zora

- *Mabel is a descendant of Ajax de Velt through his son, Cole*

Castle Hydra Floor Plan

Cutaway View

Floorplan View

Ground Floor / Vault

Entry Level

Second Floor

Third Floor

"Castle Hydra"
also known as "The Hydra"

The Legend of Blackrock Castle
(home to Clan Moriston)

On the banks of Blackrock
I found my true love
Like a mist from the sea
She called to me
Until my heart was mine no more
Into the black
The misty black
My true love, through the rocky door
To be heard from nevermore

~ c. 11th century, author unknown

The Meeting of Lares and Mabel

(Excerpt from Highland Born)

Camerton Abbey
Year of Our Lord 1315

P RETTY AND PERFECT, with golden-red hair and eyes of green, Lady Mabel Coleby Douglas-de Waverton peered from the window of the fortified carriage she and her mother were riding in, spying the rambling, rather large abbey in the distance. It was early morning on a fine day after weeks of rain, and the sky above the abbey was streaked with purplish, bruised clouds. Against the backdrop of the sky and the bright sunlight, it made for dramatic scenery.

"Is that it, Mama?" she asked, pointing to the monastery on the rise. "Camerton?"

Mabel's mother, Lady Irene, leaned over to see what her daughter was pointing at. "Aye," she said after a moment. "That must be the one. Your brother is somewhere in that monastery, and we must bring him home."

Mabel didn't ask why. She didn't ask questions. She knew

her wayward brother, George, had ended up at the monastery because he'd been traveling far from where he'd told his parents he would be and ended up breaking a leg when his horse spooked. He'd been in a remote area of Cumbria, to the southwest of Carlisle, and he'd been taken in by the priests at Camerton Abbey. A physic had been summoned, the same physic who had sent word to Lord and Lady de Waverton on George's mishap. George, in fact, hadn't sent them word at all, and Mabel had heard her father raging about her vagabond brother with no sense of responsibility. He was so angry that he sent his wife and daughter, one hundred soldiers, and two wagons to fetch George.

And that was why they were here.

Truly, Mabel was glad for the adventure. Nothing much happened in her rather sheltered life, and her father wasn't a social man, so friends and visitors were infrequent at their home of Wigton. That was in great contrast to her brother, who loved to visit and loved to travel. George the Elder, their father, didn't even like to venture out of his home, so that was why he'd sent his wife and daughter. It hadn't been because he was too angry to come, but simply that he could not come.

But George the Elder's refusal to travel was Mabel's gain. And it was probably better for her brother, whom she loved. He was sweet and kind and thoughtful, but her father was correct—he had no sense of responsibility. He was bright, but he didn't want the stress and troubles of the lordship he would inherit someday. That meant he traveled around, visited friends and family, and spent his father's money wherever he went. George the Elder paid his son's debts begrudgingly and threatened not to pay anything more that his son incurred.

But he always did.

This was simply another one of George's follies in a long line of them.

Mabel and her mother hadn't spoken much on the journey from Wigton to Camerton. It had been an overnight journey, and they'd spent the previous night in a tavern where everyone seemed to either be drunk or fighting. Mabel thought it was all great fun, but her mother wasn't under the same impression. In fact, it had put the woman in a sour mood, so there hadn't been much conversation in general.

As the carriage lurched over the muddy road that was more puddle than actual road, the rain began to fall again from those purple clouds. It was brief, just enough to dampen the men, who peered at the sky with discontent. The carriage hit a particularly deep rut and got stuck, but Lady de Waverton refused to get out of the carriage because it was so muddy, and she and Mabel remained in the carriage as the soldiers managed to free them from the hole.

After that, the dirty carriage lurched and bumped all the way to the abbey.

"Mama," Mabel said, a little green because of all of the swaying and violent bumps. "May I please get out and walk the rest of the way? It doesn't seem to be so muddy here at the top of the rise. All of the water seems to have run down the road."

Irene caught a glimpse of the big abbey ahead. They had already entered what looked like a small village area, with small cottages and fields of cabbages and turnips. She could see it along the side of the road along with men working them, more than likely pledges or wards of the abbey.

"I do not think so," she said, peering at the edge of the road. "It is still quite muddy."

Thinking she might become sick, Mabel hiked up her skirt

to show her mother the boots she was wearing. "I am properly attired," she said, taking a deep breath. "I really must walk before I become ill."

With that, she pushed her shoulder into the door of the cab, and it swung open. She was out of the carriage before her mother could stop her. She was in a heavy wool traveling dress, one that came with breeches underneath for protection and comfort, and they were tucked into her boots. Mabel began walking, holding her skirt up to keep it out of the mud as she headed off across a field on a diagonal toward the abbey.

"Mabel!" her mother called after her. "Go straight to the abbey! Do not stray!"

There weren't many places for her to stray to. Mabel simply waved her mother off, trudging across the field, trying to shake off the motion sickness. The soldiers didn't follow her because they could see her clearly as she walked through the field of cabbages. They simply followed the carriage as Mabel crossed the field toward the abbey. Fortunately, it wasn't too terribly muddy here because it was at the top of a rise. Off to her left, a few men were working the cabbages, harvesting them because they were quite large. The wind was starting to pick up a little, blustery after the rains, and Mabel fought with her skirts to keep them from blowing around. She was paying attention to her dress, not where she was stepping, and she ended up slipping on a slick spot and going down on her arse, twisting her ankle.

"Damnation," she said.

Hand to her aching ankle, she looked off toward the road only to see that it must have angled away from the abbey before coming around again to the entry. The escort was moving away from her. Realizing there was going to be no help from her father's men, she tried to get to her feet, but her ankle hurt a great deal. Still, she managed to stand, putting most of her weight on her good ankle, as a deep voice spoke from behind.

"I saw ye fall, m'lady," he said. "Did ye hurt yerself?"

Startled, Mabel turned to see a big man with shoulder-length dark hair and dark eyes. He wasn't much older than she was, and she realized with a twinge of interest that he was quite handsome. But he was dressed in clothing better suited to a peasant and carrying a farming implement in one hand. In fact, that twinge of interest turned into one of suspicion, because he'd come up behind her and she'd never heard a sound.

That made her leery.

"If you think to assault me, know that all I have to do is scream and you'll have a hundred furious soldiers down upon you," she said. "Put the shovel down."

He did, immediately. "I dinna mean tae startle ye," he said. "'Tis only that I saw ye fall. I thought ye might need help."

She tried to take a step and almost went down again. "It would seem so," she said. "I have evidently hurt my ankle."

The man moved close to her, going to one knee as he lifted her skirt to get a look at her ankle. Before Mabel could protest, he put his big hands around her booted ankle and gave a gentle squeeze.

Mabel yelped.

"Ah," he said, peering up at her. "I think ye have, indeed. Can ye put any weight on it?"

She shook her head. "I do not think so," she said, trying to use the injured joint, but she ended up nearly tumbling onto him as she walked. "Damnation. Utter *damnation!*"

He grinned at her, a charming gesture. "I've never heard a lady use such language."

She frowned at him. "And you probably never will," she said. "Unfortunately, I have a mouth like my father, and he swears constantly."

That made his grin broaden. "'Tis nothing tae be ashamed of, m'lady," he said as he stood up. "It simply means ye're passionate about the things that mean something tae ye."

She eyed him, finally breaking down in a reluctant smile. "It means my mother is constantly admonishing me," she said. "She does not share your view."

His eyes were twinkling at her. "I know something about a parent not sharing a child's view," he said, his smile fading. "My father dinna share mine, either. And if it wouldna be too bold, I'll introduce myself. My name is Lares."

That was indeed a bold move, as he suggested. Introductions were made with mutual acquaintances or friends or family, but since there was no one of that position around, perhaps it wasn't bold as it was necessary, so at least they would know whom they were speaking with.

"My name is Mabel de Waverton," she said, looking him over. "You're Scots?"

"Aye."

"Are you a farmer?"

He shook his head. "Not by trade," he said. "But by circumstances."

She wasn't sure what he meant. "What circumstances?"

He gestured toward the church. "I live there," he said. "Everyone must have a task. This is mine."

She thought she understood. "Then you are a priest," she said. "Are you even allowed to speak with a woman?"

He was shaking his head before the words were out of her mouth. "I am *not* a priest," he said. "I'm a ward, although the spineless bastards would be very happy tae see me take my vows."

His eyes widened when he realized he had sworn in front of her, and she giggled. "You have a mouth like my father, too," she said.

He put up his hands in apology. "Forgive me, m'lady," he said. "But I suppose we have that in common—we speak passionately about things."

She was smiling openly at him. "I do not think that is a bad thing," she said. "More people should say what they feel. The world might be better for it."

He chuckled. "You think so, do ye?" he said. "I think if the Scots said what they thought, we'd have constant wars, all across Scotland."

She giggled again. "I suppose you are right," she said. "Isn't it men saying what they feel that starts wars in the first place?"

"That is my belief."

Distant shouting caught their attention, and they both turned to see that the de Waverton carriage had made its way to the front of the abbey. Irene had climbed out and was shouting at her daughter, waving an arm.

Mabel waved back.

"That is my mother," she said, not entirely happily. "She is waiting for me."

Lares could see that. "Have ye come on business?"

She shook her head, trying to put weight on the ankle again but faltering. He grabbed her arm so she wouldn't fall, bracing his other arm around her waist to keep her upright as she tried to walk.

"Thank you," she said in reference to his help. "To answer your question, we are not here on business. We are here to collect my brother, George. Do you know him?"

Lares held her as she took another step and ended up hopping because she couldn't put any weight on her leg. "George?" he said curiously. "Is he a priest?"

"Nay," she said, coming to a halt because she couldn't walk any further. "He broke his leg and the priests have tended him. We've come to collect him."

That brought recognition. "Ah," he said. "*That* George. The lad in the dormitory. Aye, I've spoken tae him, but he calls himself Georgie. He's quite lively, which is something that vexes the priests, I think. But I've enjoyed him."

Mabel appreciated the kind words about her brother. "He's a darling man," she said, but her smile soon faded. "I hate to trouble you, but could you tell my mother I need help? She'll send a couple of soldiers to assist me."

Lares' response was to bend over and swiftly pick her up. Abruptly aloft in the man's arms, Mabel grasped his neck for support, realizing very quickly that their faces were quite close together. Now she could see him up close, and he was a prize specimen. She had been startled by his action at first, but now that she was in his arms, something else was happening.

A sweet little flutter, deep in her belly.

She rather liked it.

"No need for the soldiers, m'lady," he said as he continued across the field. "'Tis my pleasure tae help Georgie's sister, though I will admit I'm sorry ye've come tae take him home. He was a bright spot in an otherwise lonely life."

"I'm sorry we must, but he should go home."

"Of course he should," Lares said. "I simply meant I'll miss speaking tae him. But I suppose it doesna matter, because I'm going home as well."

"Are you?" Mabel said, trying to ignore the giddy trembling in her belly. "When do you leave?"

"Soon," Lares said. "The priests know they must release me now that my da has died. I've been called home."

"Is that so?" Mabel said with some concern. "I'm sorry that it will be a sad homecoming for you."

They were nearing the edge of the field, and Lares could see Mabel's mother waving frantically to a few soldiers, pointing to her daughter. They started heading in their direction.

"Not a sad homecoming," he said quietly, eyeing the soldiers who were still some distance away, but by nature he had an aversion to English soldiers. "Truthfully, I'm glad tae be rid of this place. I'm glad tae have the opportunity tae live a normal life again and not exist at this wretched purgatory."

"Has it been so awful?"

He looked to the abbey and its dark, tall walls with moss growing on the north side of the building. "Awful enough," he said. "But, then again, I will return tae my family's home, which isna much better."

"Where is it?"

"Far tae the north, in the Highlands," he said. "A place called Castle Hydra."

She was curious. "That's quite a name," she said. "Why is it called that?"

He shrugged. "No one really knows," he said. "It has always been called that. The home we live in has been there for hundreds of years, but before that, there was a wooden fort built by the tribes who used to inhabit the land. It sits on the edge of an inlet that leads out tae sea, and my father thinks they called it the Hydra because there really was a sea serpent in the inlet in days long past. He thinks the original building on the site used tae be a temple to the serpent. But who truly knows how things get their name? Men are strange creatures sometimes."

Mabel nodded. "True enough," she said. "Then your home has been in existence for many years?"

He nodded, looking at her with those dark, twinkling eyes. "My ancestors are Romans," he said. "Ye've heard tale that the Romans once conquered the English? They tried tae come tae Scotland, but we ran them off or forced them tae live among us. Those are my ancestors. They built the temple tae the serpent. And they settled the land and married intae the tribes."

She smiled faintly. "I had a tutor who spoke of the Romans and the Greeks," she said. "But I do not remember much about them."

He was forced to turn away from her so that he could watch where he was going now that they were near the end of the field. "'Tis nothing for a finely bred lass tae know," he said. "The Romans were conquerors. They came tae the shores of England and Scotland, back in the old days, and they forced men tae serve their empire."

"Sounds fearsome."

He gave her a half-grin. "We are."

"Is that where you get your name? I've never heard it before."

He nodded. "All men in my family are given Roman or Aragon names," he said. "The Romans we descend from were men from Aragon. Therefore, our son will have a name of my choosing. Possibly after a Roman king or an Aragon prince."

Her eyes widened, and she couldn't help the snort that escaped. "*Our* son?" she said. "Are we having a son together, then?"

All he did was cast her a sidelong glance, grinning, and

Mabel's heart nearly beat right out of her chest. Something about that expression suggested he meant what he'd said, and, strangely, she believed him. She wasn't sure why, but she did. Few were actually men of their word, but Mabel suspected Lares was one of them. Out in the middle of a lightly traveled area of Cumbria, working in a field of cabbages, was a man who spoke the truth.

He meant every word.

Pondering that very thing, Mabel was prevented from answering because the soldiers were upon them at this point. Her father's heavily armed men had come to collect her, and she batted them away.

"Leave me alone," she scolded them. "He's perfectly capable of helping me."

The soldiers weren't happy about it. Irene wasn't happy about it. But Mabel tightened her arms around Lares' neck and grinned at him as a gaggle of soldiers stood by, unsure what to do. By this time, there were a pair of priests who had come forth to greet the visitors, and they were all watching with various expressions of concern and outrage as Lares carried Mabel out of the field and headed toward her mother.

Lares wasn't unaware of the battery of condescending stares, either.

He knew he was going to get an earful.

"I fear our acquaintance is coming tae a close, m'lady," he said, his gaze on the mother in particular. "'Twas an honor tae meet ye, and I'll miss George when he leaves. Should I wish tae call upon ye, where do ye live?"

Mabel looked at him. She found that she was quite sorry they would soon be parted. "Slow your walk," she said quietly. When he looked at her curiously, she smiled. "The faster you walk, the faster you must put me down."

A smile spread across his lips, and he immediately slowed. "That was a bold suggestion, m'lady."

"Then walk quickly if you do not agree."

His dark eyes studied her. "I slowed down, didn't I?"

Mabel chuckled. "You did," she said. "But my mother will be furious that I've spoken to a farmer. Look at her—she is already having fits."

"Would she have fits if ye spoke with an earl?"

Mabel wasn't sure what he meant. "Of course not," she said. "But that is different. A man of higher standing and she'd probably throw me into his arms herself."

The smile on his lips grew. "I said I wasna a priest," he said. "Nor am I a farmer, but that is my task here at Camerton. I was sent here by my da because… Well, it doesna matter why. But know that I'm not a priest nor a farmer. I was born my father's heir."

"What does that mean?"

He told her.

︵ॐ︵

"HE'S A *WHAT*?"

Irene was close to being irate as she watched the tall, handsome man in peasant clothing carry her daughter toward the abbey entry. She'd demanded to know who he was, but a few words from the priest had her turning to the man in shock.

"Say that again," she demanded. "He's the *what*?"

"He is the Earl of Torridon." The priest, a thin man with bad teeth, was looking at her rather fearfully. "That young man who has been working our fields."

Irene's mouth popped open, briefly, in astonishment. "The

Earl of Torridon is working your fields?"

The priest seemed nervous as he spoke. "Lares dun Tarh has only just become the Earl of Torridon," he clarified. "We received word two days ago that his father has passed away, and Lares was his heir. He is now the earl and, as such, is preparing to return home."

Irene's astonishment took on a hint of interest. She returned her focus to the tall, dark-haired man emerging from the field of cabbages with her daughter in his arms, and she could see all manner of possibilities. Not that she wasn't selective about whom her daughter should marry, but Mabel had been difficult when it came to finding her a husband. At her age, she should be betrothed at the very least, but she wasn't. Any man that came to call upon her, either by his own initiative or by invitation, had been found wanting in Mabel's eyes. She was bright and stubborn, and had a very strong idea about the man she wished to marry.

Irene, however, wasn't so selective. If she could garner a titled lord for her daughter—an earl, no less—then she would do it. She would do what it took.

Even if the earl was Scots.

"Tell me about him," she said to the priest just as Lares and her daughter came out of the field. "Why was he here at the abbey? Does he mean to be a priest?"

The priest shook his head. "Nay, my lady," he said. "As I said, his father him sent here after the lad was caught trying to marry a lady without permission, but also…"

He trailed off, causing Irene to look at him curiously. "Also what?"

The priest was hesitant as he lowered his voice. "He was sent here to save his soul," he muttered. "He was caught summoning demons, and his father sent him here to purge the demons from him. Rumors said that he was becoming Lucifer himself. But since his arrival two years ago, he's slept little, read the Bible for hours every day, and worked the fields rigorously to purge the devil from him. God shall prevail in the end."

Irene's expression had a hint of horror to it as she listened. "Nonsense," she finally scoffed. "There are no demons in that man."

"We have worked hard to ensure that there are none, my lady."

"He looks perfectly normal to me."

"I hope so, my lady."

Irene wasn't sure what more to say to that. Her daughter and the man in question, now an earl, were coming closer, and as they drew near, Irene went out to meet them.

"What happened?" she said to her daughter. "Did you fall? You foolish child, I told you to be careful. I knew you would hurt yourself."

Mabel had little patience with her mother. "I slipped in the mud and twisted my ankle a little," she said. "But I assure you, I'm perfectly well."

"If you are well, then let me see you stand."

"I'm not *that* well."

Irene growled in frustration. "First your brother, now you," she said dramatically. "We are here to bring your brother home because he broke his leg, and now you are injured as well. Your father will be quite angry!"

Annoyed, Mabel squirmed with the intention of climbing out of Lares' arms, so he lowered her to the ground carefully. She stood on both feet, but the truth was that she was mostly balancing on her left foot.

"See?" she said. "I can stand. I will be completely well by the time we return home, so you needn't worry about Papa. Right now, we should be more worried about George. Have you asked to see him?"

Irene hadn't. She'd been so concerned with her headstrong daughter that the very reason they were here had completely slipped her mind.

But she wasn't going to admit that.

"Of course I have," she said, turning to the priest. "Why have you not taken me to my son yet? I demand that you take me to George immediately."

The priest had no idea what she meant, and he looked at her with surprise first and then fear. "My lady?" he stammered. "Your… your son?"

Irene threw an imperious finger toward the abbey. "I *told* you," she said, though she knew full well that she hadn't. "We've come for the young man who has broken his leg. I am Lady Irene de Waverton, and my son is inside the abbey. Take me to him immediately."

The priest darted inside with Irene following. Mabel was left standing there, or rather balancing there, as everyone seemed to be moving into the abbey. As her father's soldiers wandered back over to the escort, she looked at Lares.

"I do believe they have left us alone," she said.

The corners of his mouth twitched. "It would seem so, m'lady."

"Would you be so kind as to help me inside?" she said. "I hate to ask, but I fear that I lied to my mother when I told her that I was well. My ankle hurts a great deal."

Lares had suspected as much. "We should tend tae your ankle before it grows worse," he said. "If ye'll allow, I can help."

Mabel smiled at his kindness. "You've helped quite a lot already," she said. "But mayhap you can help me inside. I should like to see my brother."

Without a word, he bent over and picked her up again, carrying her into the dark, cool innards of Camerton. It smelled of cold earth and dust, and of the incense the priests were so fond of that came from mysterious places across the sea. While Lares was fairly certain he could become quite used to his arms around Mabel, she was thinking that she could become quite used to being carried around. By him. As he followed the voices into the dormitory where George was exclaiming his delight at seeing his mother, Mabel found her gaze lingering on Lares, only to flush and turn away when he caught her staring at him.

It was a game they played more than once. She would look, he would catch her, and before they entered the dormitory, he was looking and she caught him. Lares had gone from a simple rescue mission to a game of interest fairly quickly.

And so had Mabel.

But no more interested than Lady Irene. She didn't even care when Lares entered the dormitory carrying her daughter for a second time. Nay, she didn't mind at all because before the day was through, she'd come to know Lares dun Tarh and the tale of his remote, but evidently rich, earldom. By the next morning—for they did remain at the abbey overnight—she was to return home with two very important things: her son for one and a betrothal for the other. Lares dun Tarh had surrendered without a fight.

When their first son, Aurelius, was born a year later, and a second son, Darien, not quite two years after that, it was the beginning of the legend of Lucifer's Highland Legion.

PROLOGUE

Blackrock Castle
On the Firth of Cromarty, Scotland
Year of Our Lord 1350

"Tell me that ye will come with me, sweetheart. We'll start a life anew, just the two of us."

They were in an outbuilding away from the great hall and keep of Blackrock Castle, an enormous bastion of power that sat upon a rocky outcropping overlooking the sea. The winds were cold this night, keeping men inside, which was perfect for their situation. They didn't want anyone interrupting them, especially when he was able to nestle her down in the dried grass that had been collected for the animal's winter feed and have his way with her. Currently, that meant a hand up her skirt, where he was stroking the unfurling flower between her legs. As he suckled on her tender earlobe, his fingers worked magic below.

"We'll have a grand life," he continued. "We'll live wherever ye want tae live. Edinburgh? Glasgow? If ye dunna want tae live in the big city, then I'll tell my da tae give me my inheritance and we'll find someplace quiet, just for us."

She was thinking about his request. She truly was. Luke Cannich had a way of making her see things his way, and he had for months now. Ever since he'd been betrothed to her sister. She'd known him longer than that, but she hadn't had much contact with him until his betrothal to Eventide. *Evie*. Emelia loved her sister, but she also lusted after Luke, who had secretly wooed her with all the grace of a rutting bull. She was the eldest, after all. The heiress. Her dowry was spectacular and she was the one who would inherit Blackrock.

Luke knew this.

And he wanted it.

Emelia cried out when he inserted a finger into her wet, quivering body. A second finger went in and she gasped again as he suckled her earlobe hard, trying to seduce her as only he was capable of.

"Tell me ye love me, Emelia," he whispered. "Tell me ye'll leave with me and we'll live the lives that we want tae live. Not the lives our parents tell us that we should."

He was starting to mimic the thrusting of lovemaking with his fingers, and Emelia was very nearly lost. How could he expect her to think straight when he did such wicked things to her? Speaking of wicked, what they were discussing was wicked.

Terribly wicked.

Many people would be affected by it.

"I want tae," she breathed. "But what of Evie? What of my sister?"

He didn't let up on her, thrusting his fingers, only now he was starting to move down her neck with his mouth. She knew where that would lead. Once he started fondling her breasts, she'd be lost.

"Only I can do this tae ye," he growled. "That big lug, Darien, canna bring ye the pleasure that I can. Only *I* can do this tae ye."

He was starting to pull her bodice down. "Darien dun Tarh is mannerly," she said weakly. "He's very handsome."

"He's got a streak of white in his hair like a fool!"

"Say what ye will, but he's a beauteous lad," she said. "He's also my betrothed."

That had Luke yanking off half her bodice, tearing one of the seams, in his quest to get at her breasts. "So he's beauteous, is he?" he said, his mouth clamping down on a nipple and suckling her so hard that it brought pinpricks of pain. "Do ye let him do this tae ye?"

Emelia was nearly incoherent. "He doesna try," she said. "He tries tae be respectful."

Luke removed his fingers, tossed up her skirts, and lowered his breeches. "Listen tae me, Emelia Moriston," he said angrily, placing his phallus between her legs but not entering her just yet. "I am the only man worthy of ye. Darien dun Tarh is the son of Lucifer, and he's unworthy of ye. My people are descendent from the Picts, and we've bled and lived for Scotland for generations. Do ye want yer children tae carry the blood of Satan or the blood of a Scots?"

Emelia was looking up at him with a rather dazed expression. "Darien's father is the Earl of Torridon," she said. "He's not Lucifer!"

"He's a former priest!" Luke said, pushing his manhood into her. They'd had this argument before and it enraged him every time. "Ye would be married tae a man whose father surrendered tae the devil. Surrendered his priesthood, and now his progeny are as tainted as he is. I'll make a better husband for ye, I swear it."

With that, he thrust into her and she groaned with pleasure, spreading her legs wide and welcoming him deep. Darien dun Tarh might have been her handsome betrothed, but Luke Cannich was her lover. And *what* a lover. A mouth and manhood that was only meant for her, even though Luke was betrothed to her younger sister. Poor Eventide. A sweet, beautiful girl. Most said far more beautiful than Emelia, and that was perhaps why Emelia had no real guilt in allowing Eventide's betrothed to seduce her. Luke liked *her* better.

Anything to one-up her sister.

Emelia let Luke make love to her, but with him, it only lasted a minute or so. He had a substantial manhood but absolutely no endurance. When he finally reached his climax and spent himself on the dried grass around them, he grabbed Emelia by the jaw and forced her to look at him.

"Then it is decided," he said firmly. "We'll flee and go tae Edinburgh. I can find work somewhere and we'll live well until we decide what tae do. Are ye with me, lass? I couldna stand the pain if ye werena with me."

"I'm with ye," Emelia assured him, still panting from their encounter. "But when? Ye know that I'm tae marry Darien at the end of the week."

"I know," Luke said, squeezing her jaw so hard that it left marks. "And we must plan carefully. If we leave the night before the wedding, then everyone will be too drunk tae follow us. We'll leave when the feasting starts and that will give us all night tae get as far away from them as we can. Can ye be ready?"

Emelia sat up, pushing her skirts down. "Aye," she said. "It'll be difficult packing a satchel and trying tae keep it from Evie, but I can do it."

"And bring all the money ye have. We'll need it."

"Do ye not have any?"

He stiffened. "I have money," he said, pulling his breeches up. "But, as I said, we'll need all the money we can get tae start a new life. What about your dowry?"

"What about it?"

"Can ye get tae it?"

She thought on that, picking grass out of her dark, curly hair. "I dunna think so," she said. "I dunna know where my da keeps most of his coin. He hides it."

Luke grunted. "Then take what ye can," he said unhappily. "Make sure Evie doesna know. Ye'll have tae keep it secret."

Emelia nodded. "I can," she said. Then she smiled at him. "I can hardly believe it. We'll flee this dark place and live in the light. We'll dance every night and drink as much as we want and no one will stop us."

Luke finished securing his breeches. Some called them braies, but his mother was English and he'd grown up with a mixture of Scottish and English phrases and loyalties. But the one thing he did stay true to was the greed of his father. The man had a strong heritage, but he'd managed to drink away any money that had been left to him, hence the marriage betrothal to Eventide Moriston. Luke had a large, run-down pele tower to inherit, but there wasn't much to it other than the land and the livestock. Luke's father had managed to keep that part of it hidden from Eventide's father. As far as Fergus Moriston knew, the Cannich clan was well off.

But it wasn't.

Hence, Luke's need for the heiress.

Even if he *was* stealing her away from one of the most powerful families in the Highlands.

"Then ye'll be ready for me," he said, standing up and pulling her with him. "We'll leave this place and never look back."

He was leading her toward the ladder that would deposit them into the stables below. "We'll find a cottage by the sea," she said, telling him what he'd already heard several times before. "A little cottage with a hearth and a dog. I do want a dog."

He paused, grunting as he looked at her. "That's another mouth tae feed, lass," he said. "Wait until I find a way tae make money before we take on more than just ourselves."

Emelia clung to his arm with both hands. "But a little dog will be no trouble," she said. "And cherries. I want baskets of them."

He began his trek down the ladder, helping her down after him. "Let's worry about getting free before we speak of dogs and cherries," he said. "But make sure ye bring money with ye. Dunna forget."

Emelia took the last step of the ladder before ending up on the stable floor. "I willna," she said, still holding his hand. She took a moment to gaze up at the man, a brawny blond with a strong body that smelled of musk. "Promise me we'll be happy, Luke. Promise me that our lives will always be full of laughter and happiness."

He smiled faintly. "Always, lass," he said with quiet assurance. "We'll know nothing but joy."

Emelia beamed. "It will be difficult not speaking of this," she said. "I want tae shout it tae the world."

He shook his head, kissing her swiftly on the lips. "If ye speak a word of it, yer da will lock ye in a chamber and throw away the key," he said. "Ye must not tell a soul. Promise me?"

She nodded quickly. "Of course I willna," she said. "I

havena yet. I simply meant that I feel like shouting tae the world. I'm so happy."

He gave her hand a squeeze before pulling away. "And there'll be more happiness tae come, but not until next week," he said. "I'll be back before the wedding and we'll go."

He was starting to move toward the rear of the stable, where there was a window he could flee from. His usual escape hatch for these encounters in the stable. Emelia followed after him.

"And I'll be ready," she said, slipping in some horse dung that hadn't been shoveled away. "I love ye, my bonny lad."

He was already halfway out of the window. "Remember that when I return," he said, refusing to repeat the sentiment because the truth was that he didn't love her. He just wanted her. "Off with ye, now. Go back tae the keep."

Emelia nodded, waving at him as he slipped through the window and into the dusk beyond. They were in a walled fortress, but the walls weren't particularly high and there was an old iron gate on the west side that led to the fields beyond. Blackrock hadn't seen a siege or a warring action in decades, so it wasn't heavily guarded.

Perfect for a lover who liked to slip in and out of the place at his pleasure.

Emelia could see him flee over the wall and then into a grove of trees in the distance. That was where she lost him. But it didn't matter.

She'd see him again soon enough.

Leaving the stable, she headed for the hall because it was approaching supper and she'd be expected to help. She loved her family, but she hated the work. Her father was tight with his coin, so they didn't have the servants that they should. Fergus expected his daughters to work and lead productive lives.

Perhaps that was good for some girls, but not Emelia. Luke promised her a life of happiness and leisure, where she wouldn't have to work and where love would be the most important thing in their lives.

Her life, anyway.

She pushed aside the face that Luke seemed to have different goals than she did. He seemed concerned with the money and drinking, while she was concerned with fun and joy. She was certain she could bring him over to see her way of thinking. She was willing to stake her future on it—a future that didn't include the wife of a second son of the dun Tarh clan because she was going to take the man her sister wanted.

In the end, she'd come out on top.

Fighting off a smile, Emelia headed into the hall.

PART ONE:
DARIEN
ON THE BANKS OF BLACKROCK

CHAPTER ONE

One week later

"I SHOULD HAVE known." An older man with a crown of fading red hair was seated in a hall used by his ancestors, littered with a century of dust, symbols of power, and memories. "Luke Cannich is a bold lad with a wandering eye, and it wandered tae Emelia. How could I not have seen it?"

He shook his head in disgust, downing a big swallow of ale made from fermented pears that packed quite a punch. But it was a punch he needed at the moment.

Better from the liquor than the man seated across from him.

Lares dun Tarh was that man. He'd arrived with his son for a wedding and ended up walking into a situation that happened to other people—never to his family and most especially not to the son who was perhaps the most important one of all.

Darien didn't deserve this.

It was all Lares could do to keep from exploding.

"Tell me from the beginning, Fergus," he said with more patience than he felt. "Tell me how ye discovered that my son's betrothed has run off with her sister's intended."

He raised his voice ominously toward the end of his sentence, causing his eldest sons to look at him with concern. Aurelius, his heir, had come all the way from Northern England for the wedding of his brother, and he was eyeing Lares as if waiting for the man to leap from his chair and throttle Fergus. Estevan, or Stevan as he was known, was the third-eldest brother, a man who tended to fight first, ask questions later, and he was fully in support of his father tearing the hall apart, and Fergus with it.

And then there was the very groom himself.

Darien *an geal*, or Darien the White, he was called because of a big white streak of hair at the top of his forehead. He'd also been called Darien the Destroyer on occasion because he could be a firebrand. He was unafraid to speak his mind, which sometimes got him into trouble, but he had the skill with a sword to back up anything that came out of his mouth. He was big and fast and had fists like hammers.

Truth be told, Lares was very concerned about Darien's reaction to all of this.

So was Fergus.

"You wouldna believe me if I told ye," Fergus said, wiping a hand across his weary face. "I canna say that I entirely believe it, but the evidence is clear. It all started when my wife wanted special cheese for the wedding that a woman in Inverness makes, but she wanted it fresh. I sent some of my lads tae Inverness yesterday tae fetch it, and they saw Luke Cannich entering the city just as they were leaving with the cheese. But they saw a woman with him, one who ducked intae a shop when they saw her. It was a woman who looked like Emelia, but they dinna think anything of it until Emelia was nowhere tae be found this morning. We searched everywhere for her, including her chamber and the entire keep, but it was as if she had vanished. Then the lads returned with their tale. It doesna take a smart man tae put the pieces together and realize Emelia went with Luke. 'Tis not as if we dunna already know of the Cannich's lusty reputation when it comes tae women."

Lares sighed heavily, finally looking at Darien to see how the man was handling the news, but he was shockingly quiet about it. He certainly wasn't acting like a jilted groom.

But that could change any second.

"And what have ye done about it?" Lares demanded. "Have ye sent men after her?"

"Of course I have," Fergus said, irritated and emotional. "I had men riding tae Inverness as soon as we realized what had happened. They're probably turning the city inside out looking for her even as we speak. They'll burn the damn place down if they dunna find her."

"Has anyone asked Cannich's father?" Aurelius spoke up. Big and dark, like the rest of the dun Tarh brothers, he was a wise voice in the chaos. "Reelig Cannich should know where his son is."

Fergus looked at him. "Reelig arrived before ye did," he said. "He's gone back home, but he said that he dinna think much of Luke's absence until he came tae Blackrock and I told him what my men had seen. I must admit that it seemed as if Reelig wasna surprised."

Lares frowned. "He *knew* Luke was going to run away with Emelia?"

Fergus shook his head. "I dunna think he knew, exactly," he said. "But we all know that Luke has an eye for the ladies and likes tae spend money on them. Reelig said that Luke once spoke of the unfairness that he wasna betrothed tae Emelia because she's my heiress. She'll bring the wealth of Blackrock with her, as ye know."

Lares' frown deepened. "Was he in love with the lass, then?"

Fergus snorted. "Luke Cannich is only in love with himself," he said. "'Twas with misgivings that I betrothed Evie tae him, but the bad outweighed the good. He'll be clan chief someday. Moy Castle is a powerful stronghold, and it makes a good alliance."

"So all the signs were there that the man had his eye on Emelia, yet no one did a thing about it." Darien finally found his voice, his gaze riveted to Fergus. "I suppose if I think about it, I should have been suspicious, too, because every time I came tae Blackrock, he was here. He was probably here when I wasna here, too, and he was probably wooing Emelia even then. Am I speaking the truth?"

All eyes in the chamber were focusing suspiciously on Fergus, who could feel the weight of their gazes. It was an effort not to shrink away.

"What do ye want me tae say, Darien?" he said. "Moy is closer than the Hydra. Luke was here more frequently than ye were, but I'm trusting the man. I'm assuming he had honor. I thought he came tae see Evie."

Darien's square jaw flexed faintly. "It seems tae me that he never paid much attention tae his betrothed," he said, that legendary rage building slowly in his veins. "I canna remember a time when he seemed tae pay more attention tae her than he needed tae, which is a shame considering Eventide is the more beauteous sister. Luke had the beauty and I had the heiress, only now he seems tae have wanted what belongs tae me."

Fergus' expression was tight with outrage. "Are ye saying ye think my Emelia is homely?"

"I am saying her sister is more beautiful," Darien said in a statement designed to cut. He figured he'd already been grievously insulted by the entire situation and Fergus deserved what was coming to him. "Face the truth, Fergus. Emelia would flirt with a goat if she thought it would look in her direction. She flirted with me so heavily that I felt dirty. Dirty because everything out of her mouth was supposed tae seduce or flatter me. Never any words of wisdom or even kindness. In fact, in all the times I've been around Emelia and her sister, I never once saw Emelia show any kindness tae Evie, either. She was cruel and nasty, and Evie simply accepted it because she is not only the more beautiful sister, but she seems tae be the kinder one as well."

"Darien," Lares said quietly, warning in his tone. "Easy, lad."

Darien glanced at his father. "Why?" he said, his anger building steam. "Fergus knows what he has in his two daughters. Ye know what he has in his two daughters, only ye pledged me tae the heiress because ye wanted me tae have Blackrock. Ye wanted me tae have the Moriston money. But I've heard the rumors about Emelia and I know her father has, too. Every man around knows that Emelia hasna kept herself pure."

"That's enough," Fergus boomed, bolting to his feet. "Ye'll not speak of my daughter that way."

Darien looked at him, unintimidated. "Ye mean the daughter who was betrothed tae me but has run off with another man?" he said. Then his eyes narrowed. "She's been gone since yesterday, meaning she has been with Luke throughout the night. Do ye think she's still kept herself pure for her betrothed? I can tell ye that given Luke's reputation, and Emelia's, she's warmed his bed and then some. And it's probably not the first time."

Lares was up, pulling Darien away from Fergus, who was balling his fists. The man's face was positively red with rage. Aurelius grabbed his brother, pushing him at Estevan, who took hold of Darien and forcibly escorted him out of the chamber before the situation deteriorated into blows.

"Go," Estevan said, pointing to the yard beyond the hall. "Go for a walk and cool yer blood."

Darien shrugged. "No need," he said. "I've said what I needed tae say."

"Ye said enough tae start a war."

Darien shook his head. "Nothing I said was untrue," he said. Then he sighed heavily. "Mayhap Da willna be so quick tae force me intae a betrothal the next time. I told him what I thought of this one, but he was convinced Blackrock was a fine enough prize for the risk."

"What risk?"

"The risk of marrying a woman I dinna want tae marry."

Estevan shook his head with some regret. "Ye made that very clear, lad," he said. He pointed to the yard again. "Go for a walk."

"I think I'll go home."

"Ye'd better not," Estevan warned. "Da will have yer hide if ye leave. 'Tis supposed tae be yer wedding in two days. I wouldna vacate so soon if I were ye."

Darien glanced at him. "Why not?" he said. "If Fergus' men find Emelia and bring her back tomorrow, do ye truly think I'd marry the woman after she'd run off with Cannich?"

"Are ye thinking of avenging yerself on Cannich?"

Darien shook his head. "Nay," he muttered. "I probably should simply tae save my honor, but the truth is that the man did me a favor by taking Emelia with him. If I ever see him again, I'll buy him a drink."

Estevan snorted. "Ye *truly* dinna want tae marry the lass?"

Darien sighed heavily. He'd been fairly ambivalent about the betrothal since it was announced those months ago. He hadn't shown any great excitement *or* great aversion, and given his reputation for speaking boldly, that was saying something. It was simply that he figured there was nothing he could do about the situation, so he'd kept his mouth shut. He hadn't wanted to embarrass his father by appearing ungrateful, but now that Emelia was gone, there wasn't any reason to hold back.

Nay... he *didn't* want to marry her.

He never had.

"No fortune in the world could make me want tae marry her," he said after a moment. "I was going tae go through with it because that's what Da wanted. Not because it was what *I* wanted. She is petty and vain and shallow. Not someone I want for a wife. Let her be Cannich's problem now, because she's no longer mine."

With that, he headed away from the hall, perhaps going for that walk that Estevan had recommended. It was abundantly clear that he wasn't broken up over the situation in the least. If anything, he seemed relieved, which was surprising because Darien had never shown much enthusiasm one way or the other about the betrothal to Emelia Moriston. As he'd said, he was simply doing his duty.

But that duty had come with a complication.

A bride that had run off with another groom.

Thinking his brother had dodged what could have been a very bad situation, Estevan headed back into the hall where one father was trying to calm down another.

But the situation was only going to get worse.

CHAPTER TWO

SAINTS BE PRAISED!

Those were her thoughts and had been since she'd been told, early that morning, that her betrothed had run off with her sister. If ever two people deserved one another, it was Emelia and Luke. Selfish was where they began. No one knew where they ended, but the two of them were going to find out rather quickly. It was difficult to determine just who was the most self-centered out of the two of them, but her opinion was that Emelia was the worst of the pair.

She ought to know.

She'd grown up with the woman.

Eventide St. Brigid Moriston was the youngest of the two daughters of Fergus and Athole Moriston, and probably the only person in the family with any real brains. Fergus drank, Athole suffered from any ailment she could imagine, and Emelia was so caught up in what she wanted and how she intended to get it that not one person in the Highlands looked upon the family with any serious respect. The only redeeming quality of Blackrock Castle was the fact that Fergus was clan chief and had a good many lads who answered any call to arms, even though the area had known peace for years. Fergus was very concerned with alliances, however, which was why he made sure to pledge his daughters strategically when the time came.

In Eventide's opinion, however, there was only one groom worth the asking.

She had always thought that Darien dun Tarh was the real catch. Luke Cannich had been smooth and flattering, a silver-tongued devil if there ever was one, but he was as shallow as a mud puddle. Just as dirty, too. There was no substance to the man, and Eventide had known that since childhood because she'd known Luke as long. Given that Moy Castle was fairly close to Blackrock, and their fathers were friends, she'd come into contact with Luke more than her share. He'd paid attention to her until he tried to stick his hand up her skirts and she hit him in the face. He'd ended up with two black eyes and a story of how a horse had kicked him.

But Eventide knew the truth.

She'd known the truth still when her father pledged her to him.

God, what a miserable moment that had been. Emelia, being a year and a half older, had ended up with the prize of Darien, while Eventide had been stuck with that blond-haired scoundrel. But her father had been pleased with the situation, so, like any dutiful daughter, she'd played along. All she could see was a dismal future with a husband she didn't even like, but it seemed to mean so much to her father. He had been more pleased with the betrothal than she.

Therefore, this morning had been an answer to prayer.

Her prayer.

Even now, she was standing in the kitchen yard that was

located outside of the main castle walls. The castle itself was on a rise, overlooking the Firth of Cromarty, so there were several levels to the castle itself. The kitchens and ovens were outside of the walls, down a flight of steps, but situated amongst some rocks that had acted as a foundation for another set of walls specifically for the kitchen area. Part of it had a roof, but the chicken coop was mostly open. They were built against the northern kitchen wall, nearly the length of it, and that was where Eventide found herself on this day, thanking the saints that her buffoon of a betrothed had run off with her sister as she tended to some new chicks that had hatched the previous day.

Truthfully, she hadn't felt this good in months. But given the fact that her father was devastated by the situation, she made sure to keep her feelings to herself.

Playing the brave woman jilted by her betrothed was all she could do.

The wind was whipping in off the firth on this day, blowing hair across her face as she finished with the chicks. There was an enormous brood hen willing to tend to them, so she left them warm and cozy and called to one of the kitchen servants, making sure the woman knew which chickens to kill for supper. Some of the hens had stopped laying eggs and were destined for the stew pot. Finished with her duties at the chicken coop, she wiped her hands off on her apron and headed up the stairs that led through the doorway in the castle walls.

It was busy today because people were arriving for the coming nuptials. There was a field to the south of the castle where, already, houses were setting up encampments. Eventide paused, lifting her hand to shield her eyes from the sun, watching the men at the gate as they spoke with more guests, recently arrived.

"M'lady?"

The voice came from behind, and she turned to see Darien standing there. Tall and strong, with impossibly wide shoulders, the man couldn't have been more handsome had he tried. He had luscious, dark hair, wavy, and the unique white streak on his forehead that gave him his name—

Darien the White.

Eventide thought it was more like Darien the Glorious.

"Darien," she said, lowering her hand. "I'd heard ye arrived with yer family."

He shrugged. "Only my da and two of my brothers," he said. "My mother and the rest are due tae arrive tomorrow, but we came early tae… celebrate. It seems there is no reason tae do so now."

He'd brought up what they both knew, and Eventide felt as if she needed to apologize to the man. It was her sister who had run off, after all. And her betrothed. She was tied to this more than he was, and even if she was glad they'd run off, she still harbored some guilt when it came to Darien because she knew something no one else did—when they searched her sister's chamber, she had noticed that a satchel was missing. She hadn't told anyone because it was confirmation of Emelia's flight. Perhaps there was part of her that really didn't want her father to bring Emelia home, because if she came home, Luke came home. And she'd be forced to marry him.

Therefore, it was better not to speak up.

It was better for everyone to think Emelia had simply vanished… never to return.

"I wish I knew why Emelia did what she did," she said after a moment. "I will apologize for my sister. Ye dinna deserve this."

He shook his head. "Dunna worry about me," he said. "I should apologize tae ye."

"What for?"

"Because Luke Cannich should be horsewhipped for what he's done," he said. "Ye're a good lass, Evie. I've known ye long enough tae know that. What Luke did was shameful. The man is a fool."

Eventide regarded him for a moment. She couldn't tell just how upset he was, to be truthful. He seemed… morose. Resigned. Even reconciled? Was it possible the man's own embarrassment at the situation was causing him to focus on her as someone who'd had more of a wrong committed against her? Certainly it would take the attention off him, but if she was being perfectly honest, she had never, in all of the months her sister had been betrothed to Darien, seen the man show any overt affection or attention toward her sister. Darien had been polite and attentive, smiling appropriately, showing what thoughtfulness was necessary, but she never got the sense that he was madly in love with her sister. The only sense she ever got was that he was being dutiful.

Like her.

Simply dutiful.

But she suspected if she didn't show some disappointment, it might give away the fact that she was relieved about the whole thing.

"Ye're kind," she said, eyes downcast. "But please dunna be concerned with me. What happened tae me is small compared tae what happened tae ye. So many people are arriving for yer wedding feast, and I know my da is humiliated by the whole thing. I hope… I hope ye dunna feel that way. Emelia has always been impulsive. I'm not sure this means she tried tae hurt ye more than she simply wanted tae do what *she* wanted tae do. But I feel as if I should have seen this coming."

Darien's dark eyes were lingering on her, studying her. "And ye never saw any sign of it?" he said. "She never showed any interest toward Luke?"

Eventide nodded. "She spoke of him," she said. "She told me I was fortunate because he was so handsome. I suppose if I think on it, there were times when he'd come tae visit me but I would see him speaking with my sister, out in the ward. Just the two of them. I never thought anything of it. Emelia never said anything about it. Honestly, if they are having a conversation that I am not part of, should I think they are discussing running off together?"

Darien shook his head. "Nay," he said. "Ye're trusting that both are people of honor."

"Did Emelia ever mention anything tae you about Luke?"

He had to think on that. "Nothing that should make me suspicious," he said. "Though last month when I visited, she spoke of a desire tae travel and mentioned that Luke was going tae take ye tae Paris for yer wedding trip. She was envious of that and wanted me tae take her also."

"What did ye tell her?"

"That I have business tae attend tae before we can travel."

Eventide lifted her eyebrows. "I suspect she dinna take kindly tae that."

"Nay," Darien said firmly. "Emelia doesna like being denied."

Eventide knew that was putting it mildly. She also noticed that, for the first time, Darien seemed weary. He was trying to make a good show of not being humiliated by the situation, but she didn't think that was the case.

Perhaps he was more affected than he let on.

"Ye're an important man, and she knew that," she said. "She simply dinna want tae let on. Though I'm sorry one Moriston sister has wronged ye badly, mayhap ye'll let the other sister show you the hospitality of Blackrock? Ye've had a long ride from the Hydra. Have ye eaten?"

Darien shook his head. "Not yet."

Eventide swept her hand in the direction of the hall. "Then let me feed ye," she said. "'Tis the least I can do."

Darien's gaze moved to the hall, its steeply pitched roof, the smoke curling from the chimney, and he shook his head. "My da and yer da are in the hall," he said. "I dunna think they want us there right now."

Eventide didn't miss a beat. "Then come with me," she said, turning in another direction. "I'll find ye a quiet place."

Darien did. He followed slightly behind the young woman who barely came to his sternum, but oh… what a woman she was. She had long, wavy hair past her buttocks, dark auburn in color, but he could see the flecks of gold in it brought out by the sunlight. Whereas Emelia had brown hair, straight and fine, and a not-unhandsome face with clear skin and blue eyes, Eventide had skin the color of cream and a dusting of auburn freckles across her nose. She had the biggest blue eyes Darien had ever seen, enormous and clear, with a fringe of long lashes all around them. She also had lips shaped like a rosebud that, when parted, revealed straight teeth like a row of pearls.

As Darien had told Fergus, Eventide was the beauty of the family.

That opinion had not changed.

She also had a round figure, with full breasts and round hips, something that was quite pleasing to look at. Darien found it difficult not to look at them now as she walked slightly ahead of him. He remembered Emelia telling him that Eventide had a taste for sweets, something that evidently gave her that round figure, but he didn't care.

He thought it was delightful.

"Since our fathers are in the hall, the solar will be empty," Eventide said as they mounted the stone steps into the keep. "This will be a quiet place for you tae eat and rest."

He followed her into the dark, cold solar, a small chamber that was crammed with chairs and tables and lined with books on shelves. It smelled of smoke and dust, and as Darien brushed off one of the chairs, Eventide went straight to the hearth and began to stack the kindling.

"I think ye're in luck today," she said. "The cook has made fried cakes with her cloud cream. If they're not all gone, I'll bring ye some."

"What's cloud cream?"

Eventide paused to make a beating motion with her hand. "Cream that has been beaten and fluffed," she said. "Cook adds honey tae sweeten it. It's delicious."

Darien nodded, silently agreeing. He was going to sit down, but when he saw that she was trying to light a fire, he went to the hearth and got down on his knees. "Here," he said. "Let me do this. Ye shouldna dirty yer hands for me."

Eventide let him take the flint and stone from her, looking at the man as he concentrated on sparking the kindling. He was so close to her that she could smell him. Like leather and horses. *God, he's beautiful,* she thought. Everything about him made her heart race, and to realize what her sister had done to the man made her furious. Beyond furious, actually. It was enough to bring tears of anger to her eyes, and she sat back on her heels, watching him focus on the fire, thinking that she would throttle her sister the next time she saw her.

If she ever saw her again.

She didn't realize she was sniffling until Darien looked up at her with concern.

"What's the matter?" he asked.

Quickly aware that she had tears on her cheeks, she wiped them away hastily and stood up. "Nothing," she said. "I'll see tae yer meal."

He reached out and grasped her wrist before she could get away. "Wait," he said softly. "Dunna go, lass. I know today has been a difficult day for ye. If anyone understands that, I do."

Eventide broke down in tears. She didn't know why she should, because she had been feeling fine all morning, but something about Darien's stoic acceptance of a situation that surely must have been grossly humiliating to him had eaten at her, finally breaking through the shell of self-protection she'd kept over herself. As he held on to one wrist, she furiously wiped her eyes with her free hand.

"Ye dunna understand," she said, unable to keep her mouth shut about it. "*I* dunna understand, but I do know that I dunna weep for the reasons ye think. I dunna weep because Luke left me. I should be shouting for joy because of it."

Darien stood up, brow furrowed. "What do ye mean?"

She continued wiping her eyes as she gently, but firmly, pulled her wrist from his grasp. "Dunna mind me," she said, struggling to compose herself. "I'll bring yer meal. Please sit and rest. I'll return."

She was gone before he could say another word. Puzzled, and concerned, Darien did as he was told, claiming the chair he'd originally intended to sit in, but all the while he was thinking about her words.

I should be shouting for joy because of it.

Was it possible she felt about Luke the way he felt about Emelia?

He wondered.

The fire in the hearth began to gain steam as he sat there and pondered the situation, but along with those thoughts, he was feeling his fatigue. He and his father and brothers had spent a little more than two days traveling from the Hydra, their family home on the shores of Loch Torridon. It was an enormous structure, perhaps one of the largest in the Highlands, a stone behemoth built over old wooden temples constructed, in centuries past, to worship a sea serpent that lived in the loch. At least, that was the tradition passed down from generation to generation. Darien had lived there most of his life and had never seen a hint of any serpent, but he knew as well as anyone that the Highlands of Scotland were a mysterious place that could hide any manner of beastie.

Mysterious or not, it was his home.

The very land was the blood in his veins.

"Here ye are!"

Jolted from his train of thought, he looked at the doorway to see both Aurelius and Estevan standing there. Before he could reply, they entered the chamber, looking for food or wine or anything to sustain them. Aurelius gave up his search fairly quickly and headed to the fire, holding out his hands to warm them, but Estevan was still rooting around.

"Food is on its way," Darien said. "Sit down and warm yer bones. I'm still feeling the chill of the ride."

There was a long chest near one of the windows and Estevan lay down on it, stretching out his big frame. "A long ride for nothing," he muttered. "God's bloody Bones, Dee. I couldna feel more pity for ye than I do. I'm sorry for ye, brother."

Darien watched Estevan settle down and close his eyes before turning his attention to Aurelius. "Well?" he said. "Have Da and Fergus come tae blows?"

"Not yet," Aurelius said. "But it would be better that we let them speak in private. There is a lot tae say between them."

Darien scratched his chin, his gaze returning to the hearth, where a healthy fire had taken root. "I would imagine so," he said. "Not the least of which is even if Emelia is returned, I'll not marry her. I'll not touch another man's leavings."

Aurelius eyed his brother. He had his own seat of Lydgate Castle, far to the south on the English border, so he wasn't home very often these days. Perhaps no more than three or four times a year, less now that he and his wife had a son. He didn't like to spend time away from his strapping boy, Alvarez, who was his spitting image. But he knew enough about what was going on at the Hydra, and Scotland in general, because both Darien and his father sent him frequent messages about it. They were involved in Scotland's rule, and Aurelius, having married an English lass and assumed an English title, was involved on the English side.

But this marriage that Darien found himself committed to was something Aurelius had questioned since the beginning. Lares spoke of it and what a great alliance it would be, but Darien had said nothing—unusual for the brother who wasn't usually at a loss for words. Scotland's politics aside, Darien's silence on the marriage issue had been telling. Estevan had confirmed, whispering to him while they were in the chamber with their father and Fergus.

Darien didn't want his bride.

He never had.

"Darien, ye know I'd never speak against Da," Aurelius said after a moment. "But I know."

"Know what?"

"About this betrothal," Aurelius continued quietly. "Estevan told me what ye said about it, that ye never wanted it. We've known the Moriston family for years and, quite honestly, I never thought the eldest daughter was a good match for ye. I understand why Da brokered the contract because, strategically, the marriage would serve a purpose."

Darien looked at him. "It's not an issue now," he said. "I'll not take her back."

"Even if Da insists?"

"Especially if he insists," Darien muttered. "*He* wanted this betrothal. Not me."

"But ye were going tae go through with it."

"Of course I was," he said. "I tell ye what I told Stevan. I was going tae go through with it because that's what Da wanted. Not because it was what *I* wanted. The truth is that Emelia is petty and vain, and not someone I want for a wife."

Aurelius looked at his brother, understanding the situation. Darien was being a good son. He was doing what his father wanted. But Emelia's disappearance had given him an excuse to back out.

Perhaps it was for the best.

"What do ye intend tae do now?" Aurelius asked quietly. "And is there anything I can do for ye?"

Darien raked his fingers through his dark hair, disturbing the white streak on his widow's peak. "Nay," he said, sounding less defiant but wearier. "But I thank ye for asking. Coming tae Blackrock today made me feel as if I was coming tae my own execution. Married tae someone like Emelia, someone I'd have tae leave alone for weeks and months at a time while I went about my business, was a potential nightmare. I knew I couldna trust her. I knew that from the start. Running off with Cannich simply proves it, and I must say that I am greatly relieved. The last thing I need is tae have a wife I must worry over."

Lying on the chest against the wall, Estevan started to snore loudly. Both Aurelius and Darien chuckled at the sound.

"He still sounds like an old boar," Aurelius said. "I will admit that I've missed that."

Darien glanced over his shoulder at Estevan. "The man can rattle the roof off the keep," he said. "I dunna think I will miss it."

"Ye say that now."

That had Darien looking at his brother, deflecting his thoughts from his current situation. "But ye're happy, Bear?" he said. "All Mother can speak of is how happy ye are. When yer son came this past year, she said she'd never seen ye glow as ye do now. I must admit that I see it, too."

Bear. That was Aurelius' nickname to the family because when he and Darien had been toddlers, Darien tried to say "brother," but it came out as "ba-bear" and the name stuck. It was a term of endearment, but also a show of love and respect between two brothers who were perhaps the closest of the group. Eight brothers could be chaotic at times, but Aurelius and Darien had always been tight, the leaders who held the siblings together. They knew each other better than anyone, and Aurelius heard the curiosity, or perhaps even the longing, in Darien's voice when he asked the question.

"She's right," Aurelius said softly, a twinkle in his eye. "I've never been happier than I am now. Ye'll have that opportunity someday, Dee. Now simply isn't the right time."

"Or the right bride," Darien said, rolling his eyes. But he quickly sobered as he looked at his brother again. "I know I spoke unkindly of Valery when ye first met her. I've apologized for it before, but hearing how happy ye are makes me regret my unkindness even more. I hope ye know how much I adore yer wife. She's a great lady."

Aurelius smiled, thinking of the woman he loved more than anything else in the world. "I agree with ye," he said. "And the man that was unkind those years ago doesna exist anymore. Ye've grown, Dee. Ye've matured intae an astonishing man right before my eyes. With everything ye've undertaken for Robbie Stewart, I couldna be prouder of ye."

Robbie Stewart. Now they'd broached a greater subject that affected their lives. Aurelius was speaking of Robert Stewart, the High Steward of Scotland, who had been appointed by the Scottish Parliament to replace King David whilst the man was in captivity. Aurelius had brought up the crux of the involvement of Darien, and himself, in the dynamic and explosive politics between the Scottish and the English Crown.

That was where the dun Tarh brothers were forced to part.

It was tradition in the Earl of Torridon's family, for centuries, that the eldest dun Tarh son foster in an important English household. Lares had done it and Aurelius, as the firstborn male, had also. He had spent fifteen years in England, fostering at Berwick Castle and Winchester Castle before being knighted by the Earl of Warenton, head of the powerful de Wolfe family. Mabel, Aurelius' mother, was from the de Velt family, another formidable family in the north, and they had married into the House of de Wolfe long ago, so de Wolfe and de Velt were considered family by the Earldom of Torridon.

But it made things the least bit complicated.

And that complication was now. Aurelius was part of Edward III's court, and an integral part of the imprisonment of King David, who had been defeated in the Battle of Neville Cross and taken captive. That had put Robert Stewart on the throne, his being high steward, and Darien was entrenched in Robert's court as one of his advisors.

Each man had inside information.

Each man had his loyalties.

"Robbie is a difficult man," Darien said after a moment. "And he is indicating that he'll not support the money the nobles are currently attempting tae raise tae ransom David. Have ye heard any talk of that?"

Aurelius shook his head. "Nay," he said. "Edward hasna mentioned it. What makes ye think they willna support ransoming their own king?"

Darien glanced at Estevan again, making sure the man wasn't listening, even though he trusted him. But what he had to tell his brother was explosive. He'd been waiting for this moment for several months, knowing he'd see Aurelius at his wedding. They hadn't traveled to Blackrock together—they saw each other for the first time last night when they met up outside of Inverness. Usually, they employed trusted messengers to relay their information, but in this case, he hadn't wanted to put this in writing.

It was that serious.

"Robbie wants Berwick returned tae the Scots," Darien muttered. "I have it on good authority that he intends tae ruin the ransom of David, and the promised hostages in exchange for his freedom, because he is negotiating with the French tae ally with him when he moves tae capture Berwick."

Aurelius' eyebrows lifted. "The French on English soil?"

"The French helping the Scots regain Berwick," Darien said, a knowing gleam in his eye. "A Scots-French alliance against the English. That'll destroy everything, Bear. David is a dead man if that happens. Edward thinks he has leverage against the Scots by holding David, but Robbie is in secret negotiations with English enemies."

They were prevented from further conversation when Eventide suddenly entered the chamber, followed by three serving women bearing trays of food and drink. Aurelius had a look of shock on his face while he mulled over what he'd been told, as Eventide had the servants set the food down on the big table cluttered with her father's things.

"I hope this is tae yer liking," she said, pouring out cups of ale as Darien rose wearily to inspect the food. "Stew with chicken and greens, boiled mutton, and fruit pie."

Darien took the cup of ale that she extended to him. "Yer hospitality is generous, m'lady," he said. "Thank ye."

Eventide smiled timidly. "Given the unkindness showed tae ye by my family, 'tis the least I could do," she said. "Please enjoy. When ye're ready tae retire, please send for me and I'll show ye where ye'll sleep."

"Is it the same place I've slept in past visits?" Darien asked.

She nodded. "Aye."

"Then ye dunna need tae escort me," he said. "I can find it. My brothers, too?"

Eventide looked at the well-built brother standing near the table. The other brother was sleeping like the dead on an old chest. "Aye," she said. "Yer brothers, too. And yer father."

"I dunna think I've had the pleasure of an introduction," Aurelius said, recovering from his shock enough to show his manners. "Will ye introduce us, Dee?"

Darien indicated Eventide. "This is Eventide Moriston, Emelia's sister," he said. "M'lady, this is my eldest brother, Aurelius."

Eventide dipped into a polite curtsy. "I've not had the opportunity tae welcome ye tae Blackrock, m'lord," she said. "Ye arrived with yer father and went straight intae the hall."

Aurelius nodded. "There was much tae discuss," he said, stating the obvious. There was no use avoiding it. "May I extend my sorrow at what has happened? It not only affects my brother, but it affects ye, too. I am appalled for ye. Luke Cannich is a dastardly man."

The smile on her face faded and she averted her gaze. "Please enjoy yer food," she said, unwilling to discuss the situation. "If I can be of further assistance, please send for me."

She was gone before anyone could say a word to her. Darien watched her go, feeling some sorrow at her reaction to his brother's words. Aurelius, too, could see that his sympathies weren't well met.

"I dinna mean tae chase her away," he said. "I hope I dinna offend her."

Darien shook his head. "I dunna think ye did," he said. "I had a brief conversation with her earlier and she apologized for her sister quite a bit, but when it came tae Luke… She has the same feeling for him that I have for Emelia."

Aurelius looked surprised. "She doesn't want tae marry the man?"

Darien waggled his dark brows. "Let's say there doesna seem tae be any love lost," he said. "'Tis a difficult situation."

Aurelius grunted as he reached out to scoop up some of the stew into a cup. "Cannich left *that* lass for her sister?" he said, shaking his head. "Though we've known the family, I've never met the daughters. Emelia must be magnificent if that's the one he left behind."

Darien's attention moved to the empty doorway as if he still saw Eventide standing there. "Emelia is as plain as snow," he said. "But Evie… She's like the sun. Glorious."

There was something in his tone that caused Aurelius to look at him curiously. Before he could say anything, however, Lares was suddenly in the doorway.

"Ah," he said. "Here ye are. Stevan, get up!"

Estevan was snoring his head off, and Lares charged into the chamber, kicking his son's booted feet. That had Estevan startling himself right off the chest as Lares turned to Aurelius and Darien.

"'Tis war," he said quietly. "Fergus and I have decided that Reelig Cannich must pay for his son's actions. Our honor is at stake, lads. We ride for Moy Castle."

Estevan picked himself off the floor, rubbing his eyes, as his older brothers faced their father. "Now?" Aurelius said, surprised. "But we need men. Ye only brought twenty men with ye, Da, and I brought about the same. We cannot lay siege tae Moy with forty men."

"It willna be forty men," Lares said, looking at Estevan. "Stevan, ye'll ride back to the Hydra and gather the men. Call them in from the Highlands. We'll need as many as ye can muster in a day because I want ye tae return tae Blackrock within the week."

Aurelius and Darien glanced at each other in concern. "Da, if ye wait, Cannich will have time tae fortify his position," Darien said. "Do ye truly think he doesn't know we're coming? Why do ye think he went home this morning?"

Lares frowned. "It canna be helped," he said. "The man deserves what's coming tae him. He's wronged both Fergus and me."

"Agreed," Darien said. "But it will take too much time tae summon men from the Hydra. Ye'd do better tae seek men from Foulis Castle."

Lares looked at him sharply. "Padraig Munro?" he said. "Foulis is a half-day's ride from here."

"And he's allied with MacKenzie, as we are," Darien said. "Old Padraig can bring ye a thousand lads tae overrun Moy."

Lares had a gleam in his eye as he considered the possibility. "Padraig's mother and my mother were cousins," he said. "The man is kin."

"Aye, he is. And he likes a good fight."

That made Lares' decision for him. He turned to Estevan once again. "Ride for Foulis," he said. "Tell Padraig what has happened and request men. We have a man tae punish."

Estevan nodded, glancing at his brothers before he quit the chamber. He was an excellent fighter, but more the diplomatic type—he would rather find a peaceful resolution and fight as a last resort—but could see that Lares was determined to punish Reelig.

Not that he really blamed him.

With Estevan on the move, Lares turned to Aurelius. "Yer mother and sisters and the rest of yer brothers should be here by tomorrow," he said. "Ride out tae find them and turn them back for the Hydra. If there is tae be battle, I dunna want them here."

Aurelius scratched his head. "Ye know that Mother will want tae come," he said. "I canna keep her away if she doesn't want tae turn away."

Lares sighed heavily. "Yer mother is the light of my soul, but she's a stubborn woman," he said. "Do what ye can, Aurelius. Try tae turn her back."

Aurelius knew that was impossible, but he tended to agree with his father. He didn't want his mother and sisters at a castle involved in military action. As Aurelius headed out to find his mother's incoming party, Darien looked at his father.

"Once ye capture Moy, then what?" he asked. "And what if Fergus' men find Cannich and drag him back here tae face his sins?"

Lares caught sight of the ale and went to pour himself a measure. "One of Fergus' men has returned tae say they combed Inverness and couldna find them," he said. "They're moving on tae Glasgow."

Darien watched his father drain nearly half the pitcher, debating whether or not to speak up. There was much on his mind, much he hadn't spoken of to his father, but they were alone now.

No time like the present.

"What's the purpose of bringing them back?" he asked quietly. "I willna marry her, Da. I'll not marry Cannich's leavings."

Lares didn't seem particularly surprised by that statement. "She's yer bride, lad," he said. "Legally and by God, she belongs tae ye."

"I dunna want her," Darien said. "I never wanted her. It was bad enough tae agree tae the marriage when we'd all heard the rumors about her. Like Cannich, we knew she had a wandering eye."

"She's rich," Lares said flatly, looking at his son as if daring him to argue with that. "She's very rich, and when Fergus passes on, ye'll inherit Blackrock, her herds, and the title. Ye'll be Laird Shandwick."

"I dunna want it," Darien said calmly. "Not if I have tae marry Emelia tae get it."

Lares sighed heavily. He wasn't exactly rising to the argument, but he wanted his son to think about the situation more logically than he was. "Do ye not understand that I'm doing the best I can for ye?" he said. "Dee, ye'll not inherit anything from me. It all goes to Aurelius. I'm trying tae bring you a fortune and a title, lad. I'm sorry it has tae be with the likes of Emelia, but it will be an important alliance. And ye'll have a title and respect. Do ye not want that?"

Darien grunted unhappily and turned away. "The cost is too high," he said, letting some emotion slide through. "Did ye stop tae think that I may want a marriage with a woman I like? Ye married for love. So did Bear. Now I'm not allowed tae?"

Lares went to his son, putting a gentle hand on his shoulder. "We all hope tae marry for love," he said quietly. "But the truth is that it rarely happens. Emelia may not be the perfect prospect, but she brings a great deal with her. A man can overlook quite a bit with such a fortune."

Darien looked at him, frowning. "And how much respect for myself do I have if I marry a woman who has run from me?" he said. "She's shamed me, Da."

"Fergus willna break the betrothal," Lares said, divulging what he'd been trying to hold off telling him. During his argument with the man, Fergus had made that clear. "He will bring her back and ye'll marry her. We'll lay siege tae Moy Castle and it will belong tae ye. Ye'll have a massive amount of property, Darien. Two castles and land that will take you an entire day to reach one end of it? Ye'll have tae take comfort in that, because Fergus willna let ye escape the betrothal. The woman is yers whether or not ye want her."

Darien stared at him a moment before closing his eyes as if to ward off the reality of the situation. He turned away, unable to reply, but he didn't have to. Lares could feel his disappointment and disgust.

"Take heart, lad," he murmured. "And mayhap ye'll grow tae like her. If ye try. If not… if not, then spend your time away from her and count yer money. Lose yerself in Robbie's court and never come home. Life is what ye make of it, Dee. Ye can either spend yer life miserable… or not."

With that, he turned back to the food while Darien sat heavily in the nearest chair.

Wishing the earth would open up and swallow him.

CHAPTER THREE

"YE MUST PUNISH the whole family. What that lad has done tae humiliate us is unforgivable!"

The cry came from Athole Moriston.

It was a sorrowful scene in the bower belonging to Lady Shandwick, the Lady of Blackrock, a chamber crammed to the rafters with possessions, useful or otherwise, because Athole had made it so. She bought things she needed and things she didn't, collecting them simply because she wanted them. It was a sickness, some thought, but no one ever questioned her hoarding habits, least of all her husband. It kept the woman out of his hair, a woman who was sick or feeling unwell or being dramatic every day of her life because she wanted to be the center of attention. That was simply Athole's way.

Something Emelia and Eventide had grown up with.

Eventide never gave her mother's propensity toward spells or fits any credence. She hadn't since she'd been a girl. But today, she couldn't blame her mother for being upset about Emelia. In fact, she had come to see to her mother to make sure the woman wasn't about to hang herself from the rafters, but she ended up sitting in a corner of the cluttered chamber while her mother sobbed into a kerchief and her father spoke of going to battle. Everyone was handling Emelia's departure differently.

Fergus wanted to start a war because of it.

Now, it was a matter of family honor.

"I agree that we have been humiliated," Fergus said steadily. "And we'll have our vengeance. Lares will bring his army and his big sons and we'll raze Moy in a day, Atha. Rest assured."

Atha. The tender nickname he used for his wife, who seemed to perk up at the very mention of vengeance. "Good," she said, nodding furiously. "'Tis good to hear that ye will avenge our daughter. My poor Emelia. Where did he take her?"

She was off again, weeping over her missing daughter, and Fergus was showing signs of deteriorating along with her. He'd been strong all morning, in the face of the news and in the face of an angry Lares, but watching Athole go to pieces was wearing on him. He'd avoided actually thinking of what Emelia must be suffering, but now...

Now, he was thinking.

And he didn't like it.

"I have men searching for her," he said to soothe his wife. "I'm sure Luke dinna hurt her. Why should he? He's no reason tae. They've run off and are probably hiding somewhere, warm and safe. But we'll find her, Atha. I promise we'll find her."

In the shadows, Eventide was watching her father console her mother. It only fed her disgust for her sister's actions. Emelia was causing a very big problem, something that was trickling over to people who hadn't done anything to deserve it.

Like the Cannich clan.

"What about Reelig and his family?" she asked, no longer able to remain silent. "*They* dinna do this, Pa. Luke did. So ye'll take their home and possibly even their lives for the sins of one man?"

Fergus looked at her. "They raised a poor son."

"And ye raised a poor daughter." When Fergus' eyebrows shot up in outrage, Eventide came off the stool. "Papa, ye know I'm right. Ye know that Emelia chases any man she pleases and behaves like a dog in heat. She's done it ever since she grew breasts, and ye never did a thing tae stop her. All ye did was punish the men she preyed upon, and that has tae stop."

The mention of breasts and his failure to acknowledge his daughter's behavior had Fergus flustered with embarrassment. "Ye'll not speak that way about yer sister," he scolded. "I know ye're upset, Evie, and ye have every right tae be, but—"

"But *nothing*," Eventide said, furious that, once again, her father was defending her errant sister. "There is nothing ye can say about this because Emelia has no defense, and ye know it. If I had my guess, I'd say she convinced Luke tae run away with her, not the other way around. But still, ye'd punish him and his family? 'Tis not right, I say. If anything, the dun Tarh family should be laying siege tae Blackrock for what Emelia has done. *We* should be punished!"

"Evie!" Athole gasped. "Still yer tongue, girl. Ye'll not speak tae yer father like that."

Eventide rolled her eyes at her mother. "'Tis yer fault as much as his," he said. "Ye coddled and spoiled Emelia until she was drunk with the knowledge that she could do anything and ye wouldna punish her. Whenever she and I would fight as children, it was always 'poor Emelia' and I was the one who felt yer wrath. Ye treated her like a queen and I was the pauper, and now ye're going tae punish others for *yer* lack of discipline when it came to Emelia. We're all paying the price for it."

Fergus went to the door and opened it. "Get out," he said

quietly. "I would speak tae yer mother alone."

Eventide didn't move right away. She moved her gaze between her parents, knowing that somehow, someway, they'd convince themselves that this wasn't their fault.

It happened all the time.

Frankly, she was disgusted by it.

"And, once again, ye refuse tae acknowledge ye have a whore for a daughter," she said, her tone like icy steel. "This has been going on for far too long."

"I told ye tae go."

Eventide started to move, but slowly. It was frustrating being the only person in her family with any sense of reason. "Did my mother tell ye that we took Emelia tae Inverness last year tae find a physic who would provide her with pennyroyal and birthwort?" she said, divulging something in the heat of anger she probably shouldn't have. "Do ye know what that's for, Pa?"

Athole let out a shriek as Fergus looked confused. "Eventide, ye promised ye'd never speak of it," Athole cried. "Get out! Get out before I take a stick tae ye!"

Eventide did. She left the room, knowing she'd planted a seed of bewilderment in her father's mind that her mother was going to have to explain. Athole would try to get around it, but in the end, she wouldn't be able to. She'd have to explain to her husband that her eldest daughter had been impregnated and didn't know who the father was.

Yet another one of Emelia's lies.

She'd told her mother she'd been raped, but Eventide knew that wasn't true. There was a particular man in the next village over, a man who had done business with Fergus, who had a cock the size of a stallion's, according to Emelia. The man was married, but Emelia had bedded him several times just because she liked the size of his manhood. He was more than likely the father. But Emelia had played to her mother's stupidity, and sympathies, and the situation was buried when the abortifacients had done their work.

Another thing that had been hidden from Darien dun Tarh.

It simply wasn't right, any of it, but Emelia was an heiress and her station in life seemed to erase all her sins. Eventide had kept her mouth shut about her sister and her many vulgar adventures, but there were things Fergus didn't know and probably should. The man should be fully aware of the kind of woman who was tasked with carrying on Blackrock's legacy.

A woman who had run off with her sister's betrothed.

Not that it mattered.

It never had.

ଓ

SOMETHING WAS MOVING next to him.

Still in Fergus' small solar in the keep, Darien had been sleeping in a chair. Head back, eyes closed, he was snoring louder than Estevan had been, only he refused to acknowledge it. It was always much more fun to tease Estevan about it because he grew so furious, so quickly. No one in their right mind would tease Darien because he tended to throw his fists around, and no one wanted to get hit by a hammer. But even in his sleep, his senses were alert, and when the body moving near him brushed his hand, he suddenly grabbed them.

The cup in his hand tumbled to the floor and a gasp of fear filled the chamber.

Darien found himself looking at Eventide. He'd grabbed her hand so hard that he thought he might have broken bones, so very quickly, he sat up and began rubbing her hand.

"Forgive me," he said. "I could hear ye but I dinna know who ye were. When ye touched me, I thought it might be a threat."

She smiled weakly. "I should have known better," she said. "I was coming down from my mother's bower and heard ye snoring. I—"

He cut her off, but in a jesting manner. "Stop right there," he said. "I dunna snore."

She fought off a grin. "Do ye call me a liar, then?"

"I dinna. I simply said I dunna snore."

Eventide tried not to chuckle. She began to look around the chamber. "Ye may be right," she said. "We have an enormous boar out in the kitchen yard, and it's possible I heard him, even through these stone walls."

"That must be it."

"Then I stand corrected."

He eyed her as he continued to rub her hand. "Well and good that ye realize it," he said. "Continue yer tale. Ye were coming down from yer mother's bower and…?"

Eventide had been focusing on his big hand as it rubbed her small one, something she could easily be swept away with, so it was a struggle to return to her train of thought. "And I saw ye sleeping," she said. "Ye had a cup in yer hand that was nearly falling tae the floor, so I went tae take it."

He grunted. "And it fell anyway, because I'm clumsy," he said, looking at the cup on the floor and the dregs it had spilled. But his focus shifted and he found himself looking at her hand. He stopped rubbing. "Better?"

She pulled the appendage away from him, gently. "Aye," she said. "Ye dinna have tae do that."

He sat back in the chair, smiling at her. "Of course I did," he said. "I nearly broke yer hand, lass. I am sorry for it."

She shook her head. "No need," she said. "But I thank ye just the same. Now, would ye not be more comfortable in a bed than in my father's chair?"

He leaned his head on the back of the chair. "I'm perfectly comfortable here," he said. "But I thank ye for yer concern."

She nodded. "Of course," she said. "Anything ye need, I'll move heaven and earth tae help ye."

"I appreciate it."

She smiled timidly, nodded, and headed for the chamber door. It felt like the conversation was over, at least for him, but she still had questions.

She wanted to know something.

"Is it true that ye are going tae battle?"

She uttered the question as she paused in the doorway, turning to look at Darien. He still had his head back on the chair, staring up at the ceiling.

"Is that what ye've been told?" he asked after a moment.

She nodded. "My father told me," she said. "Was it yer decision?"

Darien's head came up, and he looked at her. "My father and yer father made the decision," he said. "I was not consulted."

"But they did it for ye, did they not?"

He snorted and looked away. "They did it for themselves," he said in a low voice. "Tae save family pride. Tae punish Reelig Cannich for his son's actions."

"And ye dunna agree?"

He looked at her again. "It seems I'm not given a choice," he said. "Not surprising, considering I've not had a choice since this whole situation began."

"What situation?"

"The betrothal," he said. Then, realizing he might have said too much, he simply shrugged. "Everything. Even a man like me can have some decisions made for him by his father."

Eventide remained in the doorway, her hands clasped, but the more he spoke, the more nervous she seemed to become. By the time he was finished speaking, she was wringing her hands as she came back into the solar.

"Are ye telling me that yer betrothal tae my sister was not yer choice?" she asked.

He looked at her, wondering why she'd come so close to him. Not that he minded looking at those gorgeous blue eyes at close range, but she seemed uneasy.

"My father made the arrangements, just as yer father made the arrangements tae Cannich," he said. "That is what parents do. They ruin their children's lives in the name of alliances. Christ... I dinna mean to imply that the betrothal tae yer sister ruined my life, only that it was... unexpected. I'm sure yer sister has good qualities."

"Nay, she does not," Eventide suddenly said in a burst. When he looked at her in surprise, she realized she could no longer remain silent. Swiftly, she dropped to her knees beside the chair and gazed up at him beseechingly. "If ye truly wish tae marry her for the title and the money, then I cannot fault ye for that, but ye should know the kind of creature ye're marrying. God forgive me, m'laird, but if ye value yer sanity and life, then ye'll run. Ye'll run fast and far and refuse tae marry my sister if my father does manage tae bring her back. She'll ruin ye!"

He furrowed his brow, caught off guard by her swiftly uttered words. "What's this?" he said, reaching out to clasp her hands as they gripped the arm of the chair. "What are ye talking about, lass?"

Eventide drew in a deep, unsteady breath. "Emelia will seek tae ruin ye," she said. "I've known her all my life. She has no kindness, no compassion, no thoughtfulness. She only knows what she wants, and she'll walk over yer grave tae get it. She's had many lovers in the past, m'laird. She'll not go tae yer marriage bed a virgin, and, in fact, if she manages tae conceive, ye'll never know if the child is yers or someone else's. Ye seem like a fine man, Darien dun Tarh, so I am telling ye… dunna marry her. No matter what my father says, or what yer father says. Ye dunna deserve a woman like that. Ye'll never know a moment's peace."

With that, she quickly bolted to her feet and raced for the chamber door, but Darien leapt to his feet as well.

"Lady," he called, running up behind her. "Wait! Dunna go. Please."

He grasped her before she could get through the door, but she was in tears when he stopped her. He could see it. As he gently tried to pull her back into the chamber, she resisted.

"I canna say more," she said, sniffling. "I shouldna said what I did, but I canna stand by and watch her ruin ye. She's a viper, m'laird. She spreads her legs tae any man she has a fancy for."

Darien had her by both hands now, very carefully pulling her back into the chamber. "Dunna be afraid," he said. "I willna tell anyone what ye told me, least of all yer father. But ye're telling me that Emelia has been bedded by other men?"

Eventide nodded. "Aye," she said. "Ye can break the betrothal based on that alone. And ye canna go make war upon Moy Castle because I'm positive my sister seduced Luke. The family doesna deserve tae be punished."

He let go of one hand so she could wipe her face, but he was still pulling her into the chamber. "Come," he said in a soft, deep voice. "Sit down. Ye've worked yerself intae a state, lass, but there's no need."

It was true. She had. Eventide allowed Darien to lower her onto a chair next to her father's table while he took a knee beside her, holding her hand. His features were full of concern as he watched her struggle to compose herself.

"Of course there's a need." She sniffled, wiping her eyes. "I shouldna have told ye about my sister, but I simply couldna stand by and watch her ruin yer life. I've watched ye court her all this time, and ye've always been kind and understanding with her, but ye'd leave Blackrock and then she'd run off to bed one of my father's men. Everyone seemed tae know it but ye."

Darien was surprisingly calm. "That's not entirely true," he said. "We've known yer family for years. Our da and yer da are allies. We've heard the rumors."

Eventide stopped weeping and looked at him in surprise. "Then why did ye agree tae the betrothal?"

He sighed heavily. "Because my da seemed tae want it so badly," he said. "I have seven brothers, but only one inherits. The rest of us must gain our fortune or titles by marriage, so my father felt he was doing the right thing by me. Even though yer sister has run off, he still feels that way. He still wants me tae marry her when she's returned."

Eventide shook her head, her eyes wide. "Ye must tell him what I've told ye," she insisted. "But please dunna tell him it was me. He'll tell my da, and there will be trouble if he knows."

Darien regarded her a moment. "What do ye mean?"

"My father is not shy when it comes tae punishment."

"He willna beat ye, will he?"

She lowered her gaze. "He did when I was younger," she said honestly. "When Emelia and I would fight, I would always be blamed. My parents favor my sister, so in any squabble, I was always the troublemaker whether or not I really was. My mother would take a switch tae me. I've the scars tae prove it."

He was concerned. "She would not beat ye now, at yer age?"

"She'll probably send me tae a convent."

"Truly?"

"Aye," she said. "But I'm heading there already because if my sister is returned, that means Luke will return. And I'll refuse tae marry him, so away tae the convent I go."

Darien didn't like the sound of that at all. It had taken a good deal of courage for her to tell him about her sister, and he appreciated that immensely. He'd never really known Eventide except what he'd observed on a cursory level, and the short interactions he'd had with her from time to time, so today was his first real experience with her. She seemed desperate to do the right thing, to protect him against her sister. It could have been jealousy, but he didn't think so. As he'd told her, he'd heard the rumors about Emelia, enough to know that Eventide wasn't making them up. But more than anything, her information seemed to underscore what a horrific situation this was for him, so much so that the sister of the woman he was supposed to marry was telling him to run.

If only he could.

Trying not to feel despondent, he shifted, ending up on his bottom next to the chair, still holding her hand. After several long moments, he shook his head in bewilderment.

"It seems as if the two of us have quite a situation on our hands," he said.

Eventide wiped at the last of her tears. "It seems so," she said. "But ye see why ye canna go tae war against Cannich. The problem is much deeper than that."

He nodded. He'd moved from simply holding her hand to caressing her fingers absently, as if it was the most natural thing in the world. As if he'd been doing it all his life. A comfort level that he'd never let himself feel before, nor had Eventide.

An inherent feeling.

Warmth.

"It may be deeper, but yer da and mine are only seeing one facet of it," he said. "They are addressing the humiliation of Luke taking Emelia. Even if she took him, he will be blamed. His family will be blamed. Vengeance must be satisfied."

"Ye cannot stop it?"

Darien shook his head. "Nay."

"And if ye dunna go tae war?"

"Then it shames my father," he said. "As I said… this is quite a situation. A complicated one."

"What will ye do?"

He looked at her, gazing into eyes the color of a warm summer sky. The woman had such an ethereal quality to her that the more he looked at her, the more she took his breath away.

But those thoughts had no place in the situation they found themselves in.

It could only complicate things.

"I dunna know," he said quietly, squeezing her hand. "I suppose I have a good deal tae think on."

Eventide was prevented from replying when her father abruptly walked past the open solar door, caught sight of them inside, and quickly retraced his steps. Now standing in the doorway, he pointed at Darien sitting on the ground, holding Eventide's hand.

"What's this?" he said. "What's happened?"

Darien knew he'd been caught doing something he probably shouldn't have been doing—being just a little *too* familiar with his betrothed's sister. But he didn't panic. He stood up and gently released Eventide's hand.

"The lady was upset, m'laird," he said. "We were… commiserating. Since we are both suffering through the same situation, I thought I could give her some comfort."

Fergus believed him. He had no reason not to. He came into the solar, looking at his daughter with some concern, even though his original intent when he came downstairs was to find her and lecture her about her unkind words about his sister. But even Fergus knew the situation was taxing on them all. He was genuinely trying to be sympathetic.

"Then ye're kind tae do so," he said to Darien. "I know it is an imposition, but could I ask ye tae stay with Evie until she's feeling better? Today has been quite a shock for her. I dunna want her tae be alone tae fret on the course her future is taking."

"What course is that, Pa?" Eventide said as she looked up at him. "Darien's is taking the same course. We've been betrothed tae two selfish people who dunna care who they hurt."

So much for Fergus being sympathetic. His features hardened. "I willna listen tae ye speak ill of yer sister again," he said. "If ye canna be civil, then ye'll go tae yer chamber and stay there until every word out of your mouth is not some sort of condemnation for Emelia."

Eventide stood up. "She deserves it," she said strongly. "She deserves all that and more."

"Then go tae yer chamber until ye can behave yerself."

Eventide's jaw twitched with fury. She wagged a finger in her father's face. "If ye said that tae Emelia once in a while, mayhap we wouldna be in this predicament," she said. "Instead, ye bully me just like ye always do. *I'm* not the problem, Pa. I wish ye understood that."

With that, she stormed out of the solar, leaving Fergus embarrassed and Darien getting a picture of just how poorly Eventide was treated around here. He had seen it before, especially when Emelia was being cruel to her sister, but he was seeing it quite plainly now. In fact, he was coming to see everything at Blackrock a little differently since his conversation with Eventide. Fergus turned to face him.

"Ye must forgive the lass," he said, forcing a smile. "She's passionate about her feelings in the best of times. This has her casting blame where she shouldna."

Darien frowned. "She is casting it at Emelia," he said. "That is exactly where the blame *should* be. Unless Luke carried her out of here kicking and screaming—which everyone would have heard—then she went willingly."

Fergus' features tightened. "I see ye've been speaking tae Evie about her sister," he said. "Ye canna believe what she tells ye."

"Why not?"

"Because it's not true."

"Shall I go around and ask yer men about Emelia and get the truth about her, since you have tried to cover it up?"

Fergus' cheeks flushed with rage. "Darien, I know ye're upset, but I'll not listen tae ye slander my daughter."

Darien didn't rise to the man's anger. In fact, he seemed to cool, his dark eyes lingering on Fergus.

"Not tae worry," he said, turning for the solar door. "I'll

discover the truth for myself."

"I would suggest ye not stir up any trouble."

Darien paused by the door. "As Evie said," he muttered, "*I'm* not the one causing trouble around here. But there are things ye're hiding about Emelia, and unless ye're ready tae tell me the truth, I'll discover them for myself."

"Do it and I'll involve yer father."

"Good," Darien said. "I think he should be involved. I think he should know that he pledged his son to marry a woman who is rumored to be unchaste."

Fergus' jaw was flexing furiously now. "Did Evie tell ye that?"

"I think everyone but me knew that," he said. But then his eyes narrowed. "And if ye think tae punish Evie for what ye think she might have done, know that I'll not take kindly tae it. Leave her alone. She's been through enough."

"Ye canna tell me how tae discipline my daughter."

"I can and I will. Touch her and ye'll not like my response."

Fergus didn't have any more to say about that, mostly because they were at an impasse and he was on the verge of being humiliated by Emelia's betrothed. He'd avoided it so far, but now it was coming from an unexpected source.

And he knew Eventide was behind it.

He simply turned away, letting Darien leave the solar without another word. But once the man was out of the solar, Fergus made plans for his errant daughter.

Eventide was going to feel his wrath no matter what Darien said.

Chapter Four

Foulis Castle

"Estevan dun Tarh!"

The shout came from the direction of the keep just as Estevan dismounted his steed. It had been an easy ride to Foulis Castle, though it was approaching sunset, so he knew he'd be spending the night here. But it didn't matter. He hadn't seen Padraig or his sons in quite some time, and by the time he turned around, Padraig rammed into his belly with a shoulder, threw his arms around Estevan, and lifted him right off the ground.

It was like being smothered by a bear.

Estevan was a big man, so the fact that a man twice his age was lifting him off the ground was some feat, indeed. But the man's big shoulder was right in his gut, and he could hardly breathe as Padraig tossed him around joyfully.

"Christ, Padraig!" Estevan said, finally pushing off the man's head to break his grip. "Ye're going tae kill someone with that greeting."

Padraig wasn't deterred in the least. He laughed heartily, grabbing Estevan by the head and kissing his cheeks. Just when

Estevan managed to peel the old man off him, he was hit from all sides by two Munro sons, both of them delighted to see him.

"Estevan!" Calum Munro shouted in Estevan's ear as he threw his arms around him. "It's been years, lad! Where have ye been keeping yerself?"

Estevan was sandwiched between Calum and his younger brother, Guthrie. He simply stood there, suffering through their hugs and kisses, suffering through those hugs until he could hardly breathe. He was afraid they were going to break his arms the way they had him pinned, and then he'd be of no use to anyone.

"Lads," he muttered, his lips twisted because Calum was pinching his face. "If ye dunna let me go, ye're going tae break bones."

"We're simply glad tae see ye, Estevan," Calum said without moving his pinching fingers. "Are ye not glad tae see us, too?"

"Release me, ye fools, or I'll wipe the ground with ye."

That had Calum and Guthrie and Padraig laughing uproariously, but they did as Estevan asked and let him go. Grinning weakly, Estevan had to shake some feeling back into his arms before he could return Padraig's embrace.

"Ye're a ridiculous old man, Padraig Munro," he said. "If I dinna like ye so much, I'd light yer farts on fire and happily watch ye burn alive."

That only drew more laughter from Padraig. "Ye're a kind man, lad," he said. "Thank ye for sparing my life."

"Ye're welcome."

"Tae what do we owe the honor of yer visit?" Padraig said. "Ye dinna send word ahead. Why not?"

Estevan gestured toward the hall. "Feed me and I'll tell ye," he said. "I've come with news of a situation we need yer help with."

That wiped some of the humor off Padraig's face. "Oh?" he said. "Serious?"

"Serious enough."

"Is yer father well, laddie? That's all I care about."

"He's quite well."

"Good," Padraig said. "Then drink my ale and tell me all about it."

The old man had a solid grip on Estevan as he pulled him toward the hall of Foulis. It was a long, skinny hall with two access points, and once Estevan entered, he could see that it looked like a typical Scottish hall, with old rushes on the floor, dogs scattered about, and a firepit in the middle. Smoke escaped through vents in a roof that had enormous timbers spanning the ceiling.

As they neared the table on the far end of the hall, Padraig began shouting for food and drink. Male servants dropped what they were doing to comply, men who had been sweeping the hearth and repairing the legs of one of the tables, among other things. Estevan sat heavily, as it had been a fast ride from Blackrock, and removed his leather gloves.

"This place gives me comfort," he said.

Padraig sat across from him. "Why is that?"

Estevan looked at him, a twinkle in his eye. "Because it never changes," he said. "I find comfort in that. I remember coming here as a wee lad, and it seems tae me that it has hardly changed at all."

Padraig looked up at that soaring ceiling. "It was the same when I was a lad, too," he said. "It has been the same since the days of my father, Jamison, and probably well before that."

"Ah," Estevan said, "the Red Lion. The great Jamison Munro. I've seen my father weep only twice in his life, and one of those times was when he received word of Jamison's passing. He was quite fond of him."

Padraig smiled faintly. "As was I," he said. "I miss him."

"And yer mother?"

Padraig motioned in a southerly direction. "When my father passed, she returned tae Four Crosses Castle on the Welsh Marches. 'Tis where she was born, and she had a desire tae return, so she did. She's still there."

"Will she ever return tae Scotland?"

Padraig shrugged. "Who can say?" he said. "She and my father were very close. His death hit her quite hard. I think she plans tae return someday, but being here reminds her of him, and that is painful for her."

"Understandable."

Drink appeared along with trays of cheese and apples and bread. Padraig sat back, watching his sons grab at the food and Estevan pour himself a healthy measure of ale, before speaking.

"Now," he finally said, "what brings ye tae Foulis, Estevan? It must be something serious if ye've ridden all the way from England."

Estevan took a couple of gulps of the ale before replying. "Originally, I came for Darien's wedding," he said. "It is supposed tae be tomorrow."

"*Supposed* tae be?" Padraig said. "It sounds as if he's not getting married."

"He's not," Estevan said flatly. "His bride ran off with her sister's betrothed. That is why I've come."

Padraig looked at him in horror. Even Guthrie and Calum stopped shoving food in their mouths, looking at him in surprise.

"Darien's bride was abducted?" Padraig said in outrage. "By whom?"

Estevan shook his head. "'Tis not so easy as all that," he said. "It appears that the bride was a willing participant. She ran off with her sister's intended, a lad named Luke Cannich. His family lives at Moy Castle. Even now, her father has men out combing Inverness and roads south looking for the pair, but meanwhile, he and my father have decided that Clan Cannich should pay for the sins of their son. He's sent me tae ask ye for men to lay siege tae Moy Castle. The situation is a mess, Padraig. My father asks for yer help."

Padraig could hardly believe what he was hearing. "Who's the bride's father?"

"Fergus Moriston."

Calum and Guthrie started to snort and hiss as Padraig spoke. "Moriston," he muttered. "I know Fergus Moriston. The bride wouldna be Emelia, by any chance?"

Estevan looked at him, puzzled. "Aye," he said. "But how did ye know?"

Padraig was reluctant to say, but Calum wasn't. He answered without hesitation. "Because Emelia took a liking tae me some time ago," he said. "There's no easy way tae say this, Estevan, but there was no keeping Emelia out of my bed. I thought she was in love with me, but she wasn't. She simply wanted tae toy with me, a poppet tae cast aside when she grew weary. I asked for her hand but her father denied me. He had bigger game in mind."

Estevan groaned with realization, slapping a hand to his forehead. "Darien," he said—what they were all coming to figure out. "How long ago was this, Calum?"

"About a year."

"That was around the time she was betrothed tae Darien," Estevan said miserably. "But I dunna understand. Ye're the heir tae Foulis. Ye're a fine prize, Calum."

"But he's not a dun Tarh," Padraig said quietly, eyeing Estevan. "And Lares wants me tae help him punish the family of the man Emelia ran off with?"

Estevan had the distinct impression that Padraig was going to deny him. "Aye," he said softly. "That is his request."

Padraig didn't say anything. He lowered his gaze for a moment, pondering the request, before glancing at Calum, who was looking at his father expectantly.

"Well?" Calum said. "Of course ye're going tae lend yer support."

Padraig sighed heavily. "Calum…"

"Dunna be ridiculous," Calum said, waving his father off. "This is Lares who is asking. Ye support the man, do ye not? He's an old friend and ally. It doesn't matter *why* he needs assistance. What matters is that he does. And ye're going tae give it tae him."

Padraig listened to Calum's plea on Estevan's behalf. He wasn't surprised because Calum was loyal that way, but he also thought the man's heart had been broken by Emelia Moriston. Perhaps he'd been wrong about that. But there was no denying this was quite an awkward situation.

Still, Calum was correct about one thing—Lares was an old friend and ally, and Padraig would do anything for him.

Even lend the man his army in defense of a woman who'd broken his son's heart.

Or not.

"Aye, I am," he finally said before looking at Estevan. "How soon does Lares need the men?"

"As soon as possible. My da is out for blood."

"I can give ye about a thousand lads in the next couple of days."

"Thank ye," Estevan said sincerely, but he was eyeing Calum as he spoke. "It seems this is a strange situation for ye, Calum, and for that, I am sorry. I dinna know about ye and Emelia."

"I know," Calum said, waving him off. "Dunna be troubled. 'Twas bad enough what she did tae me, but tae run out on Darien is unforgivable. How is he taking the situation?"

Estevan was careful in his answer. "Shocked, like the rest of us," he said. Then he returned his attention to Padraig. "My da will be in yer debt for this."

Padraig was nodding even as he drained his cup. A stream of ale ended up running down his chin, and he wiped it away with his hand when he set the cup down.

"I'm glad tae do it," he said, but his focus turned to Guthrie. "Guth, I want ye tae send messengers out intae the hills tae summon the men. If we are tae leave in two days, then we must get the word out. Start the signal fires. We must prepare."

Guthrie was on his feet, heading out of the hall even as more food and ale was being brought in. The sun was going down and the feasting was about to commence for the inhabitants of Foulis as the castle closed up for the night.

For Estevan, he had what he'd come for.

Moy Castle would soon feel the wrath of a groom scorned.

CHAPTER FIVE

EVENTIDE WASN'T ENTIRELY sure she had ever seen so many men in one place.

Hundreds of Highlanders had arrived over the course of the past two days, ever since her sister had fled with Luke, and it was clear that her father and Lares were building an army to do what needed to be done against Clan Cannich.

It was like an army from hell.

Men in long tunics, dirty, with swords and spears and clubs, had been filing into Blackrock's ward to set up encampments so that on this cold and bright evening, the air smelled heavily of smoke and piss. All of those men relieving themselves in the bailey caused the ground to turn to mud, and the stench was enough to make her eyes water. She finally had to secure the oilcloths over her windows to keep out the smell. And no amount of begging her father to keep the men away from the living quarters had made a difference.

The men were there to stay.

Because these were unfamiliar men and some tended to be rough, Eventide remained in the keep, which was bolted from the inside, for her own safety. All of the female servants were in the keep as well. The only time they were allowed to go outside was to help with the evening meal, and they were moderately safe because the kitchen was tucked behind the keep, away from the bailey. But once their chores were finished, back into the keep they went for safety.

It was like living in a prison.

But something else was happening on this evening that was of note. Aurelius arrived just before sunset, riding escort with fifty or more Highlanders and a carriage built of iron and wood. News reached the keep that Darien's mother had arrived. As Eventide went to greet the guests, her mother saw her and ordered her back to her chamber. Eventide was forced to retreat as Athole assumed her chatelaine duties. Even though Aurelius had told his mother about the runaway bride and even tried to turn her back for home, she wouldn't budge. She was still coming, one way or the other. Therefore, Lady Torridon entered Blackrock's keep with great displeasure. Unable to handle the woman's foul mood, Athole was forced to send for her rebellious daughter.

Reinforcements were needed.

Eventide thought she would be assisting her mother, but that wasn't the case. The moment she entered the small solar, her mother pleaded illness and fled, leaving Eventide to deal with the displeased guests. Facing three women who were looking at her in various stages of curiosity and annoyance, Eventide smiled weakly.

"Welcome tae Blackrock Castle," she said. "Forgive my mother for her swift departure, but she's a weak soul and this situation has upset her terribly."

A woman with carefully coiffed, faded red hair tucked into an elaborate wimple fixed her with a gripping stare. "And you are, my lady?"

She had an English accent. Eventide faced her politely. "I am Eventide Moriston," she said. "I am the youngest daughter of Fergus and Athole. Emelia is my older sister."

"The one who ran away with yer betrothed," the youngest woman spoke up. She was young, perhaps thirteen or fourteen years of age, but she was quite a beauty already, with her mother's red hair and dark, flashing eyes. "My name is Zora. Darien is my older brother. And that's Lilliana, my sister."

She was pointing to an exquisite young woman who was perhaps ten or more years older than Zora. Lilliana dun Tarh had dark, silky hair and a delicate face, and when she stood up, Eventide could see that she was shorter and more petite than Zora was. She came straight to Eventide and reached out, taking her hand.

"Forgive Zora," she said in a sweet, sultry voice. "She is young and foolish. When we were told what happened, she imagined it to be some romantic adventure, but I understand that it is not. There is nothing romantic about losing a betrothed."

She spoke like her mother, with a cultured English accent. Regardless, Eventide wasn't sure what to say. "It was certainly unexpected," she said hesitantly. "I'm sorry ye had tae come all this way for nothing, but we'll do our best tae ensure yer comfort while ye're here."

"That would be appreciated," Lilliana said.

Not to be left out, Zora grasped Eventide's free hand. "Tell me about yer betrothed," she said. "Did he leave a note for ye? Or did he steal yer sister away without a word?"

"Zora," the older woman snapped softly. "Stop asking such inappropriate questions. Come over here and sit down and be quiet."

Zora sighed at her mother's command and let go of Eventide's hand, making her way back to the woman and dragging her feet the entire way. When she plopped down in a chair, head hanging, the older woman continued.

"I am Mabel dun Tarh, Lady Torridon," she said quietly. "Will you sit, my lady? I should like to hear what happened from you. I only have Aurelius' version of events, so please tell me why my son will not be marrying your sister. Your mother could not seem to explain it adequately."

Mabel dun Tarh. Eventide knew of the woman. She'd heard her parents speak of her, as Darien's mother. Something about ruling with an iron fist. She was certainly in control of her daughters and spoke in a way that made Eventide want to obey her as well. Promptly, she found a seat and faced the Countess of Torridon.

"This morning, we discovered my sister tae be missing, m'lady," she said. "Some of my father's men saw my betrothed, Luke Cannich, in Inverness and thought they saw my sister with him. With the two of them missing, we've come tae the conclusion that they ran off together."

Mabel was listening seriously. "And why would they do this?"

Eventide sighed. "Because both Luke and my sister are known tae have a wandering eye," she said. "Luke has the reputation of having many conquests, and so does my sister. If ye knew them, m'lady, then you would come tae the same conclusion we have. Somehow, my sister seduced Luke and convinced him tae take her away from here. She never liked Blackrock, anyway. Now she's found someone to give her the life she wants."

Mabel sat there for a few seconds, digesting what she'd been told. The wheels of thought were turning in her mind. When the wait began to grow awkward, she finally turned to Lilliana.

"Take Zora and go outside the door," she said, pointing to the panel. "Close the door and stand there. Do not leave. Do not try to listen in. Do you understand me?"

Lilliana nodded and went to grab the hand of Zora, who didn't want to leave the chamber. She had the curiosity of a cat and didn't like the fact that a conversation was going to go on without her. But Lilliana managed to get her out of the chamber and shut the door. Once the panel was closed, Mabel spoke.

"I want to understand something clearly," she said quietly. "You said your sister has had many conquests?"

"Aye, m'lady," Eventide replied.

"What do you mean by that?"

"I mean that she's no stranger tae a man's bed, m'lady."

Mabel's eyes narrowed. "That's what I thought you meant," she said. "And your father was aware of this?"

Eventide nodded. "Aye, m'lady," she said. "He is well aware, as is my mother."

"I see," Mabel said calmly, but if the fire in her eyes was any indication, the calm demeanor was only on the outside. Something big was stirring inside of her. "And you are telling me this not out of spite, are you? Because your sister fled with your betrothed?"

Eventide shook her head. "I am telling you because it is the truth, m'lady," she said. "I never wanted tae marry Luke Cannich, so I suppose my sister did me a favor. But I dunna like what she's done to Darien. He dinna deserve such disrespect and humiliation."

It was clear that Mabel was lost in her own thoughts and

opinions, but she managed to nod her head. "Nay, he did not," she said. "Do you know where he is?"

"I can fetch him for ye, m'lady."

"Please do," she said. "My husband, too."

Eventide stood up, opening the door to Lilliana and Zora, who were standing right outside as their mother had instructed. As the two younger women entered the chamber, Eventide spoke directly to Mabel.

"Please dunna stray from this chamber for now, m'lady," she said. "There are a thousand men in the ward, and the women are instructed tae remain in the keep tae stay out of their way. I'll send servants in with food and drink."

Mabel nodded. "Thank you, my lady."

Eventide shut the door, scurrying to the entry door, which had been bolted after Lady Torridon and her daughters entered. After throwing the two big iron bolts, she pulled the panel open as it creaked back on its hinges. The door was so old that even the wood creaked. In front of her lay the ward, full of men camping out, and the stench of human habitation caused her to pinch her nose. She kept an eye out for Darien or even Aurelius, but there was no sign of them.

Just a sea of men.

Against her better judgment, she left the keep and went in search of them.

The sun's warm rays illuminated her way as she made her way toward the stables. She wasn't sure where to look, so she thought she'd try the stables, since there were dozens of horses there, including Darien's, so it was a place to start.

Off to her left was the kitchen yard, and she could see the cook and a couple of the female servants working swiftly. A few of her father's men were in there with them, presumably as protection. Since Blackrock hadn't seen action in years, they hadn't had the burden of an unfamiliar army, even if they were allies, so the entire experience was a new one for them. Were they being overly cautious about protecting the women? Possibly.

Possibly not.

Because of all the animals in and around the stables now, the ground was muddy with water and urine. Eventide was wearing sturdy boots, the only pair of shoes she had other than some soft leather slippers her mother had given her, and she didn't particularly want to soil them. Someone had spread grass and old rushes on the path leading into the stable to combat the mud, so she scurried over to the entryway, noting there were men inside the stable. It was relatively dark inside, so she had to enter in order to see who it was.

Immediately, she could see that it wasn't anyone she knew. They hadn't seen her, so she quickly turned around and headed for the door. But somewhere behind her, someone was shouting.

"Lass! Where are ye going?"

Eventide kept walking. "I am looking for my father."

"Who's yer father?"

"Fergus Moriston."

She was nearly to the stable door when someone grabbed her by the hand and yanked her back into the depths.

"Ye must be old Fergus' daughter," the man said seductively, shoving her back against the stable wall. "I've heard about ye, lass. Have ye come looking for another conquest? I'll make it simple for ye."

He smelled of filth and mildew because the woolen tunic he wore was damp. Eventide didn't even get a look at his face. She didn't want to. But he was tall, because her face was nearly pressed into his chest as she tried to pull away.

"Let me go," she demanded. "Do it now and I'll not tell my father ye grabbed me."

The man loosened his grip but didn't let her go completely. He simply stood back a little and looked her over. "Ye're a beauty," he said. "Turn around and let me see the back of ye."

Eventide yanked her hand away from him, daring to gaze up into his features. He was young, and not unhandsome, but she wanted no part of him.

"I'm not a mare tae be inspected," she said, trying to move around him. "Get out of my way."

He blocked her path. "Ye have fire," he said. "I like that. And I know lads who have tasted that fire, so why do ye refuse me? I've heard ye like a good time. I'll give ye one."

It began to occur to Eventide what he meant. *Who* he meant.

Emelia!

The woman's loose morals were no secret locally, but now her reputation had evidently spread. Clearly, this young buck wanted a piece of her, and if she hadn't been so frightened, Eventide would have been furious.

"I'm the *other* sister," she said frankly. "Look around ye, lad. Do ye see all of these men here? They're going tae battle because the sister ye're looking for, the one ye've heard of, has caused the trouble. Now, get out of my way. I'll not tell ye again."

Realization flickered over his features. "Who is yer sister?"

"Who did ye think I was?"

"Fergus Moriston's daughter."

"He has *two* daughters," Eventide said. "I'm the younger daughter. Emelia is the eldest."

"Emelia," he said as if he recognized the name. "I think I heard that her name was Amy."

Eventide shook her head. "Emelia," she repeated. "And she's the one who has caused all of this mess, so go about yer business and leave me alone."

He was back to smiling seductively at her. "One sister is as good as the next," he said, reaching out and trying to grasp her again. "Dunna be afraid of me, lass. I'll not hurt ye."

Eventide was trying to stay out of his range. "Ye'll not touch me," she spat. "Get out of my way, I said. If ye dunna, I'll scream and everyone will come running."

Clearly, he didn't believe her. He suddenly moved toward her, and Eventide pealed off a piercing scream before he grabbed her and tried to kiss her. Panicking, she managed to get one hand free before he threw her into a bear hug. She shoved a finger into his eye. That had the desired effect, because he howled and released her, but only briefly. As she tried to run, he grabbed her by her hair and she screamed again, throwing her fists as he tried to trap her arms.

Somehow in the process, he managed to pierce her lip with his tooth, or perhaps her tooth. Eventide wasn't certain, but she could taste blood. She could also taste more fear than she had ever known. He was closing in on her, trying to cover her mouth with his, and because he had a good grip on her head, she couldn't avoid him. But she could bite, and she did, clamping his lip as hard as she could until he roared with pain and released her. But the moment she tried to run, he cuffed her on the side of the head.

Down she went.

Dazed from the blow, Eventide was helpless when he fell on top of her and began fumbling with her bodice.

"Ye'll be sorry ye did that," he growled. "This could have been pleasant for us both, but now ye'll simply have tae let me have my way with ye."

Eventide screamed again, but he slapped a hand over her mouth. She could feel him grabbing at her dress, trying to tear it off her. But that all ended when he suddenly lurched, his full weight collapsing on her, and his hand fell away from her mouth. Eventide drew in a ragged, panicked breath, trying to move out from underneath him, but someone dragged him off her. As she scrambled to get away, she could hear a voice in the dimness.

"Easy, Evie." It was Darien. "Easy, lass. Did he hurt ye?"

She was on her knees, nearly digging through a wall to escape, but Darien's soft, concerned voice had her quickly pausing. She turned to look at him, seeing that he was close but hadn't touched her. She was panicked enough without him grabbing for her, and he knew it. In a heap several feet away lay the man who had attacked her.

He had blood coming out of his ears and nose.

Eventide burst into terrified tears.

"Nay," she sobbed. "He... he dinna hurt me. But he tried."

Darien knelt down in front of her, reaching out to gently cup her face. "Ye've got blood on yer mouth," he said. "Did he strike ye?"

She was weeping uncontrollably. "Aye," she said. "He thought I was Emelia. He said he'd heard about me and wanted... He said if I wanted another conquest, he'd make it easy for me."

Darien grunted in disgust. He glanced at the man he'd brained with the butt of his sword, but Eventide's sobbing had his attention. She was absolutely terrified. As a man with great empathy that he usually kept buried, he found that he couldn't hide it when it came to Eventide. He could feel her fear. Not knowing what else to do, he carefully pulled her into his embrace and held her as she wept.

"He'll not trouble ye again, I promise," he said, his big hand in her hair, holding her head against his chest as his arms held her tightly. "Are ye sure he dinna hurt ye?"

Eventide was pressed up against him, quivering. "Nay," she said. "But had ye not come when ye did, he would have."

"I came because I heard ye scream," he said. "I was over by the smithy's stall. I thought it might have been a horse in distress at first, but I heard ye a second time, so I came tae see what it was. What are ye doing out here?"

Eventide was clutching him, gripping his tunic, and she wasn't even aware of it. She was simply clinging to safety, and that safety happened to be Darien at the moment.

"Yer mother is in the keep and wants tae speak with yer father," she said, finally lifting her head to look at him. "She asked if I would send for him."

"But why not send a servant?"

"Because I couldna find one. They're all busy."

That was true. Blackrock was a hive of activity at the moment. Realizing she had ventured out because his mother wanted to speak with his father didn't sit well with him.

"My mother could have waited," he said, frowning. "She dinna have tae send ye out into a sea of men tae look for my da."

"She dinna send me out intae a sea of men," Eventide said, finally loosening her grip on him so she could wipe her nose. "She simply asked me tae send for yer da."

"Did ye at least tell her ye were forbidden tae wander the

ward?"

"Of course not," she said. "She seems unhappy as it is. I dinna want tae irritate her further."

He lifted a dark eyebrow. "Irritated, is she?" He shook his head. "We'll see about that."

Taking her by the hand and leaving the Highlander he'd clobbered still lying in a heap, Darien led her out of the stable and toward the keep. There were men everywhere, some paying attention to him and some not, and he kept a protective grip on Eventide because most attention was on her. She was hard to miss with that mass of glorious red hair. He took her all the way up the old stone steps that led into the keep, and when he asked where his mother might be, she pointed at the closed solar door.

With more force than necessary, he threw open the door.

Lilliana and Zora gasped as the door smacked back against the wall. Mabel sat up straight, her eyes wide at Darien, who was still holding on to Eventide. He pulled her forward, however, so his mother could see the blood smear on the corner of her mouth.

"Mother," he said through clenched teeth. "I want you to see what yer demands tae see Father have cost Eventide."

Horrified, Mabel stood up and went to her. "What happened?" she asked.

Darien was genuinely trying to keep his temper in check. "Ye know that there are a thousand Highlanders outside," he said. "That is why ye and Zora and Lilli are in here—tae keep ye safe from them."

Mabel inspected Eventide's cut lip. "I know," she said, eyeing him. "What is your point?"

Darien was forced to let go of Eventide's hand because Mabel was directing the woman into a chair. "My point is that due tae yer impatience, ye sent this lass out intae a field of men, one of whom attacked her," he said. "Ye know that Da would return tae ye at some point, but ye couldna wait for that, so ye would jeopardize Evie's life just tae have yer wants fulfilled?"

Mabel stiffened. "I did no such thing," she said. "At least, not knowingly. I asked to have your father summoned. I did not tell her to go out into the ward looking for him."

Darien's eyes narrowed. "She's yer hostess," he said. "Of course she's going tae do yer bidding tae ensure it is done."

"But—"

He cut her off. "There were no more servants in the keep," he said. "Rather than disappoint ye, as her guest, she took it upon herself tae carry our yer wish. And she was attacked for it. So I've come tae tell ye not tae do that again, not while we have a thousand unfamiliar men in the ward. I'll send Da tae ye, but ye could have waited. Ye *should* have waited. There is nothing so important that it could not have waited."

Surprisingly, Mabel didn't snap back. Her gaze moved from her son to Eventide with a most regretful expression.

"It was not my intention to put you in danger, my lady," she said quietly. "I am truly sorry if you were injured. I hope you will allow me to tend you."

Eventide wasn't so sure about a guest taking the role of helping her. "It would be ill-mannered for me tae allow it," she said, smiling weakly. "Ye're our guest, after all. I truly dinna think anything would happen if I remained away from the ward, but someone mistook me for my sister. It happened quickly."

That brought Mabel's attention back to Darien. "The sister," she hissed. "That is why I wished to speak with your father. Were you aware of Lady Emelia's reputation when your father betrothed the two of you?"

Darien was coming to understand why his mother had sent for his father. Clearly, someone had told her something beyond the polite overview of the situation, which was Emelia fleeing with her sister's betrothed. In fact, Aurelius had been as ambiguous as he could be when he told his mother what had happened, knowing how upset she would be. But Mabel, true to form, had done some digging on the absent bride.

And she was livid.

"I was aware of her reputation," Darien said after a moment. "But if ye want tae know if Da was, ye'll have tae ask him."

That didn't ease Mabel in the least. "Rest assured that I will," she said sternly. "But you… you knew, yet you did not refuse this marriage?"

Darien's irritation at his mother was easing a little. "What could I say?" he said. "Tae refuse would be tae shame him. And I am not in the habit of shaming my da."

Mabel shook her head in disgust. "He shall hear about it from me, then," she said. "I cannot believe he would pledge you to a woman with a less-than-savory reputation."

"Dunna be too angry with him," Darien said, an odd stance considering how angry he had been at his father, too. "I'm a second son. I willna inherit. He was trying tae secure me a future and a fortune."

Mabel knew that. "But a woman like *that*?"

Darien sighed sharply. "Mam, he has seven sons tae provide for," he said. "Not every marriage is going tae be perfect. Not everyone can have what you and Da have, so just… leave him alone. He was only doing what he felt best."

She regarded him carefully. "You are defending him."

He averted his gaze. "I've already told him that if they manage tae bring her back, I'll not marry her," he said. "We've had our words about it, but I willna change my mind."

Mabel showed visible relief. "Good," she said. "At least I will be able to sleep tonight knowing that. But now I hear you are going off to war to punish the family of the man your bride ran away with?"

Darien held up his hands in a gesture of surrender. "That was decided by Da and Fergus Moriston, so dunna lecture me over it," he said. "As I told Da, the man did me a favor by ensuring I would not marry Emelia, so I genuinely have no quarrel with him. But Da says that I am shamed, as is Fergus, so the men gathered in the ward are the army that will raze Moy Castle in the name of vengeance."

Mabel wasn't happy. "That's what your brother said, more or less."

"Speaking of brothers, I've seen the rest of the lads outside," Darien said, changing the subject because he didn't want to get into a verbal tussle with his mother more than he already had. "I should go to them, but I came tae tell ye not tae send any more women outside. Evie was lucky that I heard her when I did."

As he'd hoped, Mabel's attention shifted back to Eventide, still sitting in the chair and looking at both of them with big, concerned eyes.

Mabel forced a smile.

"And I'll take good care of her," she said, reaching out to put a gentle hand on Eventide's head. "Darien, will you send a male servant to me, please? I need things, and since no women should venture outside the keep, I'll need a man to do it."

Darien's gaze was fixed on Eventide even as he answered his

mother. "Aye," he said, but he went to Eventide and took her soft hand in his. "I am glad ye weren't terribly hurt. My mother will take good care of ye now."

Eventide simply nodded, watching him kiss her fingers and give her an encouraging smile before he quit the chamber. She remained in the chair, her thoughts lingering on Darien even as a male servant appeared and Lady Mabel took charge of the situation. The woman knew exactly what to do and how to do it, and Lilliana and Zora jumped at their mother's bidding. When it should have been Eventide tending to her guests, circumstances saw the guests become the caregivers. She still wasn't entirely sure how she felt about that, but she did know one thing—

Darien dun Tarh was heavy in her thoughts, no matter how much she tried to shake him.

Perhaps she wasn't trying very hard.

Perhaps she didn't want to.

CHAPTER SIX

THEY DIDN'T PUT up much of a fight.

Moy Castle, a squat and fortified bastion with walls several feet thick and a broad, short pele-tower keep in the center, didn't have any men guarding it when the Munro and dun Tarh and Moriston army arrived. In fact, it seemed as if the castle was vacant, which spooked the men. *Ghosts,* they said. It had been Darien, Aurelius, Estevan, and younger brother Kaladin who thundered into the ward to seek out any men that might be hiding.

They found them.

There were several outbuildings on the eastern side of the ward that contained a few dozen men, who came charging out the moment Kaladin put his hand on the door latch to open up their hiding place. Kaladin, the brother known as "Baby Bull" because he was big and fearless—and, at times, reckless—had nearly been trampled when the tide of Scotsmen rushed him and knocked him down. Had it not been for Estevan, who fought off the horde so Kaladin could get to his feet, the young man might have very well been smashed into the muddy earth.

After that, it was a short-lived fight. The remaining Cannich men were savage in their fighting, but they were wildly outnumbered. Aurelius and Darien were in the middle of it, with Aurelius commanding the battle inside the ward. Since it was tradition in the dun Tarh family that the eldest son be fully knighted, Aurelius was the only true knight in the entire battle, even though all of the brothers had been trained in the English fashion. They fought like knights and they mostly dressed like knights, but against Highlanders who used different weapons from mounted English knights, that could be dangerous.

This case was no exception.

The Cannich men had spears and clubs. The spears were longer than the reach of the broadswords that the dun Tarh men used. Since all of the brothers were in attendance—Aurelius, Darien, Estevan, Caelus, Kaladin, Lucan, and Leandro, with Cruz, the youngest brother, occupied with squire duties—there were seven very big, English-dressed warriors in the heat of the battle.

Lucan and Leandro, who had only recently been permitted to fight in full English form, tended to be the most aggressive and were early in the fight, but a Highlander managed to clobber Leandro's left knee with a spiked club. He bled profusely, not knowing how bad the damage was until Aurelius ordered them all off their horses because the Cannich men had brought out at least two crossbows, one of which barely missed Caelus. On mounts as they were, they made big targets, so they came off their steeds, and Leandro could hardly walk with his smashed knee. That had his father pulling him out of the fight to keep company with Cruz, which thoroughly enraged Leandro because he'd only been fighting like a knight, in full regalia, for about six months.

The younger dun Tarh lads had fragile egos.

But the truth was that the fifty or so men they'd caught hiding couldn't last long against the thousand men that had come to raze their castle, so the battle ended in less than an hour. The Cannich men put up a good fight, but in the end, they were simply outmanned. That had the bulk of the army moving into the immense ward of Moy, cheering the fall of the castle and raiding it for anything they could get their hands on. Though the castle seemed rather run-down, any clothing, food, weapons, or tools were taken by the victorious troops.

The dun Tarh men stood on the stone steps of the keep, watching it happen.

"Have they made it intae the keep yet?" Lares asked.

Aurelius shook his head. "Nay," he said. "We managed tae seal it before they started their raid."

"Everything in it goes tae Darien. Do ye understand?"

He said it to all of his sons, who nodded their heads. All but Darien. He looked behind him at the very strong, compact keep that was only two stories in height, and the stone steps led to the second floor.

"They knew we were coming," he said. "I'd wager that Cannich took everything he could carry. I doubt there's much left in the keep."

"Doesna matter," Lares said. "It belongs tae ye. So does the castle. Small comfort for a stolen bride, but when she's returned, the two of ye can live here. 'Twill be yer home."

Aurelius cast a long look at his brother, who was still looking at the keep. Knowing Darien's position on the betrothal, and the bride, he waited for the response and prepared to put himself between his brother and father if things got heated.

Darien's response wasn't long in coming.

"I told ye, I willna marry her," Darien said, finally turning to look at his father. "I told ye I was not fully supportive of laying siege tae Moy Castle. Ye've known my position all along, but still, ye lay siege tae a castle I dinna want and try tae shove that whore and this betrothal down my throat. When I speak, do ye not listen?"

Those were fighting words, and a shock to the younger brothers, who hadn't been privy to any of this prior. Aurelius caught Estevan's eye and discreetly tilted his head in the direction of their brothers, silently telling the man to clear them out. Estevan was already one step ahead of him, pushing Caelus, the Baby Bull, and the rest of them down the steps, telling them to start clearing all the outbuildings and making sure there was no one, or nothing, left. That gave them something to do as Darien squared off with Lares.

And it wasn't going to be pretty.

"Mayhap I dunna listen tae ye when ye speak tae me with such disrespect," Lares said, flexing his jaw with irritation. "And I certainly dunna expect ye tae speak like that in front of yer brothers."

"Then listen tae me," Darien snapped, stamping a big foot. "I dunna want this castle. I dunna want Moriston's daughter. I've got a life waiting for me in Edinburgh with Robbie and his court, so I willna let ye force me intae this marriage. I was willing tae in the beginning, but no more. I willna marry a woman with a reputation like that."

Lares began clenching his fists. "Her father willna break the betrothal," he said. "I told ye that. I've told ye all of this."

Darien didn't care. "I wonder what Mother will think of this?" he said. "She knows about Emelia's reputation. Yesterday, she sent Evie tae summon ye about it, but Evie had a mishap and Mother forgot tae ask you what you knew. But if ye insist on this, I'll pull her intae the situation and we'll see what she has tae say about her son marrying a whore."

Lares flinched in Darien's direction, but Aurelius was there, putting his hands on his father's chest to keep him at bay. "Dunna do something in anger ye'll regret," he said in a low voice. "But ye know he's right, Da."

Lares looked at Aurelius, stricken. "Now ye side with him?"

Aurelius nodded. "In this case, I must," he said. "While I realize ye were trying tae gain lands and a title for Darien, ye took the woman that no one else wanted tae marry because they knew of her reputation. That's why Fergus agreed tae a betrothal so quickly. That's why he's willing tae give Darien everything he owns and then some. He thought he'd never offload that used sow of a daughter."

Infuriated, Lares pulled away from his eldest son, eyeing Aurelius and Darien with a great deal of hostility.

Unfortunately, he knew he was cornered.

He trusted Aurelius and Darien. They'd never given him bad advice. Darien was a wise soul, a man who was part of the Scottish royal court as an advisor, a counselor. There was great turbulence these days, something men like Darien were trying to keep control of. There was a great deal of pressure on him. But as Lares had told him, he was trying to broker an advantageous marriage for him, one commensurate with his position at court. Fergus Moriston, Lord Shadwick, was a man with land and wealth. That was all Lares had been focused on. Because of it, however, he'd ignored the rumors about the man's eldest daughter. He'd been so focused on getting the title and wealth for Darien that he'd ignored the cost.

His sons wouldn't let him ignore it any longer.

"Da," Darien said, forcing himself to calm. "The chances are that Luke and Emelia dinna run off simply for the sake of upsetting everyone. They ran off for a reason, and if I could guess, I'd say it was because they wanted tae be married. They were unhappy with their respective betrothals, so they ran away tae be married. They are probably married as we speak, meaning the title and the wealth belong to Luke Cannich. Even if Fergus protests, the church willna allow an annulment. The marriage will stand."

Lares knew that. It had been in the back of his mind since the situation started. He was gearing up to come back with a strong argument, but he'd only look like a fool if he did. He couldn't deny the obvious. After a moment, he simply shook his head.

"Then Fergus can withhold the money," he said. "Not the title, because that will belong tae Cannich by law, as will the properties, but the one thing Fergus can withhold is the money. He can give it tae ye for the trouble ye've been caused. I'll demand it. And ye'll keep Moy Castle, lad. It's a dun Tarh property now."

Darien had to admit that he was relieved that his father was finally starting to see the light. That took his anger down considerably. Leaning against the wall behind him, he removed his helm and wearily wiped his brow.

"Nay," he muttered. "Have him give the money tae Evie. She's earned it. I only had tae deal with Emelia, but she had tae deal with Emelia *and* Luke. Poor lass."

Lares, who had been hanging his head in defeat, suddenly lifted it. "If ye have Moy Castle, then ye have property," he said, thinking aloud. "If ye marry Evie, then ye'll have the money, too. Fergus would be satisfied because both of his daughters have married."

Darien heard him, but it took him a moment to realize what he was saying. As he looked at his father in surprise, Aurelius spoke up.

"Evie is a much better match," he said. "She's certainly more beautiful, and her manner is not like her sister's. She doesna have a loose reputation. The kind of wife a courtier would proudly display."

Darien pushed himself off the wall and lifted his hands. "Wait," he said over the chatter of his brother. "Why are ye talking about this?"

Lares seemed excited about it. "Because it's a solution tae the problem," he said. "Moy is now yer property. I give it tae ye. Marry Evie and she'll bring the money with her. I'll insist on it. Would ye be agreeable tae marrying Emelia's sister, lad?"

Darien froze, hands still up, looking at his father and brother as if they'd lost their minds.

Would ye be agreeable tae marrying Emelia's sister?

That was probably the most important question he'd ever been asked. *Would* he? That flame-haired beauty with the enormous blue eyes had his interest. There was no doubt about it. He was attracted to her. She was a good girl, one he had easy conversations with. He could imagine speaking to her every night for the rest of his life.

Would he consider her?

Truth be told, he'd consider no one else. He didn't know why he hadn't thought of it sooner.

"Aye," he said after a moment, lowering his hands. "If Fergus is agreeable, then I am."

Those few words lit Lares up. The man went from defeated to elated in a matter of seconds. As he fled down the stairs to look for Fergus, who was somewhere among the hordes of men in the ward, Aurelius turned to Darien.

"Do ye mean it?" he asked. "Are ye truly agreeable or are ye just trying tae keep the peace?"

Darien looked at him. He couldn't help the twinkle in his eye or the faint smile on his lips as he thought on the prospect of marrying Eventide Moriston. That sweet, lovely woman would indeed be something to be proud of.

And perhaps more.

"I mean it," he muttered.

Aurelius believed him completely.

CHAPTER SEVEN

"DRINK!" LARES ROARED.

Fergus slammed more ale down his throat.

The two of them were sitting on the wall of Moy Castle—literally. They were seated on the wall walk, their legs hanging over the side, with a twenty-foot drop below them where the ground sloped into a lake that was full of little creatures who were making noise against the backdrop of the night. Between them sat a scratched earthenware pitcher that had been full of the strongest drink Lares had ever tasted. They'd found it in the vault of Moy when they were looking for things to take with them, a drink that seemed to be fermented from pears or apples or something that made it terribly strong, with a hell of a bite to it.

But it would do the job it was designed to do.

It would convince Fergus that Eventide was meant for Darien.

"God," Fergus grunted, wiping his mouth with the back of his hand. "What *is* that stuff?"

"Why? Do ye not like it?"

"It tastes like lightning! My stomach will think I'm punishing it!"

Lares laughed loudly, slapping Fergus on the back. "That's because ye are," he said, pouring more into Fergus' dirty cup. "Drink it. We've much tae celebrate this night."

Fergus lifted the cup and looked at it as if unsure he was ready to pour that molten fire down his throat again. "So," he muttered, "ye want Evie for Darien, do ye?"

Lares sighed heavily. "The truth is what I told ye," he said. "He'll not take Emelia, even if yer men return her. He says he'll not take Cannich's leavings. Can ye blame him?"

Truthfully, Fergus couldn't, but he wasn't ready to admit it yet. "Damnation," he growled. "That damn lass is always getting intae trouble. But now she's done it. She's done it good."

Lares nodded, drunkenly clanking his cup against Fergus' in agreement before downing the contents and grabbing his throat when it burned. "Christ," he said hoarsely. "Look at my neck. Did that stuff burn a hole in it?"

Fergus peered at his neck. "Nay," he said. "'Tis the same wrinkled neck it always was."

Lares frowned. "My wife likes it just fine," he said. "And speaking of wives, do we have an agreement? Darien says Evie is a good lass. She'll make a fine wife for an important advisor tae Robert Stewart. She'll have a good life, Fergus. Better than she would with Luke Cannich."

Fergus wasn't hard pressed to agree. "I know," he said, feeling his liquor. Plainly, he was drunk. "I knew he wasna good enough for her, but she needs tae wed. And I wanted her near me. Is that so bad?"

Lares put his arm around the man's neck in a companionable gesture. "Nay," he said. "Of course ye want tae keep her close. She's yer youngest."

Fergus nodded, thinking on the flame-haired lass who was the only decent person in the entire family. "She is," he said. "Emelia was the troublemaker and always had my attention. Evie was neglected, sorry tae say, and she knows it. But ye say ye want half of Emelia's dowry because of what's happened?"

Lares nodded. "I think it's fair," he said. "Ye promised my lad a bride and wealth. Ye can still provide that. And Emelia and Luke should be punished for what they did. Surely ye canna think tae give Cannich Emelia's dowry? The lad doesna deserve it for what he's done."

"True."

"But ye dunna want tae leave them destitute."

"Nay, I dunna."

"So ye only give him half of what he's expecting," Lares said, grinning. "That will infuriate him, and he deserves it for what he's done."

"Do ye think so?"

"Of course I do," Lares said. "Why do ye think he ran away with Emelia? Because she has everything that was going tae go tae Darien. Luke knew that if he married Emelia, it would go tae him."

Fergus frowned. "'Tis true," he mumbled. "The thieving wretch. If he married her—"

Lares cut him off. "And ye know he did."

"*If* he did," Fergus continued, "then the titles and the land are his. But the money…"

Lares started laughing, slapping him on the back. "Ye control the money, my friend," he said. "Ye should give it all tae Darien. That would truly infuriate Luke!"

They cackled like hens. Fergus ended up downing more of that fire water until he could hardly see straight, but he didn't care. Eventide would marry Darien instead of Luke, and Darien would get the dowry meant for Emelia.

Seemed like a damn fine plan to him.

Darien was with Aurelius and Estevan when one of his father's men summoned him. He found Lares and Fergus still on the wall, only they were quite drunk at that point, so much so that Darien urged them off the wall so one of them wouldn't fall and break his neck. He had to help the two giddy old men down to the ward where the army was digging in for the night. Evidently, they'd located more of that liquid lightning, so the men were getting drunk around the bonfires that littered the yard.

That was when Lares told Darien that he, once again, had a bride.

Eventide.

Unlike the sensation he'd had when he was told that he was betrothed to Emelia, which was something between nausea and a genuine pain in his gut, Darien realized he felt quite happy about this announcement. Both Lares and Fergus told him that he would marry Eventide at a date and time of his choosing, and after the wave of surprise washed over him, he was left feeling overwhelmed. Overwhelmed that he would actually marry a woman he liked, someone he had respect for. Someone he was strongly attracted to. That flame-haired beauty would carry the dun Tarh name, and she would bear sons with that same flaming hair, the thought of which put a smile on his face.

How proud he'd be.

As his father and Fergus eventually passed out in the hall of Moy because of the strong ale, Darien couldn't sleep. He wanted to see Eventide and tell her what had transpired, but the night was dark and cold, so he waited until the eastern horizon began to turn shades of pink and blue before departing Moy for Blackrock.

It was a fresh, new day.

For him, a fresh, new life.

The ride from Moy to Blackrock was only about twenty miles. However, what started out as a leisurely ride turned into something at a more clipped pace because the more the day advanced, the more excited Darien became. Although he'd never received the impression that Eventide was interested in him romantically, he knew the conversations they'd had were interesting and meaningful and, at times, even warm. Eventide had a natural charm about her, something he found as alluring as her beauty. She was easy to talk to, and that wasn't a common quality. Darien knew he could be direct, and at times even abrupt, because that was the world he lived in. His life veered toward the political and the diplomatic, not military or even clan-centric like his father's. He didn't spend his days worrying about friendships or alliances or who his sons were going to marry, but he did spend his days in a never-ending chess game of politics and strategy.

He wondered how that was going to change when he married Eventide.

The truth was that he had seen men marry and how their lives became complicated by the women they'd wed. He had seen men's obsessions with their wives and how it tended to change them. He swore he wouldn't be one of those men who lost themselves in the women that they married, but given the fact he was going to marry Eventide, he could easily see how he would become obsessed with her.

Maybe he *was* going to become one of those men.

Time would tell.

He was about two hours away from Blackrock when darker thoughts began to consume him. None of this would happen if Eventide wasn't agreeable to a marriage, and there was every possibility that she wouldn't be. She had told him she hadn't wanted to marry Luke, but what if she didn't want to marry at all? What if the woman wanted to join the cloisters? What if she simply didn't like men and preferred a life of solitude? He realized he would be quite disappointed if that was her attitude, but until he could actually speak with her, there was no use in being troubled by it.

He'd find out soon enough.

It was afternoon when the walls of Blackrock began to come into view. Beyond the castle he could see the blue waters of the Firth of Cromarty, that vast body of water that spread across the land. Where he was born, along the banks of Loch Torridon, it seemed to him that the sea was wilder. He remembered seeing sea creatures sleeping on the beaches when he was a child, and he would watch them from a safe distance before chasing them off by throwing rocks.

Big, fat sea creatures with dark hides that made noises like an elk during the mating season. He remembered one year that his sister, Lilliana, brought home a baby sea creature because she thought it was cute. His mother made her take it back, only she made the brothers do it because of the danger when encountering the larger creatures. Lilliana had cried as they took her little pet away, but once they got to the shores of the loch, they realized that the mother and probably her entire family were waiting for the baby to be returned.

Darien and Aurelius had dropped off the small creature and run like the wind in the opposite direction, terrified they were about to be set upon. Memories like that made him smile, part of a childhood that was truly idyllic. So many people he knew had had horrific childhoods, but he wasn't one of them. He grew up in a house that was genuinely loving, and he'd fostered in a home that was much the same. That kind of security was something he wanted to provide for his own children, someday.

As he gazed at the castle in the distance, he found himself wishing for that future.

And a wife who loved him.

ଓଃ

"I HOPE YE slept well, m'lady," Eventide said as she swept into the room. "I've brought some food."

It was afternoon at Blackrock Castle as Mabel and her daughters roused themselves from long naps. No one had slept because of the siege of Moy Castle, not until they knew their men were safe, so after the news of victory had arrived, the women had finally allowed themselves the luxury of sleep.

Mabel, in particular, seemed to be groggy. She pushed herself up in bed just as Eventide entered with three or four female servants in tow, all of them carrying various dishes, which were deposited on a table in the middle of the chamber. Mabel and her daughters had taken the largest chamber in the keep, which belonged to Fergus, but he wasn't here to use it and Eventide had set them up in it against her mother's protests.

Athole had retreated to another part of the house.

Unfortunately, the chamber had needed some tidying because her father lived like a pig, but Eventide and the servants had managed to clean the chamber and make it comfortable for the three women. They'd even brought in another bed for Lilliana, while Zora shared the big bed with her mother. In fact, the very mention of food had Zora climbing out of bed, staggering over to the table to inspect the offering. Lilliana was a bit slower, but she smiled at Eventide as she sat up in bed.

"You are very kind," she said, yawning. "Have you been able to sleep at all?"

Eventide nodded. "A little," she said. "Tae be perfectly honest, my mother is so distressed about my father going tae war that she's taken tae bed and refuses tae rise, so I do apologize that she's not been here tae see tae yer needs."

Mabel was out of bed now, pulling on a silken robe. "I understand her distress," she said honestly. "But we are married to warriors. That means they must go to battle from time to time."

Eventide snorted softly. "My father is no warrior," she said. "Strange as it may seem, the only battles he has ever been in were in his youth. I dunna think he has fought a battle his entire adult life."

Mabel cocked her head curiously. "Blackrock has not seen any battles?"

"Not since I was born."

"Mama?" Zora said, mouth full as she stood over the table and shoved apples into her face. "When are we going home?"

The attention in the chamber was diverted to the young girl as Lilliana, having risen, urged her little sister to sit down and eat. Mabel was still over by the bed as she pulled a hairbrush out of her satchel.

"As soon as your father returns, I'm sure," she said. "There does not seem to be any reason to remain here, since there is not going to be a wedding, thank God."

As soon as she said it, she was sorry because the sister of Darien's betrothed was standing a few feet away. In fact, Eventide had been the very model of a gracious hostess during their entire stay, always making sure the ladies were well tended and warm and fed. To keep them entertained, she'd arranged for them to tour Blackrock and the small village down by the loch. She'd even arranged a visit to the local church, where the priests kept bees and there was ample honey to sample, much to Zora's delight. Eventide had done everything she could to ensure that this was a pleasant visit in spite of the circumstances, and Mabel was very grateful to her.

She'd come to like her.

"Forgive me, my lady," she said quietly. "I should not have said that. It was foolish of me."

Eventide, too, had come to like the straightforward dun Tarh matriarch. Having grown up with a feeble-minded mother as her example, it had been eye opening to watch Mabel handle her children. She ruled with an iron fist, but there was something nurturing and warm that drew Eventide to her. Even in the few days that she'd known the woman, she had come to see someone she appreciated very much.

Someone she felt that she could be honest with.

"There is nothing tae forgive, m'lady," she said softly. "I happen tae agree with ye."

Mabel gazed at her a moment, smiling weakly, before reaching out and taking her hand. "Come over here with me," she said, pulling Eventide toward the bed. "Sit down next to me. I wish to speak with you."

Eventide did as she was told. She let Mabel sit her down, then watched the woman attentively as she sat next to her. The entire time, Mabel never let go of her hand.

"Evie," she said quietly. "May I call you Evie? I heard your mother call you by that name. It suits you."

Eventide smiled. "Of course, m'lady," she said. "I would be honored."

"Good," Mabel said, patting her hand. "Now, I want you to be completely honest with me. Can you do that?"

"Absolutely, m'lady."

"What is truly going on here?" Mabel asked. "What I mean to say is—now that your sister is gone, what are your plans?"

Eventide's smile faded. "Plans?" she repeated. "For what?"

"For your future," Mabel said. "Your sister ran off with your betrothed. What do you intend to do about it?"

Eventide shrugged. "There is nothing I can do about it," she said. She hesitated before continuing. "May I tell ye something?"

"I wish you would."

"I am glad that she did."

Mabel blinked in surprise. "You are?" she said. "But why?"

Eventide sighed heavily, averting her gaze. "Because the man I was betrothed tae was a hound," she muttered. "He never met a woman he dinna like."

Mabel was looking at her with disgust. "And your father knew this?"

"He did."

"Then why did he betroth you to the man?"

Eventide shrugged. "Because he wanted the alliance," she said. "Luke Cannich's home, Moy Castle, now belongs tae my father. I dunna think that's really what he wanted, but Luke's humiliation must be avenged. Or so he says. But he dinna avenge *me*. He avenged the Moriston name and nothing more."

Mabel knew that mindset all too well. "And the dun Tarh name," she said. "Nothing would stop Lares, either. Where a man's pride is concerned, he'll stop at nothing to save it."

Eventide nodded. "I dinna want tae marry Luke," she said. "I dinna want my father tae attack Moy. This is not about me in the least."

"I can see that," Mabel said. "But Luke Cannich wasn't the only one with a reputation. Your sister has one, too."

"She does," Eventide said. "I know ye were upset that ye'd not been told. Did ye ask yer husband about it?"

Mabel growled unhappily. "Not before he departed for Moy," she said. "He deliberately avoided me."

"Will ye ask him when he returns?"

"He'll be fortunate if he leaves these walls with his hide intact."

Eventide struggled not to laugh out loud. "But surely his intentions were just like my father's," she said. "He wanted the alliance. My sister is the heiress and brings a great deal with her. Surely that is all he was thinking of."

Mabel eyed her. "You defend him?"

"I'm simply saying that men like yer husband and my father think alike."

Mabel contemplated that. "True," she said. "You are astute, Evie."

"Thank ye, m'lady."

"But you still have not told me what you intend to do about your future."

It was an uncomfortable subject for Eventide. She lowered her gaze, looking at her lap. "There is nothing I can do," she said quietly. "But I do know one thing."

"What?"

"That I'll not let my father push me intae another betrothal."

"What do you intend to do about it?"

"Join the cloister."

That answer saddened Mabel. "Oh… Evie," she said softly,

patting the woman's hand. "Please do not do that yet. Surely there is someone else you should like to marry?"

Eventide shrugged. "I canna think of anyone, and I'm fearful of what my father will do next," she said. "I could end up with a beast or a fool just because he wants an alliance."

Mabel could see her point. "You never know what is on the horizon for you tomorrow, or next month, or even next year," she said. "Do not commit yourself so quickly to the cloister. In fact, I have seven sons who are not married. You could have your pick of any one you wished, and I can promise you that they are all fine men. I do not raise beasts or fools."

Eventide looked at her. "I canna imagine ye would, m'lady."

"What about Darien?" Mabel said. "Now that your sister has fled, he is eligible. Would he be acceptable?"

It was an unexpected question, and Eventide flushed a bright shade of red, something she had absolutely no control over. The mere mention of Darien's name had her turning as red as an apple. She'd just spent the past few days worrying over the man, thinking about him, and trying not to show it. She thought she'd concealed that very well. But one mention about him from his own mother and she was about to burst into flame.

"He's an important man, m'lady," she said, averting her gaze. "He requires a marriage with a lady who can bring him a title and lands. I bring him nothing."

Mabel didn't say anything for a moment. She continued to hold Eventide's hand, perhaps contemplating that very thing. *I can bring him nothing.*

She didn't quite agree.

"I happen to believe that my children should be happy with the man or woman they marry," she said. "I realize that marriages are about strengthening families and alliances, but I think happiness should be important, too."

Eventide was listening. "Did ye choose Lares because he made ye happy?"

Mabel grinned. "You will not believe this, but I met him at a monastery."

Eventide looked up from her lap, her eyes wide. "Ye did?"

"I did," Mabel confirmed. "He had been sent there by his father for a very foolish reason, and my brother had ended up at the monastery because he broke his leg whilst traveling, so I met Lares when my mother and I went to collect him."

"Was Lares a priest?"

"Nay, thankfully," Mabel said. "But I knew within the first few minutes of knowing him that he could make me happy. And he has, all of these years."

Eventide smiled because Mabel was. "That is a lovely memory," she said. "I envy ye."

Mabel patted her hand. "May I ask you a question?"

"Of course."

"How long have you known the man you were supposed to marry?"

Eventide had to think on that. "Since we were young," she said. "He was a neighbor, an ally, and nothing more until my father decided he should be my husband."

"Did you think he could make you happy?"

Eventide's smile faded. "Nay," she said. "I never thought that."

"And what did you think of Darien when you first met him?"

Eventide reflected on that moment months ago. "I thought that he was the most handsome man I'd ever seen," she said. "I thought my sister was very fortunate."

"Have you been able to speak with him much since he has been here at Blackrock?"

"A little." Eventide nodded. "Enough tae know that he is a fine man. I told ye once my sister dinna deserve him. I meant it."

"What about you?"

"What *about* me?"

"Do *you* deserve him?"

Eventide lowered her gaze again. "I told ye that I canna give him what he needs," she said. "It would not be an advantageous marriage for him."

"I do not care about that," Mabel said. "Do you think you could be happy with him?"

Eventide's cheeks were starting to flame again as she looked at her hands. "Verily," she said softly. "But I dunna think he'd be happy with me."

"Why not?"

"Because I'm not a prestigious wife."

"That may be, but I have an idea. Will you listen?"

Eventide had no idea what to say. Was the woman truly attempting to gain her consent to marry Darien? Obviously, *she* couldn't consent. It wasn't her right. And Darien would surely be furious about it. He'd just rid himself of one Moriston sister and his mother was trying to saddle him with another? She was almost angry at the woman for trying to get her hopes up.

It was cruel.

"M'lady," she said as politely as she could, "I am sure ye mean well, but ye cannot speak for yer son. Surely... surely one Moriston sister was enough. I'm sure he's willing tae be done with the lot of us."

Mabel was watching her carefully, at the way she wouldn't make eye contact. The way she fidgeted with her fingers. Eventide was usually composed in any given situation—an admirable composure, considering what she'd been through—but when speaking of Darien, Mabel had noticed she tended to become uneasy.

She suspected why.

"Both you and my husband seem to be obsessed with Darien marrying for a title and lands," she said. "It is true that he is the second son and will not inherit from his father, but he can inherit from his mother."

Eventide looked at the woman, guarded. "What do ye mean?"

Mabel had the young woman's attention. That was a good sign. She smiled and stood up, resuming brushing her hair.

"My family is de Waverton," she said. "I am certain you suspected I was not from Scotland."

She said it in jest, referring to her obvious English accent, and Eventide smiled weakly.

"Ye have the manners of royalty, m'lady," she said.

Mabel grinned. "That is true," she said. "I do. In fact, my father is a descendant of William Longespee, Earl of Salisbury. He was the illegitimate son of Henry II, so we have royal blood in our lines. My father married my mother, Irene, and they had two children—myself and my brother, George. Oh, how I loved my brother. He was kind and warm, but he was also a troublemaker. Unfortunately, he died childless, and when my parents also died, my father's lordship passed to me. Technically, it belongs to Lares, but he doesn't care about it because it is an English title. Therefore, I'm sure he would happily give it to Darien, although it clearly has not occurred to him to do so. He was trying to secure Darien a Scottish title and lands through marriage, but since Lowmoor is a landed property title, he can just as easily give it to Darien. He would become Lord Lowmoor, and Wigton House, where I grew up, would become your home."

Eventide was staring at her by the time she was done. She simply didn't know what to say to it all. As Mabel continued to brush her hair, Eventide sat on the bed and pondered what she'd been told. Mabel seemed to think she would make Darien a good wife and was even willing to give him her family's title in place of the one Eventide wouldn't bring to the marriage. Was it actually possible?

Could this actually happen?

But the fact remained that Darien had no idea what his mother was up to. Whether or not Eventide was agreeable to a marriage, Darien and even Lares and Fergus still had to give their approval. But why would they?

She was no one of note.

With a sigh of disappointment, Eventide stood up from the bed.

"Ye've given me much tae think about, m'lady," she said. "I do appreciate yer kindness. It means a great deal."

Mabel's gaze lingered on her. She realized she wasn't going to get an answer out of the young woman, at least not yet. She could tell that the conversation had overwhelmed Eventide, and Mabel could well understand that. But this was only the first volley in the attempt of a mother to matchmake for her son.

There would be more.

"You are easy to be kind to," she said after a moment. "But I suspect you haven't had much kindness in your life, Eventide. Am I wrong?"

Eventide didn't know why, but her eyes welled with tears. She was going to weep and had no idea why. So she forced a brave smile and shook her head, quickly wiping away the tears that fell.

"Ye're not," she said quietly. "That is why yer kindness means so much tae me. I will always remember it. And ye."

Mabel went to her and kissed her on the cheek. "We'll speak more after I have dressed," she said. "Meanwhile, I should like to see your mother. Do you think we could convince her to rise from her bed and join us?"

Eventide shrugged. "Possibly," she said. "I think—"

She was cut off when the sentries began to shout at the gate. A rider had arrived. All of the women in the chamber rushed to the window, which had a partial view of the main gate. Eventide couldn't see much because Zora was in her way, straining to see what she could, but Mabel pulled her away from the window and took her place. It only took her a few seconds to see who had come.

"Darien is here," she said with some excitement. "My son has come. Praise the saints."

Eventide's heart began to pound in her chest at the mere mention of the man's name. "I will see tae him," she said, quickly moving for the door. "Shall I send him tae ye, m'lady?"

Mabel thought on that. "Nay," she said after a moment. "Take him to the hall and remain with him. I will join you there."

"As ye wish, m'lady."

As Eventide scurried from the chamber, a smile spread across Mabel's face. Perhaps a little time alone with Darien in the hall would convince Eventide that this marriage suggestion was a good one. Mabel was fairly confident that the young woman found her son attractive. She hadn't missed the violent blushing when Darien was mentioned. Now, all the lass needed was a little push by a mother who wanted to see her son happy.

Mabel rather enjoyed matchmaking.

"Mama," Zora said eagerly, "I want tae see Darien, too!"

"Not yet," Mabel said. "Finish your meal and then I want you to bathe and dress. You'll see your brother in due time."

Zora wasn't happy about the delay but did what her mother said. As she plopped back down at the table and picked up a hunk of bread, Lilliana made her way over to her mother.

"I heard what you said to Evie," she said quietly. "I think that she and Darien would make a fine match."

"Hush," Mabel said, holding up her hand in a silencing gesture. "Do you want your sister to hear? She'll run off and tell Darien and your father and God knows who else. This situation must be handled… delicately."

Lilliana passed a glance at Zora chewing her bread and cheese. "Shall I tie her up?"

Mabel shook her head. Then a devious expression crossed her features, as if she were reconsidering.

"Hide her shoes," she whispered. "I do not want her running down to the hall and interrupting Darien and Evie. They must have some time alone."

"But what if Darien has brought important news from Papa?"

"Then he'll simply have to wait to give it to me."

Lilliana understood. Fighting off a smile, she went on a covert mission to hide Zora's shoes until her mother said that it was time to return them.

They must have some time alone.

Mabel was going to buy them as much time as she could.

PART TWO:
EVENTIDE
I Found My True Love

CHAPTER EIGHT

H E'D RECOGNIZE THAT hair anywhere.
It was like a flame against the dull and drab backdrop of the ward, that fiery vision of Eventide's hair as she headed in his direction. He saw her come from the keep, and since the moment she'd appeared, he couldn't take his eyes off her.

This was what he'd come for.

This was the moment.

Not strangely, he was the least bit nervous. That wasn't something he usually experienced, so the sensation was unsettling. He'd spent the entire ride from Moy telling himself that the lady would be honored and he would be gracious about it. Eventide had been wronged and wronged again, but here he was, riding in like her savior. *It seems I am tae save ye from yer humiliation, m'lady. Aye, ye may kiss my hand in gratitude.*

Kiss his hand?

What was he—the damn pope?

He had laughed at himself for that one, but the truth was that he was nearly giddy with anticipation, and his thoughts were reflective of that. He'd viewed marriage to Emelia like a jail sentence, but marriage to Eventide was quite the opposite.

At least, he intended that it should be. He'd never thought that marriage would excite him in any way, but here he was.

God help him, he was actually excited.

Sweet Mary, please dunna let her reject me!

He came to a halt just inside the gates of Blackrock, handing his steed off to a stable servant. But his attention remained on Eventide, and when she saw he'd dismounted, she lifted her hand and waved. He waved back. Removing his heavy leather gloves, he headed in her direction.

"Welcome back, m'laird," Eventide said, smiling as she gazed up at him. "We heard that the siege of Moy was successful."

"It was."

"Did ye bring the wounded with ye?"

He glanced at the gate behind him. "There was no wounded tae bring," he said, returning his attention to her. "Honestly, Evie, I've never seen such a battle in my life. It was quite… easy."

She looked at him curiously. "Easy? How?"

He shrugged as he tucked his gloves into the belt at his waist. "There was very little opposition," he said. "What resistance there was ended up subdued early on."

"Did ye capture Reelig and the family?"

He shook his head. "Nay," he said. "They were not there. Someone must have told them we were coming."

That seemed to bring her a sense of relief. "Luke told me once that they have kin near Stonehaven," she said. "That must be where they've gone."

Darien shrugged. "Mayhap," he said. "They certainly went somewhere, because they weren't at Moy. That made things simple."

"It would seem so," she said. "I must admit that I'm glad no one was killed or captured. Ye knew I was against this from the start, so I'm glad it seemed tae be resolved without bloodshed."

"Very little," he said. "In fact, yer da and mine are still there, mopping up the remains. Old Padraig Munro dinna come tae battle, but his sons did. Estevan told me that the sons want a piece of Moy, so I suspect they're being soundly beaten by my da at this very moment because they asked for more than he is willing tae give."

"What is he willing tae give?"

His gaze lingered on her for a moment, as if there was much on his mind. "He's giving me the castle," he said simply. "*That* is what he's willing tae give, and that's why I've returned before the army. I need tae speak with ye, Evie."

She looked at him, puzzled. "Me?" she said. "Why? Have I done something wrong?"

He shook his head. Reaching out, he took her by the elbow and began to escort her back toward the keep. "Of course not," he said. "At least, not that I know of. Why? Do ye have a guilty conscience?"

She chuckled. "Not usually," she said, "but ye sound mysterious."

"I dunna mean tae be," he said. "But we need tae speak in private. Where can we go?"

"The hall," she said, pointing to the building with the steeply pitched roof. "Yer mother said that we should go intae the hall and she'd meet us there."

He headed for the hall. "And we must always obey my mother."

"I suspect she would not take it kindly otherwise."

He looked at her and started laughing. "Ye've met my

mother, have ye?"

She chuckled because he was. "I've spent the last few days with her," she said. "She's a formidable lady."

"Ye have no idea."

Eventide continued to snort as they headed into the hall, which was mostly vacant at this hour. The dogs were sleeping, strewn around the room, and a few servants were milling about and cleaning up dog feces, which Athole had always insisted upon. She was willing to let the hall be a man's domain, but she wasn't willing for it to be a dog's.

Eventide indicated for them to sit on the dais at the far end of the hall.

It was quiet here, away from the dogs and servants, and Darien politely helped her sit before taking the spot on the bench next to her. A helpful servant saw her with a guest and rushed to see if she needed refreshments. Eventide made the request and the woman rushed off to fetch it. When they were alone again, Eventide turned to Darien expectantly.

"Unfortunately, I dunna think this is the most private place for a conversation, but it will have tae do," she said. "I hope this doesn't displease you."

Darien shook his head. "Not at all," he said, but his gaze lingered on her as if he wanted to say more. After a few moments, he smiled faintly. "Ye've always been the consummate chatelaine, concerned for everyone. And I've only ever known ye tae be kind. Isn't that exhausting?"

Eventide grinned and averted her gaze modestly. "It is unkindness that is exhausting," she said. "Speaking of kindness, yer mother has been very sweet tae me."

"Has she?"

"Aye," Eventide said, nodding. "I've had the privilege of

spending the past few days with her and yer sisters, and I must say that I find all of them quite agreeable. It has been delightful."

His eyes glimmered. "My mother likes ye, does she?"

"She has been lovely."

"That is good, because she does not like just anyone," he said. "Dunna tell her I told ye that, because she'll box my ears, but I've seen her behave rather imperiously with women she doesna like."

"She has never been that way with me."

"Good," he said. "It means she approves of ye."

Eventide nodded, a somewhat sideways gesture when mixed with a shrug. "I dunna mean tae agree with ye, but I think she does," she said. "Do ye know what she said tae me today?"

"What?"

"She thinks that the two of us should marry."

Darien couldn't help the shock that rolled over his features. "U-us?" he repeated. "She told ye that?"

Eventide nodded seriously. "She says I'd make a good match for ye," she said. "Please dunna tell her that I told ye, because I think she wants tae tell ye herself. I'm telling ye because… Well, I'll tell ye what I told her."

"What did ye tell her?"

Eventide took a deep breath and lowered her gaze. "I told yer mother that ye were probably weary of the Moriston sisters," she said. "After what Emelia did, surely ye canna even consider her sister. It sounds foolish simply tae suggest it."

"Why?"

She shrugged. "Because ye probably think ye're well off tae be done with us," she said. "But I also told her that I dunna bring a title and lands like Emelia does. That makes me unsuitable. So… if she mentions this tae ye, then ye can tell her yerself. I only told ye what she said because I dinna think it right that she surprise ye with it. It's a very big decision."

Darien nodded, contemplating what he'd been told. Frankly, he was quite surprised to hear it. Astonished was more like it. His mother had suggested a marriage between him and Eventide? Either the old girl had lost her mind or she had taken a fancy to Eventide. Fortunately, he suspected the latter.

He could hardly believe it.

But along with that surprise came unease. He couldn't tell if Eventide was receptive to the suggestion or not. It appeared to him that she was trying to downplay any association with him by making it seem as if she were an unsuitable match. Either she meant it and she had no interest, or she was being humble.

There was only one way to find out.

"It *is* a big decision," he said after a moment. "In fact, that's what I wanted tae speak with ye about. Ye may find it surprising tae know that not only has my mother apparently suggested a union between us, but so have your father and my father."

Now it was Eventide's turn to be surprised. She looked at Darien with wide eyes, prevented from replying when the servant returned bearing a heavy tray of ale, bread, fruit, cheese, and something in a bowl that was white with green speckles. Darien remained silent while the servant set everything out. He couldn't help but notice that Eventide seemed to be unable to direct the woman. She seemed rather dazed. When the servant faded away, Eventide's brow furrowed as she poured Darien a cup of the strong, yeasty ale.

"My father suggested a betrothal between us?" she asked. "And he proposed it to yer father?"

Darien shook his head. "My father came up with the idea,"

he said. "Yer father agreed."

Eventide was quickly sliding into a world of bewilderment. It was written all over her face, and had she realized Darien was watching her so closely, she probably would have tried to conceal her expression a little more. But she couldn't. Lady Mabel had suggested a betrothal, but so had her husband, evidently. And now her father was in on it. Eventide had no idea how Darien felt about any of it, but he didn't seem too angry. Or frustrated. If he wasn't, she had badly judged his reaction. She'd assumed he would have been positively averse to a marriage to another Moriston sister.

But maybe she'd been wrong.

It never occurred to her that she would be.

"And what are yer feelings on the matter?" she asked, but kept talking the moment he opened his mouth to speak. "I told yer mother I'm unsuitable. A man like ye needs a prestigious wife tae bring ye wealth and lands, and I simply dunna have anything tae offer. Ye dunna need tae spare my feelings because I know what ye're going tae say. Truly, ye needn't worry. I understand completely."

He was watching her with a good deal of amusement. "Ye do?"

"Of course I do. Our parents should have never suggested such a thing."

"But what if *I'm* agreeable to a betrothal? What then?"

She looked at him, fearfully, as if she didn't want to believe him. "But ye canna be."

"Why not?"

"I told ye why."

He cocked an eyebrow. "I think ye're doing a lot of talking for me," he said. "Can I not speak for myself?"

She grew flustered. "Ye can," she said. "My apologies. When I become nervous, I talk. Sometimes far too much. I canna stop myself."

He started to chuckle. "Like now?"

"Like now."

He shook his head, snorting. "Hush, woman," he said. "Stop talking and listen. Are ye listening?"

She nodded hesitantly. "I am," she said. "I am a good listener, I promise. I am—"

He put a couple of fingers over her lips to quiet her. "*Hush,*" he said again. "Ye want tae know what I think? I think it's a splendid idea. I dinna want tae marry Emelia, but I do want tae marry ye. In spite of what ye've said, I think ye're more than suitable. I'd be honored tae call ye my wife."

His voice was low and soft. He was being gentle and kind, but Eventide was so overwhelmed that she leaned away from him, putting distance between them, and nearly leaned right off the bench. He had to grab her to keep her from falling, and when he did, putting a big arm around her to hold her steady, she gazed into his eyes with what could only be described as sheer disbelief.

"It… it's not true!" she managed to gasp.

He didn't let her go, thinking she felt quite wonderful in his embrace. "Aye, lass," he said. "I'm not sorry tae say that it is."

"Nay!"

"Do ye not want me, then?"

She swallowed hard as the truth began to settle in. But she still couldn't believe it. She pointed to herself.

"Me?"

"Ye," he said. "Answer me. Do ye not want me?"

She took a deep breath, but it was ragged and uneven. Like

she was gasping for air. "It's not that," she said. "Do I want ye? I never thought I'd ever hear that question. I never thought anyone like ye would... Are ye *sure*?"

He grinned. "I'm sure."

"Ye're not going tae change yer mind?"

"Not me," he said. "But ye've yet tae give me an answer. Will ye be my wife, Evie? If ye need convincing, I swear tae ye that I'll be a good husband. Ye'll want for nothing, and I swear that I will always be true tae ye. I'd never shame or hurt ye. We'll raise a dozen sons with yer red hair and my good looks. I'll be the envy of every man in Scotland."

Her mouth was hanging open by the time he was finished, but finally, he saw the light of warmth flicker in her eyes. That flicker was followed by a smile with a big dimple on either side of her mouth. She had the sweetest smile.

He knew he could grow to cherish it.

"Aye," she finally said. "I'll be yer wife. And I promise this Moriston sister couldna be dragged away from ye if God himself came out of the heavens and demanded it. If ye want me, ye have me. Forever."

Realizing he had her agreement did something to Darien. He began to laugh, something deep and booming. He laughed so hard that tears streamed down his cheeks, and because he was laughing, Eventide started laughing. Soon, they were laughing together like a couple of fools, weeping with joy.

Until Darien pulled her against him and kissed her.

Eventide had never been kissed before. Not like this. Luke had tried, but she'd always turned her face away from him and he ended up kissing a cheek. Other than a few boys when she'd been a young girl, little boys who liked to steal little kisses, this was her first experience with a man kissing a woman.

And what a kiss it was.

It was warm and delicious. He tasted of the yeasty ale he'd been drinking. But his lips were soft as he suckled her gently, and Eventide's heart began to pound so strongly that she swore it was about to beat right out of her chest. Her arms, as if they had a mind of their own, wrapped around his neck and held him tightly. So tightly that she was practically strangling him.

But Darien didn't seem to mind.

"I hope that did not offend ye," he whispered as his lips released hers. "Some men finish a deal with the shake of a hand. I thought we should finish ours with a kiss. It seemed appropriate."

Dazed and breathless, Eventide managed to grin. "No offense taken, laddie."

He returned her smile. "Good," he said. "Because I'll probably do that again sometime. Probably every day for the rest of our lives."

She licked her lips and loosened her grip around his neck. "Did ye ever kiss my sister like that?"

His smile faded. "We are tae be clear about one thing right now," he said. "Ye're not tae bring up yer sister like that. Not that I'm trying tae forget about her, because there's truly nothing tae forget, but simply because I want something special with ye, and we canna build that if ye keep bringing up yer sister. Do ye understand?"

Eventide nodded solemnly. "I do," she said. "I'm sorry."

"Don't be," he said. "I'll tell ye anything ye want tae know about my feelings toward Emelia, but not before, during, or after I've kissed ye. Are we clear?"

"Aye, Darien."

"Thank ye," he said. "I dunna want tae think about Emelia

when all I should be thinking about is ye."

"I understand."

She was contrite, perhaps even a little hurt because he'd very nearly scolded her, so he unwound her arms from around his neck and held her hands, kissing them.

"I'll answer yer question if ye wish," he said softly. "Nay, I never kissed her like that. I never wanted tae, and she never brought it up. All yer sister and I did was talk. Just talk. Sometimes I held her hand, but there was no affection behind it. Only duty. Evie, I never felt anything for yer sister. Surely ye know that."

Truth be told, Eventide *did* know that. But more importantly, she was feeling a little woozy. His kiss had been overwhelming, and now his big hands were holding hers ever so tenderly. She was in a position she'd never thought she'd be in. She'd been planning to commit herself to the cloister after Luke's departure, and now… now, she was getting married to the most beautiful man she'd ever seen. As she stared at his hands, her eyes began to well, and she struggled not to weep.

"What is it?" he asked gently. "Tell me why ye weep."

She tried to smile. "I dunna know," she said, sniffling. "I suppose because I'm happy. Yer mother asked me about my future, since I would no longer be marrying Luke, and I told her I would join a nunnery before I'd let my father betroth me to another man, so until this conversation, that was my future. A bleak, cold future. I feel as if I'm dreaming now."

He smiled, using his thumbs to wipe away her tears. "If ye're dreaming, I'm dreaming right alongside ye," he said. "And I wouldna let ye join a nunnery. I'd beat the door down and take ye out of there."

She chuckled. "I'll save ye the trouble and not go," she said.

But her smile faded as she gazed into his eyes. "Ye canna know what this means tae me. What I hope ye'll come tae mean tae me. Ye swore tae me that ye'd be a good husband, and I'll make ye the same promise. I'll be a good wife and try tae make ye proud, Darien. I'll try my hardest."

He leaned over, kissing her gently on the cheek. "I know ye will," he said. Then he waggled his eyebrows. "Ye know, when I came tae Blackrock for the marriage tae Emelia, I felt as if I was coming tae my own execution. I dunna wish tae speak badly about yer sister in front of ye, but I will say that I knew we would have problems. Probably too many of them for the marriage tae be a happy one. But I know that willna be the case with ye."

Eventide wiped the last of the tears from her eyes. "Nay," she said. "Ye'll never have tae worry over me. I'm as loyal as a dog. When I have the most handsome husband in all of Scotland, why would I ever look at anyone else?"

He flashed a grin. "Ye think I'm handsome?"

"The *most* handsome."

He snorted. "My brothers might take exception to that."

"I'm not marrying any of your brothers. I dunna care what they think."

He laughed softly as he pulled her into his embrace again, but he didn't kiss her. He simply held her, his gaze drifting over her hair, the shape of her face, the fringe of eyelashes around those blue eyes.

She was flawless.

"My parents married for love," he said quietly. "I'd always hoped I would, but I lost that hope with Emelia. I think I've found it again."

Her cheeks flushed, and, fighting off a smile, she laid her

head against his chest. She could smell his distinctive musk, hear his heart pounding strongly in her ear. She moved her hands to his chest, gently touching him, acquainting herself with the feel of him. There wasn't anything about the man that wasn't utterly magical.

It was the most romantic moment of her life.

"Yer mother told me how she met yer da," she said. "She said she met him at a monastery."

Darien had his eyes closed, feeling every touch, every breath she took against his chest. There was something so calm and tender about her, something that soothed his mind in a way he'd never known before. Just holding her made him feel peace. It settled him.

She was like a salve for his soul.

"She did," he said, eyes still closed. "His father was convinced he was worshiping the devil, so he sent my da there for the priests to straighten out."

"Was he worshiping the devil?"

"Nay," he said. "Ye can rest assured that I dunna come from a family of devil worshipers. But I do have a very old family with complex and mysterious origins."

"Where do they come from?"

"Hispania," Darien said. "My family descends from a Roman legion, the Hispania legion, that came tae Scotland tae subdue the Picts. Tradition says they were overwhelmed by the fierce fighters, but the few who survived married intae the tribes. Even our standard reflects that."

She lifted her head to look at him. "What's on yer standard?" she asked. "I never noticed."

He opened his eyes and looked down at her. "A red bull," he said. "Our family name is Tarh—*tarbh* in Gaelic means 'bull,' as ye know. We've had that name for over a thousand years."

She smiled faintly. "That makes yer family quite old," she said. "Not many can claim that."

"Our children will be able tae."

Her smile grew. "They'll be able tae claim the blood of the Northmen, too," she said. "My ancestors were Northmen raiders who settled in this area centuries ago. Moriston means 'dark.'"

"Then ye've just given our family its own standard."

She looked at him curiously. "What do ye mean?"

His eyes twinkled. "Yer name means 'dark' and mine means 'bull,'" he said. "Our standard will be a black bull. We'll be known as the black bull of Moy Castle."

Her expression turned serious as she sat back, putting some space between them. "Do ye intend tae keep Moy, then?"

"Why?" he said. "Is that not to yer liking?"

"I'm not sure," she said truthfully. "It's a Cannich property. Do ye not think they'll try tae get it back?"

He shrugged. "It's possible," he said. "It's equally possible my da will simply give it back tae Reelig Cannich if the man apologizes for his son's actions. My father is actually quite easy tae placate sometimes. When his anger cools about Luke and yer sister, he might be willing tae return the castle."

"Then why did he take it tae begin with?"

"Tae prove a point," Darien said. "If he does give it back, I'm not sure where that leaves us for a place tae live, but I do have a small home in Edinburgh. I live there when I'm entrenched in Robbie Stewart's court."

"Do ye spend much time there?"

"I have over the past few years."

"Then if that's where ye live, that's where I'll live, too," she said. She hesitated before continuing. "But ye should know that when yer mother was trying tae convince me that ye and I should wed, she told me that she would tell yer father tae give ye the Lowmoor title and Wigton House. That's where she grew up."

His brow furrowed. "She told ye that?"

Eventide nodded. "When I told her I was unsuitable because I wouldna bring ye a title or land, she said that yer father inherited her father's title and property when her brother died," she explained. "She says yer da doesn't care about the title because it's English, so she will tell him tae give it tae ye. Ye'll be Lord Lowmoor of Wigton House."

Darien thought on that. He'd known about the Lowmoor title, but it never occurred to him that it could be gifted to someone. He'd never cared, so he never asked. Therefore, this was a bit of a revelation to him.

"If she really intends tae convey the title tae me, that is an astonishing prospect," he said. "And a welcome one."

Eventide leaned toward him, grasping at the neck of his tunic. "Dunna tell her I told ye," she said. "Act surprised when she speaks of it."

He shook his head firmly. "I wouldna dream of betraying ye," he said, thinking on the enormous manor house near the sea. "Wigton House is impressive. When I was a child, we would visit from time tae time. My grandmother, Irene, was a serious woman with a loud voice. She always seemed quite imperious. But she would sneak us sweets after we went tae bed and then lie tae my mother about it, so we knew she loved us."

"Ye have fond memories of the place."

"Verily."

"Then it will be a good place tae raise our own family."

He hadn't thought of that until she said it. Then he grinned and pulled her into his arms again.

"That we will, lass," he said, his cheek against the top of her head. "Evie, are we truly going tae do this? Are we truly going tae get married?"

"I think we are."

"I'd be disappointed if we dinna."

"Me too."

"Darien dun Tarh! What are you doing to that woman?"

The shouting came from the hall entry, and the two of them turned in time to see Mabel entering the room, a frown on her face. She was waving a hand at her son.

"Let her go," Mabel commanded. "Get back from her. *Move!*"

Eventide had to put a hand over her mouth to keep from laughing as Darien sighed heavily, let her go, and stood up from the bench. He could hear his mother muttering as she approached the dais, and he leaned toward Eventide's ear.

"I'm telling ye now that if she tries tae box my ears, I'm running away," he whispered.

Eventide couldn't help the giggles. "What if she tries tae box mine? Will ye defend me?"

He looked at her as if she'd gone mad. "Against my mother?" he said, aghast. "Never. Ye're on yer own, lass."

Eventide continued to giggle as Mabel came to the dais, her focus on her son. "Well?" she demanded. "Why were you holding her like that? What do you have to say for yourself?"

Darien was fighting off a smile. "Lares dun Tarh and Fergus Moriston have decided that Evie and I should wed," he said. "Congratulate me, Mam. I've agreed tae it. More importantly, so has Evie."

Mabel went from outrage to elation in a split second. Not that she had been *truly* outraged to see Darien and Eventide in an embrace, but she did want to know what was going on. Now, she knew. Forget about crediting her husband or even Fergus with this success. Mabel knew this was *her* doing.

Her matchmaking had paid off, and she was damn happy about it.

By the look on Darien's face, she could see that he was, too.

CHAPTER NINE

Glasgow
Two Months Later

SHE HADN'T SEEN a blue sky since she left Blackrock. Funny how she had gotten used to a gray sky and constant storm clouds, heavy and bleak and mirroring the hopelessness that she felt. Her freedom from Blackrock had not included a scenario where she wasn't completely and utterly happy. The future she'd hoped for was full of drink and music and laughter, of spending her days lounging in a mild breeze and her nights wrapped up in Luke's arms.

But that hadn't happened.

It had been an incredibly difficult lesson to learn when Emilia realized the life she had hoped for was not the life she was going to get. Fleeing her parents and marriage to Darien dun Tarh two months ago had been exciting and liberating, and she'd had high hopes that everything from that point forward would be perfect. Luke had promised her a wonderful life, a life of love and happiness, but all she'd managed to get from him was hardship and heartache.

And it had only gotten worse.

Unfortunately, she realized her mistake just a few short days after reaching Glasgow. She and Luke had spent two weeks running from her father's men, dashing all over the Highlands and hiding in little villages, hoping to escape his clutches. Her father had been persistent in trying to find her, but fortunately, she recognized the men he sent so was able to avoid them. She and Luke had moved from Inverness to Elgin, and then south on small roads until they reached Perth. From there, they continued south and decided not to settle in Edinburgh, because she was positive her father would look for her there. More than that, Darien, her betrothed, was part of Robert Stewart's court, and they met in and around Edinburgh.

She didn't want to be seen.

So, they moved west, to Glasgow, that foul-smelling pile of humanity that was just this side of Hell. The city had a reputation for being dirty and full of disease and crime, so in order to throw her father off the scent, she and Luke had settled in a city where she was certain her father would never look for her. Fergus knew that Emelia would seek out a fine city with fine lodgings and fine taverns and markets, and that meant Edinburgh this far north. Of course, they could go further south to Carlisle or to Berwick, but that would take them into England, and neither one of them wanted to go into that vile country.

Therefore, Glasgow was to be their home.

Within a day or two of arriving, they realized that they didn't have the finances to keep them afloat in the style in which they were accustomed to. To be clear, in which Emelia was accustomed to. Luke didn't care. They had spent a lot of their money on their flight south, spending it in fine taverns and paying off the owners so they would throw Moriston men off the scent if they came too close. In fact, they'd spent far too much money bribing proprietors and, eventually, paying a hefty donation to the church in Perth so that the priest would marry them without parental permission. Emelia made the mistake of telling the priest that her parents were still alive, and that had caused the man to falter when it came to performing a wedding mass. About half the money they had with them had somehow cleared the way, and they were legally married.

But it wasn't a happy marriage from the start.

Two days in Glasgow and Luke found work down at the River Clyde, offloading merchant vessels and other manual labor. It wasn't a lot of money, but it was something, and within the first few weeks, they realized that Emelia needed to find a position as well. Since she had never worked for money a day in her life and the only servants she really knew were the ones she had commanded, there really wasn't much she could do, but the tavern where they ended up every night lost a serving wench one evening because she got caught in a fight between two patrons. The girl ended up with a broken arm and a battered body, and, seeing an opportunity, Emelia asked the owner if she could take the girl's position. Because she was well spoken and had all of her teeth, the tavern owner agreed.

The place was called The Lion's Head, and that was where she found herself working six days a week for tips. She wasn't paid anything by the tavern itself, so every cent she earned was strictly from patrons grateful for the service she provided. The tavern was heavily visited by seamen off the River Clyde, so they weren't rich by any means. All they wanted to do was eat and drink and perhaps share the bed of one of the wenches if the price was right. Since Emelia was married, and against her usual nature, she'd declined to jump into bed with them, but she wasn't beyond letting them grope her breasts or stick a hand up her skirt in exchange for a few coins.

Things that Luke didn't know about.

Quite honestly, letting men take advantage of her was completely normal for Emelia. She didn't care if they wanted to play with her breasts—some of them even wanted to suckle on her, and she would wait, bored, while they put their mouths on her nipples and stroked their male member until it became hard. She wouldn't touch them if they asked her to because, in her world, a man was there to merely service her, so they would grope her and suck on her until they were satisfied. Then they'd pay her—sometimes well—and she would go back to work and find another man who wanted to fondle her buttocks or lick her thigh. For a high price, she'd even go into a corner and let them feast on the flower between her legs, but only if it was a *very* high price.

Luke was blissfully unaware.

Because he spent all of his time down on the riverbank working like a Roman slave, he never had the time to come to The Lion's Head to see what his wife was doing. Luke worked seven days a week with hardly a break except at night to sleep, so he didn't have time to see what Emelia was up to. All he knew was that she brought in more money than he did, so after four weeks in Glasgow, they were able to move out of the tiny room they had been letting in a merchant's house down near the river and take possession of a small domicile in the city. It was a three-story building, and they were able to procure a three-room dwelling on the second floor.

It wasn't as nice as the single chamber that they had paid for in the merchant's home, but it was all theirs. The floors leaned and the ceiling had chunks of plaster that had fallen away, but at least they didn't have to depend on the merchant for food and shelter. They were able to buy a small bed, and Luke found a broken table and an empty lot a couple of blocks over, something he was able to repair so at least they had a place to sit. There was a wheelwright in the city who built furniture, and they were able to purchase a couple of chairs and a stool and a few other things to make their new dwelling livable.

Emelia was hoping that things were finally looking up a little. Their new living arrangement wasn't terribly bad, but they discovered the walls leaked when it rained and the fireplace in the main room didn't function correctly. The thing spat out smoke as much as it evacuated it, and in lighting a fire, one risked being smoked out of the place entirely.

But still, they were together.

At least, that was what Emelia kept telling herself.

The truth was that marriage to Luke hadn't been anything she had imagined. All he did was work, and when he came home, he didn't want to talk. He wanted to eat his supper and then he expected his wife in bed, where he would ravage her until he fell asleep on top of her. Then, when morning came, he would get up and go to work again. And that was the only time she saw him.

And then it happened.

Her menses stopped.

Emelia wasn't stupid. She knew that constant coupling would produce a child, eventually. She'd been pregnant once before, but her mother had taken her to an apothecary who gave her herbs and potions, and she'd passed the child away in a couple of days. She didn't want this child, either, even if it was her husband's, so she'd asked the tavern owner's wife about an apothecary, and the woman steered her to an old man near the cathedral. A *very* old man who smelled of onion had given her a coltsfoot pessary and told her to insert the pessary into her womb and submerge herself in hot water for as long as she was able. Luke had come home to her submerged in a half-barrel lined with tar that served as their place to wash. He wanted to know why she was taking a bath, and she told him.

That had started the brawl.

He wanted a son. She didn't. They'd gone around and around until he finally left before sunrise. That had been two days ago. The coltsfoot pessary hadn't done its job yet, so she'd gone back to work and made a fortune from a fat, slovenly merchant who just wanted to suck her toes. He'd sucked every one of them and given her a pound for each. By the end of the night, Emelia was wildly rich and she'd only had to let the man touch her feet, but the other serving wenches at the tavern knew what she'd done, and how much money she'd received—and before she left near midnight to return home, they'd taken broomsticks and beaten her unconscious. They took most of her money, and as she staggered home that night, bruised and beaten, she lost the baby in the gutter by her house.

For Emelia, Glasgow had been one hell of an adventure so far.

And not a good one.

It was of lost children and an uncertain future that Emelia was thinking of this night as she gazed from the window overlooking the street below. This street had the distinction of having cobblestones, but the gutters ran thick with human and animal excrement and dirty water. The smell was horrific sometimes, when the mist hung low to the ground and kept the stench from dissipating into the sky. Tonight was another of those misty nights, and she'd chosen not to return to The Lion's

Head, knowing that she'd probably endure another beating because now the wenches were on to her scent. She'd never liked them anyway, and they'd never liked her, but they'd never taken her money before. Now that they knew they could, they'd do it again.

She couldn't go back.

The night watch had lit the torches along the avenue, making it so it wasn't entirely dark as the evening settled in. Emelia was watching the street below, the limited traffic on it, thinking she'd have to go look for another position soon. Although she'd made good tips at The Lion's Head, she was a spender. If she had money, she would spend it. The three small rooms she shared with Luke were full of things she'd bought from the Street of the Merchants. Not because she needed them, but because she wanted them.

Fabric, trinkets, slippers, perfume, hairbrushes, hairpins, expensive linens for the bed, pillows, and more besides. Emelia also bought food, prepared in the tiny chamber that had a hearth for cooking and shelves that held things like flour and baskets of dried fish and dried fruit. There was even a little glass vessel she'd purchased from a woman down by the river that contained honeycomb. Emelia had a sweet tooth, and it was nearly her only comfort these days.

Comfort in a life that had gone awry.

So, she sat by the window, the glass vessel of honeycomb in her lap as she picked at it and watched the fog. She was thinking about eating some of the bread and cheese from the morning's meal when she caught sight of a familiar figure walking through the mist.

Luke was approaching.

Quickly, she moved off the windowsill and pulled the oilcloth tight. There was a weak fire in the hearth and she swiftly stirred it, watching the flame flare, before rushing into the small chamber to put her honeycomb back on the shelf. Reaching into the basket on the floor, she pulled forth the bread wrapped in a cloth and a hunk of white cheese. Just as she put them on the small table, she heard a knock at the door. Brushing off her hands, she went to answer it.

After she threw the bolt, the panel slowly creaked open.

"I wasna sure when ye'd return," Emelia said, standing back as he entered. "Where have ye been?"

Luke was covered with filth. That was usual from his job down on the riverbank, but this level of dirt was different. As if he'd been sleeping in the gutters. He smelled like it.

"Where's the ale?" he asked, his voice hoarse.

Emelia went into the small chamber and emerged a few moments later with an earthenware pitcher. Luke grabbed it from her and drained whatever was left, but when it wasn't enough, he angrily threw the pitcher into the hearth. The flame flared up as bits of alcohol sprayed.

"Why did ye do that?" Emelia demanded. "Now I will have tae buy another one!"

Standing in the middle of the chamber, he cast her a long look. "That shouldna be too difficult," he said. "Ye spend all of yer money as it is. Ye make more money than I do, but ye've got nothing tae show for it. Ye spend yer money and mine as well."

Emelia thrust her chin up. "'Tis my money," she said. "Why shouldn't I spend it?"

Luke rolled his eyes and turned away, plowing into the small chamber they used as a kitchen and, seeing bread and cheese on the table, beginning to devour it.

Emelia followed.

"Answer me," she said. "Where have ye been for two days?"

Luke's mouth was full of bread. "Where have *I* been?" he muttered rhetorically. "Ye could say I've been in the city. In fact, I went tae The Lion's Head looking for ye. I wanted tae smooth things from the argument we had about the bairn, but ye weren't there."

Emelia shook her head. "Nay," she said. "I dunna work there any longer."

"So I was told."

"Did they tell ye why?" she said with some anger. "The women there beat me and stole my money. Look at the bruises they gave me. I willna go back there!"

She held out her arms, showing him the damage, but he was still eating. He didn't even look at her.

"I know *how* ye made the money," he said. "They were more than happy tae tell me. Ye let some man suckle yer toes, did ye?"

Emelia shrugged. "He paid me a pound a toe," she said. "We would have been rich had those selfish cats not stolen my money. Will ye go back with me and beat them if they dunna give it back?"

He snorted, finally turning to her. "They also told me that it's not the first time ye've let a man touch ye," he said. "Is that where ye've gotten all of yer money, Emelia? By letting men who aren't yer husband touch ye?"

The fact that the same women who robbed her had told her husband just how she'd earned her money gave her pause. It never occurred to her that they would tell him. In fact, Luke had never been inside The Lion's Head since she started working there, so she had been confident her secrets were safe. But looking at his expression, she could see that wasn't the case. He knew, and he wasn't happy.

Cornered, she had no choice but to go on the offensive.

"'Tis yer fault," she said. "If ye were a man, I wouldna have tae earn money tae begin with."

He scowled. "What do ye mean by that?"

"I mean ye havena asked my da for my dowry!" she spat. "I've told ye tae do it, but ye delay. That's money that belongs tae ye, yet ye let my father steal it from ye!"

"He's not stolen it from me."

"Ye're a weak man, Luke Cannich," she said. "Weak and worthless!"

His jaw tightened. "Ye'll never speak like that tae me again."

"Then do something about it," she said angrily. "Demand the money from my da!"

His jaw twitched dangerously. "Do ye understand that if I do that, he'll know where we are?" he said. "He'll send men after us. He could arrest me and charge me with thievery at the very least. We must wait until the situation calms down and he's more willing tae forgive. Then I'll demand it."

She cocked an eyebrow. "That's pure cowardice."

"How is that cowardice?"

"Ye never mentioned this before ye talked me intae running off with ye," she said. "Ye never mentioned that we'd go out on our own and ye'd turn intae a coward that canna stand up tae my father and demand his due. *Our* due."

She wasn't entirely wrong. He'd been so caught up in seducing her for the money and title that the reality of their lives after they ran away hadn't really occurred to him. He thought they'd simply hide out and drink until the fuss was over. But Emelia spent money like it was water through her fingers, and soon her flaws began to outweigh her attributes. Their rosy life together wasn't so rosy, and he'd begun to realize what a mistake he'd made. By then, however, it was too late. They were married.

God… What had he gotten himself into?

"Ye know that running off the way we did could land us both in chains," he said. "I stole ye from dun Tarh. If he wants tae bring the law down on me, he can. Do ye think Darien isn't out looking for us, too? I'd rather be caught by yer father than by him."

"So ye'll let my da keep the money?"

"Unless ye want tae be caught, we canna communicate with him."

"I want the money that belongs to me!"

Luke stared at her before shaking his head, turning away in disgust. "And that's all ye ever want," he muttered. "Money. Since we left Blackrock, all ye've spoken of is money. Money and drink and excitement."

"What else is there?"

"For ye? Nothing, evidently. I see ye for what ye are."

"And what's that?"

"A whore," he said, turning to look at her. "A whore for money, a whore for men. Ye were betrothed tae one man, yet ye gave yer affections tae another—with me. I always knew what ye were, but I thought marrying ye for the title and money would be worth the price. How wrong I was."

Her mouth flew open in outrage. "How dare ye say such a thing about yer own wife!"

He shook his head, this time with more resignation. "I only married ye for the money," he said. "Dunna tell me that ye dinna know. Evie's the beauty, not ye. But that much money can make any woman beautiful, I suppose."

It was a hard-hitting blow, one that was difficult to hear, but one that didn't surprise her. Deep down, Emelia had known it all along. Only Eventide had the beauty and manners that men wanted. Sweet, pretty Evie. That was why she hated her sister so, why she was glad to take her betrothed away. But now the philandering pair found themselves in a stewpot where they could no longer conceal the truth, unpleasant as it was.

She had some truth of her own.

"Since we're being honest, ye should know that I only married ye so my sister couldna have ye," she said. "Ye're as stupid as a log, Luke Cannich, and ye're only good enough tae work in the filth of the riverbank. Ye're such a failure that yer wife has tae earn money so ye can eat."

He looked at her sharply. "I told ye not tae say that again."

"Or what?"

He looked her up and down. "I canna strike ye because it risks my son," he said. Then he cocked an eyebrow. "Or *is* it my son? Mayhap it's another man's child. I wouldna be surprised if it was."

She smiled thinly. "Ye needn't worry about that," she said. "The babe is gone. After the beating I took, yer son ended up in the gutter when I pissed him out. Good riddance, I say."

Luke stared at her a moment before smiling. It was a strange, empty smile. "I am relieved tae hear it," he said. "I dinna want a woman like ye tae mother my son. He deserves better."

Infuriated, she picked up the nearest object, which happened to be the knife used to cut bread and cheese. Wielding it as a weapon, she went after him, but he was fast. Luke dashed into their main chamber, where they lived and ate, pushing Emelia away when she came too close with the knife.

"Get out," she snapped. "Get out or I'll kill ye."

He didn't take her seriously. "And destroy someone who brings ye money?" he said. "Ye'd never do such a thing."

She slashed at him with the knife, catching him on the elbow. It drew blood. Angry, Luke charged her and, as she screamed, wrenched the knife from her hand. He tossed it back into the kitchen chamber as she slapped him with her hands and tried to kick him in the shins. Luke simply walked around the chamber, dodging her, before finally pushing her away. He pushed a little too hard, and she ended up on her behind.

Furious, she leapt to her feet.

"Ye're a worthless brute, Luke Cannich," she said. "I dunna know why I ever agreed tae run away with ye. Ye're not worth the spit in my mouth!"

Luke managed to stay out of her range as she tried to hit him again. Now, he stood over by the window that faced the muddy, misty street, watching her coil herself up in preparation for charging.

"I suppose we could go back home and lie tae our families," he said casually as she built up a head of steam. "We can tell them we weren't married. We can make up a story as tae why we ran off together. Mayhap we can tell them ye were captured by pirates and I ran off tae help ye. But knowing how ye are around men, no one would believe it. They'd know ye ran off with the pirates quite agreeably. Maybe ye let them suck yer toes, too."

There was a shout on the street below, which caught his notice. He made the mistake of taking his attention off Emelia by turning to the window and lifting the oilcloth to see what was going on. Furious with his slander, she chose that moment to charge at him, ramming into him with all of the strength in her body. Her arms were flailing, slapping at his head. Luke went to grab part of the window to keep himself from falling forward, but the old wood crumbled in his hand, and, without any way to stop his fall, he pitched out of the window and fell on his head and shoulders on the cobblestones below.

He was dead when he hit the ground.

Emelia's momentum nearly had her falling also, but she managed to catch herself. On her knees, her head hanging from the window, she could see Luke's lifeless body below. With a shriek, she scrambled to her feet and flew out of the flat, rushing down the rickety old stairs and into the misty night. Running to Luke as he lay on the ground, she rolled him onto his back only to see that he had an enormous knot on his head and the right side of his face was damaged. He also seemed to have a broken right arm. She listened for a heartbeat but couldn't tell if she heard it. She couldn't even tell if he was breathing.

She was positive that he was quite dead.

Shocked, Emelia stared at his body, realizing she'd killed the man. She hadn't exactly *meant* to throw him out of the window, but it had happened. She'd done all she could to make sure it happened.

Now, she was a murderess.

Panic-stricken, Emelia stumbled to her feet and ran back into the flat. Self-preservation consumed her—she had to get away before Luke's body was discovered by the night watch. They'd figure out what happened and come to the flat with the broken window overlooking the street.

That would lead them to her.

Her!

Emelia wasn't going to let anyone punish her for this. Luke's death was an accident. Sort of. But she knew she'd be blamed. The only thing she could do was flee, to run home. She didn't know where else to go or what else to do. She'd be forced to beg her father's forgiveness and tell him a story—*any* story— that absolved her of whatever sins she had surely committed. Running away with her sister's betrothed? *That* was a sin. Therefore, she had to think of something that didn't put her in the wrong.

Anything at all.

What if…

What if Luke had abducted her? Had forced her into marriage? Surely Fergus would believe that, wouldn't he? Surely he would forgive her for leaving, because her father always forgave her, for anything she'd ever done. Any transgression. Emelia was his heiress and she could do no wrong. He'd forgive her this time. She was sure of it.

But first, she had to get out of there.

She ran off and left Luke where he belonged… in the gutter.

CHAPTER TEN

Blackrock Castle

HE DREAMED ABOUT moments like this. Beneath him, Eventide's eyes were closed, her red hair spread out over the wooden floor like a burst of flame. Her arms were up, over her head, and her full, soft breasts were bouncing every time their bodies came together.

Two months.

Two months of a betrothal to this woman he couldn't get enough of. He wasn't supposed to be in her bed yet because they weren't officially married, but he was. He had been for about a month. That tender white skin that he feasted on, those magnificent breasts that he couldn't keep his hands off. He'd tasted, touched, licked, or otherwise fondled every part of her body, and instead of it satisfying him, he just wanted more. He bedded her as much as he could, and he'd even done it when she was on her menses. He didn't care.

He just wanted her.

This time was no different. Having been gone for the past two weeks in Edinburgh, he'd ridden through the gates of Blackrock this morning and was practically mauled by Eventide the moment he dismounted his horse. Fergus allowed them to have time some alone together in the solar, without any chaperones, and that was where they found themselves. Even now, as he thrust into her, he was a hairsbreadth away from spilling into her, and he didn't want to—not yet, anyway—but as he watched her body move underneath him, he knew he couldn't stop himself. He thrust again and again, feeling himself climaxing with the greatest of pleasure. When Eventide felt his throbbing organ inside her, she grasped his buttocks and held him against her, forcing the man to stay buried in her as he spent himself.

But Darien wasn't finished with her. He wanted her to enjoy this as much as he did. Even after he finished, he remained embedded in her and moved his hands under her hips, holding her to him as he continued to thrust into her. Eventide's body responded to him as it always did, the heat in her loins like liquid fire, growing in intensity.

A wildfire was raging.

Darien was measured and firm, and she gave herself up completely to him. He heard her swift pants and knew she was close to her release, so he shifted himself and put his fingers where their bodies were joined, probing her stiff little bud of pleasure. The moment he touched her, Eventide pealed a gasp that filled the chamber. Darien descended on her mouth quickly to muffle the sound, because her mother tended to linger outside the door and listen in on their conversations. He certainly didn't want her to hear this.

Eventide had a climax like no other.

Powerful and long. When the tremors finally died down, Darien collapsed on top of her. They were lying on one of the hides on her father's floor, the cleanest one they could find. It wasn't ideal, but it was what they had to work with. Darien cradled her tightly, and she clung to him, running her hands over him, reacquainting herself with his body after their separation. When her hands moved to his face, he kissed her fingers before speaking.

"I dunna want tae wait anymore tae marry ye," he whispered. "I want tae do it before I have tae return tae Edinburgh."

She looked at him with concern. "When are ye returning?"

"I told Robbie I'd be back next month," he said. "There are things happening that I must be part of, but I'm not going tae leave ye behind the next time I go, Evie. It nearly killed me to do it the last time."

She shifted under him, trying to find a comfortable position on the hard floor, but the movement excited him. He was still buried in her body, so, semi-aroused, he began to move in her again, gently kissing her neck as he did so. Eventide wrapped her legs around his hips, wound her arms around his neck.

"My father wanted us to wait," she murmured, groaning softly at the feel of him inside her. "It wouldna look good for me tae marry ye so soon after yer broken betrothal with my sister. Da thinks the church would frown on such a thing. Ye know he had tae discuss it with the priests in Inverness."

Darien growled and rolled onto his back. With a gasp, Eventide ended up straddling him as he held her hips against his.

"The church has no reason tae protest our marriage," he said, moving his hands from her hips to both breasts. "Yer sister lost all right tae a marriage when she ran off. I dunna see why we need to wait."

"Because it makes us both look like fickle fools tae marry one another so soon after losing our respective betrothals," she explained yet again, eyes closed as he toyed with her nipples. "If we wait, people will forget. The scandal willna be so fresh."

Darien understood that, in theory, but his hot blood didn't want to wait. He sat up, wrapping his arms around her and kissing her deeply as she remained straddling him. But his mouth trailed away from her lips, moving to her neck and shoulder.

"Move, Evie," he whispered. "Move on me, lass."

She knew what he meant. Bracing her knees on the floor, Eventide did as he asked. Slowly, sensually, she rode his manhood, grinding her pelvis against his, feeling him growing increasingly hard within her. He was able to hold his stamina better this time, indulging in the feel and smell of her, letting his feed his senses. He'd missed her so much when he was away from her that he could hardly think for want of her. That was why he'd come to Blackrock, in fact. He'd been summoned to Edinburgh by Robert Stewart but was having such a difficult time concentrating that Stewart sent him to Blackrock and told him not to return until he'd married his lady.

And that was exactly what he planned to do.

But right now, he had her where he wanted her, and he slowed his pace with her the second time around. Eventide rode him until her legs grew tired, at which time he rolled her over again and she ended up underneath him. In little time, he spent himself for a second time in an hour, soaking up every moment of the experience.

Truly, it went beyond words sometimes.

"I love ye, Eventide Moriston," he murmured, kissing her soft lips. "If ye dunna marry me soon, I'll go mad."

Eventide grinned, running her fingers through her impatient man's hair. "We'll talk tae my da today, my angel," she said, kissing him. "I wouldna want ye tae lose what's left of yer mind."

Angel. She'd been calling him that for a while now because of his nickname, Darien *an geal*. The Gaelic word for "white" sounded a little like "gal," and *an geal* when spoken sounded closely to "angel." As she explained it, Darien *was* her angel.

And she was his.

"Ye'll like Edinburgh," he said. "And ye'll have a house tae run. Not a large house, but enough of one."

She smiled faintly. "I like the idea of that," she said. "I'm a grown woman and I canna be submissive tae my mother in her own house for the rest of my life. I deserve my own."

He kissed her one last time before pushing himself off her, rocking back on his heels as he pulled her into a sitting position.

"Ye do," he said. Then he gestured at her clothes, in a pile a few feet away. "Get dressed. I plan on speaking tae yer father this very moment."

With a smile, Eventide crawled over to collect her clothing as Darien grabbed his own. He'd been in mail and tunics and boots, which he'd had to stop in the heat of passion to tear from his body. As Eventide pulled her shift over her head, followed by the simple dress of pale blue that she wore, Darien had a bit more to do with hose, followed by breeches, followed by two tunics and a mail coat.

Eventide had to help him with the mail because it was cumbersome, so she quickly finished tying off the back of her dress before rushing to assist. She pulled and tugged to straighten him out, and when she came around front to make sure the mail was straight, he grabbed her by the waist and tickled her. Screaming with delight, and perhaps annoyance, she slapped his hands away and darted out of his reach.

"Come back here," he told her. "I wasn't finished with ye."

She laughed softly as she pulled on her boots. "Not a chance, laddie," she said, wagging a finger at him. "Ye have big fingers, and they hurt."

"They dunna hurt."

"They do!"

"Ye're as whiny as a bairn."

She cocked an eyebrow as she pulled her hair over her right shoulder and started to braid it. "Is that so?" she said. "Next time, I'll dig my fingers intae yer ribs and see how ye like it."

He shook his head as he tied off one of his boots. "Ye'd better not."

"Why not?"

"Because the last time someone tickled me, it was Aurelius and I was about four years of age," he said. "I pissed myself and Aurelius never let me forget it. I dunna want tae piss myself again in front of ye."

Eventide burst into soft laughter. "I'm sure ye've outgrown that."

"I dunna want tae tempt fate."

Before she could reply, there was a pounding on the door. It startled Eventide, but Darien quickly pulled on his other boot.

"Who comes?" he demanded.

"'Tis me!" Fergus said. He rattled the door. "Why did ye bolt it? Open the door if ye know what's good for ye!"

Darien looked at Eventide, who had her hand over her grinning mouth. Her hair was smoothed, her clothes on, but when they looked at the hide where they'd made love, there was a wet spot on it. Horrified, Eventide ran to it and tried to rub it out with her shoe while Darien went to the solar door.

"I'm coming," he called back to Fergus, watching Eventide

smooth over the wet spot. "Have patience, man."

The evidence was gone, and he opened the door as Eventide went to sit in the chair near one of the small lancet windows, very casually, as if nothing was at all amiss. Or had been amiss. As if they hadn't been doing naughty things on the solar floor. Fergus charged into the chamber, frowning.

"Why'd ye lock the door?" he asked Darien.

Darien gestured to Eventide. "To keep her from running out," he said. "I've been trying tae convince her that we need tae wed before I return tae Edinburgh. Fergus, I canna stand leaving her one more time. I know ye're concerned about what others will think if Evie and I wed so soon after Emelia and Luke ran away, but have pity on me. I love yer daughter and I want tae make her my wife. Will ye agree tae a marriage before I return next month?"

Fergus put his hands on his hips, irritated, as he looked between Eventide and Darien. "I told ye why I wanted ye tae wait," he said. "Evie, did ye put him up tae this?"

Eventide shook her head. "Nay," she said. "But I agree with him. There's no reason for us tae wait any longer. We can have a priest's blessing with just the family as witnesses. We dunna need tae make a big celebration out of it. All I need is Darien and nothing more."

Fergus had heard this argument before. For the past two months, in fact. When Darien was here, he was harping on it so much that Fergus had to hide from him, but when it was just Eventide, the woman was more persistent than a gnat. He couldn't shake her. Truthfully, he was hoping to hold the pair off because of the optics their wedding would project to everyone in the Highlands—humiliated by their respective marital partners running off together, they'd rebounded into each other and a rushed marriage. He'd spoken about it to Lares, who agreed, and to Mabel, who didn't, and then to Athole, who didn't care.

But Fergus cared.

For the first time in his life, he cared about something Eventide did.

In the two months that Emelia had been gone, the dynamics at Blackrock had changed. Fergus was no longer focused on his eldest daughter, the one who always had his full attention, and in the days since Emelia had fled, he'd had the chance to get to know his youngest.

The one always overshadowed by her sister.

It wasn't that he didn't know Eventide, because he did. She was his daughter, so, clearly, he knew her to a certain extent. But what he hadn't known was how caring and thoughtful she was. He hadn't known how bright she was, that she had a wicked sense of humor that made him grin from time to time. She had been more than willing to step in and take over her mother's chatelaine duties because ever since Emelia's flight, Athole had taken to her bed and refused to leave. She had decided that she simply didn't care anymore, about anything, and spent her days locked up in her chamber.

Because of this, Eventide had been forced to assume her mother's tasks, and she had taken to them naturally. She had been educated at Saint Mary's church in Inverness, where the monks taught her to read and write and do her sums. Education was important to Fergus, and he'd made sure that both of his daughters had some level of education, although Emelia had never shown much aptitude for it. Eventide had, and since Emelia's departure, Fergus had been reacquainted with a bright daughter he'd forgotten about.

The only daughter who hadn't shamed him.

He realized that he had treated Eventide poorly because of his attention toward her sister. The past two months had seen him soften toward her considerably, and the relationship had strengthened. Because of this, he found himself increasingly willing to let her and Darien finally get married, because the truth was that there really was no reason to delay it any longer. His fears about the optics of the situation were probably unfounded, but he didn't regret telling them to wait. Eventide and Darien had just suffered through a humiliating circumstance, and there was a part of Fergus that wanted to give the couple time to make sure their desire to marry wasn't some vindictive or emotional reaction to the situation. From what he could see, it wasn't either of those things. What Eventide and Darien felt for each other had nothing to do with Emelia or Luke.

It had everything to do with how they looked at each other and the joy in their eyes when they did so.

Even now, he could see it in their faces.

"Well," Fergus finally said, scratching his neck, "Darien, yer mother seemed tae think there was no reason tae delay the marriage, but yer father agreed with me. Ye know that."

Darien nodded. "I know," he said. "And I understand the reasons behind asking us tae wait. Mayhap ye even wanted tae test our feelings toward one another, which is completely reasonable. But the truth is that I love yer daughter and every day that passes sees that love grow. I'll not change my mind tomorrow or ever. But I do want tae call her my wife in the worst way possible."

Fergus could see the longing in the man's eyes, and he broke down into a faint smile. "I understand, lad," he said.

"Will ye take her tae yer English property, then? God help me, my daughter will bear an English title. Lady Lowmoor. The shame of it!"

He wasn't serious, and both Darien and Eventide grinned at his dramatics. She went to her father and put her hand on his arm.

"Just dunna tell anyone," she said. "Tell them the truth—that Darien has a townhome in Edinburgh and that's where we live. Ye dunna have tae mention Wigton House."

He grunted. "I want tae see this big house, Darien," he said. "Is it big and grand enough for my daughter?"

Darien fought off a smile. "Twice the size of Blackrock," he said. "It's a manor home with its own chapel. And the chapel is quite large."

Fergus was skeptical. "Ye willna raise yer children there?"

"I dunna know. I haven't thought on it."

"Then *think*," Fergus said, thumping himself on the head. "Ye want tae raise Scots loyal tae Scotland. If they're born at Wigton House, they'll only be confused."

Darien cocked a dark eyebrow. "And if ye dunna let me marry yer daughter before I have tae return tae Edinburgh, ye may not have any grandchildren at all."

The tides had turned, and Fergus cleared his throat unhappily. "True," he said. Pausing, he lingered on his daughter and her hopeful expression for a moment. "If ye plan tae get married before the whelp ye're marrying has tae return tae Edinburgh, then ye'd better send word tae Lady Mabel. If ye marry without her present, ye'll never hear the end of it."

Eventide beamed. "Do ye mean we can get married?"

"If I deny ye, ye'd just run off and do it anyway."

With a squeal of delight, Eventide threw her arms around

her father. Darien went to the man, clapping him on the shoulder.

"Thank you," he said sincerely. "I'll send a missive tae my parents immediately so they can be here when we take our vows."

"How soon do ye think they can come?" Eventide asked, still holding her father. "Soon?"

Darien shrugged. "Knowing my mother, she'll be on the road an hour after receiving the missive," he said. "She willna miss it. But given that it takes a little time for the missive tae arrive and for them tae travel, I would say they can be here in a little more than a week."

That seemed to fuel Eventide's joy all over again, and she let out another shriek and kissed her father on the cheek. Letting the man go, she rushed to Darien, who pulled her into his arms and hugged her tightly. Fergus watched it all, softened by the sight of a young couple so very much in love.

"I suppose it had tae happen sometime," he said. "I knew I couldna delay for too long, but I will admit that it's been grand spending the days with ye, Evie. It makes me sorry I dinna do it when yer sister was still here. I should have paid more attention tae ye, and I'm sorry I dinna. Ye're much more interesting than Emelia."

Eventide smiled. "She's much more vivacious than I am," she said. "Da, I dunna hate her for occupying yer attention. She's my sister and I could never hate her. I hope wherever she is that she's at least happy. 'Twould be terrible to go through all of this trouble and not be happy."

Fergus didn't have much to say to that. He simply shrugged and glanced at Darien, who didn't have much to say to it either. After all Emelia had done to her sister, Eventide still couldn't bring herself to hate her.

That said a great deal for her heart.

"Well, now," Fergus said, shifting the subject as he waved an impatient hand at Darien, "ye'd better get tae writing that missive tae yer parents. If we're tae have a wedding, we need them here."

"That's very true," Eventide said, already moving for her father's big table with its vellum and writing kit. "Shall I write it for ye, my angel?"

Since she was already sitting down to write, grasping at a vellum sheet, Darien chuckled. "Go ahead," he said. "I'll find a messenger tae send it."

Eventide beamed at him as she pulled the writing kit closer to her in preparation. Fergus leaned over the table.

"Make sure ye'll tell them tae hurry," he said. "And tell Lares tae bring barrels of drink with him. We'll need it."

Darien snorted, shaking his head at Fergus' priorities for his wedding, before heading out of the chamber. Since he'd spent so much time at Blackrock over the past couple of months, he'd come to know Fergus' men fairly well. He knew that there were a couple of young Highlanders who rode like the wind, and he intended to find at least one of them to deliver the missive.

It was a glorious day outside, not terribly cool, and the sun was bright. As he came out of the keep, he glanced up at the sky, watching some birds as they flocked toward the sea. His home, the Hydra, was also on a sea inlet, so he'd grown up smelling the salt and feeling the wind on his face. He didn't get much of that in Edinburgh. It was something that fed his soul.

A soul that was whole these days.

He smiled when he thought of Eventide in her father's solar, scratching away a missive to his mother. Mabel loved Eventide, and that meant the world to Darien. Given how selective his mother was when it came to women, he was elated that she was so warm and welcoming to Eventide.

Life couldn't get any better.

"Darien!"

A shout caught his attention and he paused, turning to see Calum and Guthrie Munro heading in his direction. He grinned at the sight of the Munro brothers, who had become regular fixtures at Blackrock since the sacking of Moy Castle. In fact, it was the brothers who'd made sure Moy was manned and protected while Darien was in Edinburgh. He hadn't realized they were at Blackrock when he returned this morning, but then again, he was only looking for Eventide.

Now, he had time for his friends.

"What are ye doing here?" he asked. "Ye're supposed tae be at Moy."

Calum smiled at the man he genuinely liked. "We were," he said, quickly sobering. "But we received word from Foulis and had tae go home. My da isn't well, Darien. The physic thinks he may not be long for this world."

Darien's expression was washed with sorrow. "I'm sorry for ye," he said. "I dinna know he was ill."

"It came on quickly."

Darien could see that both brothers were struggling with their sorrow, and he reached out to grasp Guthrie's arm, giving him a squeeze of support.

"I'll send word tae my da," he said. "He'll want tae see old Padraig. And ye'll tell Fergus now. He'll probably rush over to Foulis today."

Calum shook his head. "Not today," he said. "It was a bad morning for my da. That's why we left. Mayhap tomorrow will be better."

"Will ye at least stay and feast with us?" Darien said. "Fergus has finally given permission for Evie and I tae be married right away, so I'd like ye tae celebrate that with us."

Calum smiled weakly. "Of course we will," he said. "Ye've got yerself a fine wife, Darien. I wish ye years of happiness."

"Thank ye," Darien said sincerely. "Now we've got tae find ye and Guthrie wives so our children can grow up together."

The mood lightened as they talked about the children they would have, new generations that would defeat the English and make Scotland a strong and free country. Already, Calum was trying to negotiate a marriage between his future son and Darien's future daughter, which had Darien demanding to see their accounts to determine if they were rich enough for his daughter. He was so caught up in the laughter of the conversation that he failed to see one of the men who manned the gates running for him. He only noticed when the man was practically on top of him, his voice full of panic.

"Darien!" the man said, grabbing his arm. "Ye must come!"

Darien didn't take kindly to being grabbed, but he could hear the fear in the man's voice. "Why?" he demanded. "What's amiss?"

The man could only point to the gate, which was open. There were several men there, and that was all he could see, so he took off at a run with Calum and Guthrie behind him, all of them heading for the gate. Once they reached the open panels, the sea of men seemed to part and, finally, they could see what had the man so rattled.

A sight Darien never thought he'd see again.

Emelia had returned.

CHAPTER ELEVEN

"TAKE ANOTHER SIP, Emelia," Fergus said as he held the cup to his daughter's lips. "That's right, lass. Drink it down and then breathe. *Breathe.*"

They were crowded around Emelia, who was only half conscious. She'd fainted at the gatehouse when Darien came upon her, and he'd carried her back to the keep and practically dumped her into her astonished father's arms. Now, she was in a chair as Fergus knelt beside it, trying to force her to drink a very strong spirit called *aqua vitae*, something he'd purchased from the monks at Fearn Abbey to the north. They distilled the brew in small batches, a strong and delicious drink that went straight to a man's head. It could also revive those who were weak of spirit, which Emelia was, so Fergus was practically pouring it down her throat as Darien, Eventide, Calum, Guthrie, and even Athole hovered around her. Everyone was concerned about the pale, exhausted woman.

Everyone but Darien, that was.

He had no concern, only questions.

"Emelia!" Athole had her daughter's hand, patting it furiously. "Tell us what happened, love! What happened to ye?"

Emelia was faking it. Darien was completely convinced of that because she'd looked perfectly fine at the gatehouse when he spied her, but the moment their eyes locked, she collapsed and he was positive it was just for sympathy. Just like this little show in front of him was. She wasn't ill.

She was trying to gain absolution for her sins from eager parents.

"Mama?" Emelia said weakly, struggling to open her eyes. "Is that ye?"

Athole burst into tears. "'Tis me, my dear lass," she said. "Ye've come home tae me! I knew ye would!"

Emelia's eyes finally rolled open and she began to weep. "I ran from him," she gasped. "I managed tae break free of him and ran all the way home!"

"Break free from whom?" Fergus asked.

Emelia sobbed dramatically. "Luke!" she wept. "He abducted me and forced me... he forced me tae his will. I tried tae fight him, but he beat me. I dinna want tae go with him, but he made me. *He made me!*"

She was crying loudly, hands on her face, and Athole threw her arms around her daughter.

"Ye're safe, lass," she said, weeping alongside her child. "Ye're safe now. Ye needn't worry."

"I dinna want tae go!" Emelia said again. Then she dropped her hands and looked at Darien. "I was looking forward tae becoming yer wife. I'm still looking forward tae it. I hope ye can forgive me, Darien. Luke forced me and I couldna fight him. Forgive me for being weak."

Darien just stared at her. She presented the proper picture of a distraught young woman except for one thing—she wasn't weeping tears. She was making a lot of noise, and being dramatic, and perhaps there were a few tears around her eyes, but the way she was carrying on, they should have been down her face and dripping onto the floor.

The lack of actual tears made him extremely suspicious.

"Then tell us what happened," he said emotionlessly. "How did Luke force ye tae leave?"

Emelia was focused on him as if he were the only person in the chamber. "On the day he took me, I woke up early," she said. "I knew guests would be arriving and since my mother takes ill so often, I wanted tae help. But he was waiting for me."

"Where?"

"In the kitchen yard."

"What happened?"

Emelia gestured to her head. "He hit me with something," she said. "I dunna remember anything until we were on the road, heading tae Inverness. He told me he'd kill me if I dinna keep quiet, so out of fear, I did."

Darien watched as Athole stroked Emelia's hair and finally pulled the woman into an embrace. Fergus was still kneeling next to the chair, watching his daughter, clearly enraged by what he was hearing.

Does he actually believe her?

It never occurred to Darien that Fergus would change his stance on why she'd disappeared. He'd spent weeks looking for her, positively convinced that she'd run away with Luke of her own free will. But now... now he looked as if he might be swayed.

But Darien wouldn't be.

He was going to get to the bottom of this.

"Let me see if I have this straight," he said. "Ye woke up early and went tae the kitchen yard."

"Aye."

"And Luke was waiting for ye."

"He was."

"He hit ye over the head with something hard enough tae knock ye unconscious."

"He did."

Darien lifted his eyebrows. "Don't ye think someone would have seen or heard something?" he said. "The kitchen yard has servants in it at any given time, and if Luke had tae take ye out of Blackrock, he would have had tae pass the gates. Men would have seen."

Emelia blinked, a startled gesture that told Darien she hadn't expected anyone to question her story. "I canna know who was near the gates," she said, sounding less traumatized and more indignant. "I was unconscious."

Darien remained cool, sounding neutral. "I'm simply pointing out that he couldna have taken ye through the gates. Someone would have seen."

"Then ask them!"

"We did," Darien said. "On the day ye left, we asked the gate guards and they saw nothing. Was Luke on horseback?"

"Of course he was on horseback."

Darien stroked his chin, turning away as he pondered her lies. "If he was on horseback, either the horse was in the ward, or the stables, or it was tethered somewhere outside," he said. "That means Luke would have tae carry ye tae the horse."

"What are ye driving at, Darien?" Fergus asked. He could see that the man was trying to make a point, so better he come out with it. "What are ye saying?"

Darien paused to look at the woman's father. He was clearly glad to have her back, hypnotized by her sad tale. Clearly falling back under Emelia's spell.

But Darien wasn't.

"I'm simply trying tae understand what happened," he said. His focus returned to Emelia. "Where *is* Luke?"

She hesitated, having to think on an answer, and that gave her away, at least to Darien. *She's making this up as she goes along,* he thought. *She thinks we're stupid.*

"I dunna know where he is," Emelia said. "We were in Sterling, near the river, because he worked for a man who had ships. A merchant. One day, he dinna return and I ran away. I ran all the way home."

She was starting to feign tears again and Darien couldn't stand it. He sighed heavily as he watched Athole and Fergus comfort her, thinking they were two of the most foolish people he'd ever met. But he caught a glimpse of red hair out of the corner of his eye and turned to see Eventide standing near the door.

She didn't believe any of it either.

Her gaze met his and he could see the turmoil in those blue depths. He turned in her direction, wanting to give her some comfort. He could only imagine what she was thinking now that her sister had returned. But the moment he turned for her, Emelia spoke up.

"The only thing that kept me alive was thoughts of our marriage, Darien," she said. "All I could think of was returning tae ye. I know how worried ye must have been."

Darien paused, his gaze lingering on her before he looked at Fergus. The situation had changed so drastically since Emelia's departure that surely the man couldn't expect that things would go back to the way they were.

Darien wasn't going to let that happen.

"Are ye going tae tell her of the current situation or will I?" he asked Fergus.

"What situation?" Emelia said. "What has happened?"

Fergus was greatly torn. "Not now, Darien," he said, ignoring Emelia's question. "She's only just returned. Let her rest and we'll discuss it… later."

Darien could just tell by the look on the man's face that he was in danger of wavering. The reappearance of his eldest daughter was making him weak. Her lies were breaking him down. It was the same old dynamic again, with Emelia controlling her parents, who refused to see her for what she was.

But Darien wasn't fooled.

He wasn't going to let this drag on.

"Ye need tae admit the truth," he said, a hint of anger in his voice as he looked at Emelia. "No one believes that Luke abducted ye. Ye ran off with the man and God only knows where ye've been the past two months, but I know ye for what ye are, Emelia. Ye spread yer legs tae every man who caught yer fancy and everyone knows it. Ye spread them for Luke, and when I wouldna bed ye before marriage, ye decided tae run off with him."

Emelia shrieked. "'Tis not true!" she cried. "How dare ye say such things!"

"Admit it!" Darien boomed.

Emelia screamed, recoiling, as Fergus stood up with the intention of protecting her from an enraged Darien.

"Darien, please," Fergus begged. "Let the woman have some peace before we—"

"Shut yer lips," Darien spat at him, cutting him off harshly. "Shut yer lips before ye say something we'll both regret. We had an agreement, ye and I. We all know what happened with Emelia. Ye were so convinced of her actions that ye and my father captured Moy Castle tae punish the Cannich Clan. *That's how much ye believed yer daughter ran off with Luke.* We all knew it. But I've been standing here, watching ye lose yer spine as she spouts her lies because she knows ye'll believe her. The woman controls you as surely as God controls the heavens, but she canna control me. I willna listen tae her lies and I willna marry Luke Cannich's leavings. She's dead tae me, and if ye believe her lies, then so are ye. I would think very carefully what I say tae me at this time."

He'd shouted at Fergus in a way Fergus had never been shouted at before. No one in that chamber, including Calum and Guthrie, had ever seen Darien so angry. Emelia let out a scream and burst into real tears at that point.

"How could ye say such things about me?" she wept. "'Tis not true!"

"Of course it's true." Eventide, no longer able to stand by and watch her sister manipulate everyone around her, had found her voice. "Emelia, we all know it's true. Ye've been letting men bed ye since ye grew breasts and Da has overlooked it. He tried tae pass ye tae Darien as an heiress, a woman of honor, but ye're not. Darien is right—admit ye ran off with Luke. We all know ye did. Stop lying."

Emelia looked at her sister, a woman who was usually supportive of her, and quickly turned angry. "I'll punish ye for doubting my word," she said. "I'll take a stick to ye!"

In the past, that had been true. When Emelia had been upset with Eventide, she'd taken sticks and beaten her with them until Fergus intervened. Eventide had been too passive to truly fight back, but that had changed. *She* had changed. Her love for Darien had made her brave and strong, and before anyone could stop her, she stormed up to her sister and slapped her so hard that Emelia's entire body lurched sideways.

"Take a stick tae me and I'll beat ye within an inch of yer life!" Eventide shouted. "I'll not let ye bully me anymore, do ye hear? Try tae strike me again and see what happens to ye!"

Emelia had her hand on the left side of her face, her cheek stinging from the slap. But she didn't fight back. She simply sat there, wide-eyed with shock, until she realized everyone was looking at her. Then she erupted into loud, angry tears.

"Father," she sobbed. "Are ye going tae let her do that tae me?"

Fergus was in a bind. Things were happening quickly and he was struggling to stay on an even keel. He ended up pulling Emelia out of the chair because Eventide was still close to her, close enough to strike her again, and then looked at his wife.

"Take Evie out of here," he said. "Do it now."

But Athole didn't want to go. "Nay," she insisted, trying to pull Emelia back into the chair and out of her father's grip. "My place is here, with Emelia. I'm not leaving."

Fergus growled. No one was obeying him. Everything was out of control. Before he could snap at Eventide and chase her away, Darien intervened and grasped her by the arms. Without another word to Fergus or Emelia, he pulled Eventide out of the chamber. Calum and Guthrie followed, thinking they had no business in the solar with only Fergus and Emelia and Athole remaining.

Their presence wasn't necessary in this family matter.

And what a matter it was.

As the Munro brothers made themselves scarce, Darien took Eventide out into the ward. He had his arm around her shoulders and they simply started walking with no real destination in mind.

Anything to cool off.

Anything to get over the shock.

"What does this mean now?" she said, her voice trembling. "She still thinks ye're going tae marry her. She thinks nothing has changed."

Darien sighed heavily, seeing that the gates were open and thinking they might be able to use a walk down by the shoreline. He headed in that direction, keeping a tight grip on Eventide.

"She's a fool if she thinks it hasn't changed," he said. "Her return changes nothing, Evie. I love ye as I always have and I will marry ye. Yer sister will have tae find another husband."

Eventide was genuinely trying to remain calm, but she was rattled. Badly rattled. Tears filled her eyes, and as Darien walked her out of the fortress, she let them fall. She didn't try to hide it. By the time they reached the rocky shore, her entire face was wet. Darien only saw it when they came to a stop and he turned to her.

"Oh… sweetheart," he murmured, wiping her tears off her chin. "Please dunna weep. Emelia's return means nothing tae us, truly."

"Doesn't it?" she said, sniffling. "She hasn't changed. She still lies about everything and my parents will believe her."

"Mayhap," Darien said. "But that does not change the fact that yer father has given his permission for us tae wed. And we will."

"But ye had permission tae marry Emelia first."

Darien shook his head. "I've already made it clear I wouldna marry her if she returned," he said. "That is a vow I will keep."

Eventide took a deep breath, gazing out over the rocky shore, the gray ocean. Because the currents were strong here, they tended to dredge up the sand and turn the waters gray.

"I believe ye," she said. "I dunna want ye tae think I have a lack of faith in ye, for I do. But I know how manipulative my sister can be. We need tae return tae my father right now and make sure he doesna change his mind. Emelia is good at getting him tae do what she wants him tae do."

Darien's gaze moved to the castle on the rise. "I was thinking the same thing," he said. "But I had tae get clear of that room and yer sister. I needed tae breathe and I needed tae hold ye. I can go back and face the rest now."

"Good," Eventide said, reaching out to take his hand. "I'll go with ye. We must face him together so he doesna weaken."

Darien nodded, puffing out his cheeks and exhaling sharply. "I must say that this was the last thing I expected," he admitted. "I supposed I always believed she would return at some point, but this was still unexpected. It has been such a good day until now."

Eventide held his hand tightly as they headed back toward the castle. "It was only a matter of time before she came back," she said. "It was just a matter of when. Emelia has never given her attention for any length of time tae one man. My guess is that she simply grew bored with Luke and came back with that wild story."

"That's as good an explanation as any," Darien said. "But I very much wonder where Luke is. If Emelia has come back, has Luke returned tae Moy?"

"Yer men would send word if he did."

"True enough," Darien said. "But mayhap he returned, saw strange men on the wall, and is hiding out somewhere, wondering what happened."

"Mayhap ye should send men tae search nearby towns for him."

"That is not a bad idea."

"Do ye think they really lived in Sterling?"

"Who knows? We may never get a straight answer from her."

Eventide fell silent for a moment, contemplating the situation, before continuing. "One thing ye must ask her is if she and Luke were married," she said. "Emelia was in love with the idea of marriage, and Luke… Well, the lad is greedy. He's envious of men with titles and land, so it's possible he married Emelia tae gain my father's fortune and keep it away from ye. I dunna think he'd run off with Emelia and remain unmarried tae her for two months. Why run off if he wasn't going tae marry her before ye did?"

Darien glanced at her as they approached the big, open gates. "That is a very good argument," he said. "Church registers would have such a thing, but we'd have tae know where they really went. Was it really Sterling? Or were they in Edinburgh or Glasgow?"

"Do ye want me tae find out?"

He looked at her. "Do ye think she'll tell ye anything after ye slapped her?"

Eventide shrugged. "Sisters fight," she said. "I can apologize and pretend tae be nice tae her. She usually tells me the truth."

Darien grunted, shaking his head. "I wouldna believe anything she told me."

"Probably not, but I can try."

He lifted her hand and kissed it just as they passed into the ward through the gates. "Be calm," he said. "And be strong. She canna hurt us, Evie. Remember that."

Eventide let go of his hand and came to a halt, facing him. "When she finds out we are tae wed, she will try," she said quietly. "I know my sister, Darien. She'll try tae hurt us any way she can. Dunna underestimate her."

Darien nodded faintly, deliberating the situation they found themselves in. Now that the surprise had worn off, he could focus on a plan. "Then we'll just have tae factor that in when we come tae it," he said. "For now, I think we should divide and conquer. I'll take yer father and ye see tae yer sister. Find out what ye can and then meet me in the hall later."

"I'll do my best."

He winked at her. "I love ye, lass," he murmured. "That love makes us strong."

She nodded, blowing him a kiss as he headed for the keep. He seemed so sure of himself, so sure of the situation, but Eventide felt differently. She wasn't sure in the least. In fact, she was very much on her guard.

Dunna underestimate her.

Eventide was fairly certain that she and her sister were about to engage in a knife fight.

And she was determined to win.

CHAPTER TWELVE

"THIS IS BAD," Guthrie mumbled. "Very bad. What is Darien going tae do? He's tae marry one sister, then his original bride returns."

The brothers were leaning against the wall of an outbuilding near the stables, watching the activity in the ward. They'd watched Darien and Eventide leave the gates, and they'd watched them come back in again. The couple looked very upset—and with good reason. They watched the pair go their separate ways when they returned, but still, the mood lingered.

Everything seemed dark.

Calum shook his head to his brother's question.

"I dunna know," he said. "But there's no doubt in my mind that Emelia is lying. She's all for show, that one."

Guthrie nodded in agreement. "Ye know her reputation," he said. "Everyone around here knows. That's why I was so surprised when I heard she was betrothed tae Darien. He's a good man, and she… she's like a bitch in heat."

Calum knew what his brother was talking about. Everyone in this part of the Highlands had heard of Emelia Moriston's reputation, whether or not they knew the family well.

"From what I heard, Lares made the betrothal and Darien had no choice," he said. "One doesna go against the will of Lares dun Tarh."

"But surely Lares knew the lass's reputation?"

"Only Lares can answer that, and I'll not ask him. Will ye?"

Guthrie shook his head. "Nay," he said firmly. "But what do we do now? Do we return tae Moy? Do we return tae Foulis and tell Da about this?"

Calum thought on that a moment. "I think we stay," he said. "Darien doesna have any of his family here tae help him should he need it, so we'll stay for his sake. He may have need of us."

"But what can we do?"

Calum's gaze lingered on the keep. "I dunna know," he said. "But if needs us, we'll be here."

Guthrie pushed himself off the wall, facing his brother. "What if he needs us tae get rid of Emelia?" he asked. "He's in love with Evie and he's going tae marry her, but Emelia's return will ruin those plans. What if he wants us tae get rid of her?"

Calum looked at him. "He'd do it for us."

That was very true. Darien and the dun Tarh brothers were loyal friends. Guthrie had to accept the fact that helping Darien might involve something unsavory, but he wasn't opposed to it. As his brother said, Darien would do it for them.

They were here to help him, however they could.

"Very well," Guthrie said after a moment. "Should we offer, then?"

Calum snorted. "Tae throw the lass in the sea?" he said, incredulous. "Nay, we dunna offer. But if he asks…"

"If he asks, we do."

"We do."

Now, all they had to do was wait.

⁂

SOMETHING WAS GOING on.

Emelia knew that right away. As she lay on her bed, staring up at the ceiling, she could hear her mother moving around in the adjoining chamber that belonged to Eventide.

Eventide.

Something was going on between her sister and Darien.

Emelia's return to Blackrock had been mostly victorious. Her parents had been glad to see her and more than willing to listen to her story. She knew her mother believed her and was quite certain her father would soon believe her as well. She'd always been able to convince him of whatever she wanted, true or not. Emilia felt completely at home again, amongst people she could manipulate easily. Her parents had always been weak.

She had been counting on it.

The journey from Glasgow to Blackrock hadn't been particularly full of peril. Fortunately, she'd managed to join up with a family that was traveling far to the north and allowed her to ride in the back of the wagon. She'd sat with the daughters of the family, two young girls who had been quite enamored with her, and told them stories as the caravan traveled north. Since she really didn't want to spend money to compensate these people for allowing her to travel with them, she made herself useful by entertaining the children.

That seemed to be good enough.

They left her in Inverness, and from there, it was a half-day's walk home. Blackrock hadn't changed in the time she'd been away, and she found a good deal of comfort in that, but what she hadn't expected was to see Darien the moment she came in through the gates. He was looking at her with astonishment, and for lack of a better reaction, she pretended to faint. She wanted the man's sympathy, and that was a quick way to get it. She'd been concocting her story all the way home and thought it was a good one—she intended to tell her parents that Luke had kidnapped her, thereby pushing the blame off her and onto him. As she'd hoped, her parents believed her.

But Darien and Eventide didn't.

That was what initially made her think there was something going on between them. They stood united in condemning her. But the confirmation of her suspicions was when Darien removed Eventide from the solar, putting his arm around her most comfortingly and taking her out of the keep.

That was something Emelia hadn't anticipated.

In hindsight, she should have. They'd been the two left behind when she and Luke fled, so it was only natural that they found comfort in one another. Clearly, that comfort had turned into something stronger, and that concerned Emelia.

She hadn't expected that obstacle.

But she should have.

Did she really think it was going to be so easy to simply come back into Darien's life? She had assumed he would believe her story, so she had expected that he would be grateful enough for her return that the marriage would be back on. Especially if he thought Luke had abducted her. But he didn't believe her at all and, in fact, mentioned something about razing Moy Castle. Clearly, things had gone on while she'd been away, and she intended to get to the bottom of it—but in questioning her mother, she realized that the woman didn't know much. That wasn't unusual, and often Emelia counted on that kind of thing, but in this case it was annoying.

She needed to know what was happening.

After the initial interrogation, her mother took her up to her chamber to rest, and that was where she found herself lying on her bed, staring up at the ceiling. She was physically weary but not sleepy. What she very much wanted to do was interrogate her mother again to see if she could get more out of the woman. She was thinking of doing precisely that when the chamber door opened and Eventide entered.

The claws came out.

"*Ye!*" Emelia said as she sat bolt upright in bed. "What have ye done tae my betrothed?"

Eventide remained cool in the face of a shouted accusation. They heard the door in the connecting chamber slam because Athole, hearing her daughter yelling, didn't want to get involved in any fray. That was usual with her.

"Who was that?" Eventide asked.

"Mother," Emelia said, knowing Eventide couldn't see into the other chamber because of the angle of the room. "Answer me—*what* is happening? What have ye done with my betrothed?"

Eventide cast her sister a long look before going into her chamber and bolting that door. Then she came back into Emelia's chamber and bolted that door, too. With both doors locked, she folded her arms across her chest and faced her sister.

"I'm sorry I slapped ye earlier," she said. "How are ye feeling?"

That wasn't what Emelia had been expecting. Given what happened in the solar, she'd expected more of Eventide's rage. And flying palms. The fact that she couldn't anticipate her sister left her feeling uneasy.

"Ye still haven't answered me," she said. "*What* has happened between ye and Darien?"

"I'm more concerned about what happened between ye and Luke."

Emelia wasn't used to being denied her wants. In this case, she wanted an answer to a question, and when Eventide didn't answer her, yet again, she flew out of the bed.

"I told ye what happened and ye called me a liar," she snapped. "Ye had no right tae do that!"

Eventide sighed. "Emelia, I know ye better than anyone," she said. "I know Luke dinna abduct ye. Ye'd been eyeing the man for weeks before ye ran off with him. There's nothing ye can say that will change my mind, so ye may as well stop trying. Ye ran off with my betrothed and ye humiliated me and Darien and both of our families. What I want tae know is why ye returned—did Luke grow tired of ye and throw ye out?"

"Ha!" Emelia said. "That's how much ye know. He would never—"

She stopped herself before she could say more, but Eventide latched on to it. "He would never… *what*?" she said, coming closer. "Never throw ye over? Never tire of ye? Something happened, because if it hadn't, ye wouldna be here. Did he meet someone prettier than ye? It wouldna be difficult."

Emelia marched over to her and slapped her across the face. It was a weak slap, barely moving Eventide's head. She grinned at her sister, in fact, before she answered with a devastating slap that sent Emelia sideways. Before Emelia could catch her balance, Eventide shoved her to the floor.

"That's where ye belong, ye gutter rat," she growled. "Luke never abducted ye. Ye convinced him tae run away with ye. When he got tired of looking at yer ugly face, ye came home and hoped Darien would be stupid enough tae believe yer story. Well, he doesna believe ye. He knows ye for what ye are. We all do."

Emelia was furious. She was still on the floor, but she kicked out, trying to catch her sister in the shins. "He's my betrothed," she shouted. "Ye canna have him!"

"Ye took mine. I'm taking yers."

Emelia struggled to her feet, quivering with rage. "Ye canna," she said, wiping at her mouth and realizing Eventide's slap had drawn a little blood when her tooth cut into her cheek. "He was mine first."

Eventide was losing her temper, something she'd hoped not to do. She'd hoped to ease things between her and her sister, but Emelia's instant rancor when she entered the chamber had changed that. Now she was becoming acrimonious, too, and if they kept going, there was going to be a brawl.

Eventide had to slow the situation down.

If she was to get the truth out of her sister, she had to at least pretend to be calm.

"Ye're right," she said, swallowing her rage. "I'm sorry we've been fighting since ye returned, Emmy, but we were so upset when ye left. We dinna know what tae think. And now ye're back and everything is so confusing."

She lowered her head and wiped at her eyes for effect, hoping Emelia would calm down and be more forthcoming if she thought Eventide was backing down.

But Emelia wasn't ready to calm down yet.

"Aye, I'm back," she said, still angry. "I want ye tae tell me what is happening between ye and Darien. How dare ye move in on him. He's mine!"

So much for backing down. Eventide could see that Emelia

wasn't going to calm herself, so she had no choice but to continue butting heads—only she opted to not only butt heads, but put her foot to Emelia's arse for good measure.

So much for sisterly love.

"I've decided something," Eventide said after a moment. "I've decided that I'm going tae find every man ye've spread yer legs for, including the well-hung lad who beget ye with child, and I'm going tae bring them all here tae Blackrock so they can tell Darien what kind of woman ye are. Dunna forget that I know yer secrets, Emelia. All of them."

Emelia turned red in the face. "He'll not believe ye."

Eventide laughed, without humor. "He'll believe the dozens of men ye've satisfied," she said. "Ye want tae know what's happened between me and Darien? He's met a woman who is worthy of him. He loves me and I love him, and Da has given us permission tae be wed. Ye lost the right tae have him when ye left, Emelia. He's mine now."

Emelia's mouth popped open in outrage. "Ye stole him from me!" she said. "Da couldna have given his permission tae marry! Darien is *my* betrothed."

"Not any longer."

With a scream of rage, Emelia charged her sister, but Eventide was prepared. She dodged out of the way and gave Emelia a shove, pushing her off balance and into the door. It didn't deter Emelia because she ran at her sister again, open palms flying, and Eventide was able to push the hands aside. As Emelia went off balance yet again, Eventide balled a fist and hit her squarely in the chin.

Down Emelia went.

"Now," Eventide said, standing over her sister and shoving her when she tried to get up. "If ye're finished trying tae fight with me, I want ye tae listen. Ye only have yerself tae blame for this. Darien doesna want ye. We're going tae be married and live in Edinburgh so I never have tae see yer sorry hide again. Ye canna have what ye want this time, Emelia. Ye may as well accept it. Find another husband, because Darien belongs tae me."

On the ground, Emelia kicked at her. Eventide slapped her on the side of the head and grabbed her hair for good measure, pulling hard. That had Emelia screaming again, but Eventide only pulled harder.

"Do ye understand me?" she said. "Tell me ye understand that this battle is over and I'll let go."

She pulled so hard that Emelia eventually had to concede. As Eventide left the chamber and went in search of Darien, Emelia sat on the floor and wept.

But not for long.

He was mine first!

That's what she'd said to her sister, because it was true. Darien belonged to her, and in the eyes of the church, a betrothal was nearly as binding as a marriage. Even if Darien refused to marry her, and her father had given permission for Eventide and Darien to wed, Emelia refused to surrender. She'd taken one man from her sister.

She could take another.

This wasn't over.

Not in the least.

CHAPTER THIRTEEN

The Hydra

"Kal! Fetch Caelus and come with me!"

The shout came from Estevan, calling to his brother, who was standing with a group of Highlanders as they practiced spear throwing. Bales of rope-bound grass had been set up for targets and, so far, the middle dun Tarh brothers, Caelus and Kaladin, seemed to be doing quite well. Caelus, in fact, with his long arms and long legs, seemed to be doing particularly well, and he wasn't modest about it.

But Estevan didn't have time for their foolery.

Something serious was afoot.

Sensing this, Kaladin motioned to Caelus, pulling him away from the Highlanders, who now wanted to start wagering on the spear throwing. Caelus, the tallest dun Tarh brother, wasn't happy about being removed from a sure-money situation, but Estevan didn't look pleased. Curious, Kaladin and Caelus went to see what was amiss, but Estevan waved off their questions.

"Come," he said. "Da wants tae speak with us."

The intrigue deepened.

Beneath mild skies, with a hint of rain on the horizon, the

brothers passed from the massive outer ward into the slightly less massive inner ward. The keep of the Hydra was in the middle of the inner ward, a stout, square beast of a building, one of the largest in Scotland. It didn't have a lot of chambers to it, but the chambers it did have were enormous. There was a massive hall on the entry level, one that spanned the entire width and breadth of the keep.

That was where they found Lares.

The great hall of the Hydra was also Lares' solar. The Hydra didn't have a separate solar set aside for the lord of the manor, so Lares tended to conduct business in the hall and keep all of his documents and valuables in the colossal chamber he shared with his wife. His sons could see him at the far end of the hall, sitting at one end of the dais. When they drew closer, they could see that the man had a missive in his hand.

"I brought them, Da," Estevan said. "Tell them what ye told me."

Lares was still looking at the missive. It tended to be dark at this end of the hall, so the servants had brought a bank of yellow tapers affixed to an iron sconce that was as tall as a man. It gave off a good deal of light. Lares waited until his sons sat down before speaking.

"Darien has trouble, lads," he said, looking up from the missive. "He's sent word that Emelia has returned tae Blackrock."

A collective hiss went up between Caelus and Kaladin. "She's *back*?" Caelus said, aghast. "Why? What happened?"

Lares held up the missive. "Yer brother wrote this," he said. "According to him, she returned three days ago with a tale that Luke Cannich had abducted her against her will. She has returned tae Blackrock and wants tae marry yer brother, only he intends tae marry Evie. I'm leaving for Blackrock at dawn because I have a feeling this is something I need tae straighten out with Fergus."

"Why?" Estevan said. "Are ye afraid he'll go back on his word tae Darien about Evie?"

Lares shrugged. "Truthfully, I dunna know, but I dunna trust him when it comes tae Emelia," he said. "He convinced me that she'd be a good wife for Darien once, but we've come tae see that is not the case. He told me once that if she returned, he'd not break the betrothal with Darien, but that was before Darien and Evie fell in love. If Fergus tries tae force Darien tae marry Emelia, I'm afraid what yer brother might do to him."

"What about Mother?" Kaladin asked. "Lilliana said she's very fond of Evie. Does she know any of this?"

Lares shook his head. "Not yet," he said sadly. "I wanted tae tell the three of ye because I want ye tae come with me tae Blackrock tomorrow. When I tell yer mother, I suspect she'll want tae come, too. She'll not let Fergus hurt yer brother."

The brothers nodded, looking at one another, feeling uncertainty on behalf of Darien. They could only imagine what the man was going through, so they were eager to get to Blackrock, just as their father was, in the hopes of straightening this mess out.

If only the woman had stayed away…

"Da," Kaladin said after a moment, "ye are aware that I know Luke Cannich. We were both tutored by the same priest from Inverness. The man loves women—there's no doubt about that—but he doesna have a mean streak in him. I dunna believe Emelia when she says he abducted her. That's not the Luke I know."

Lares sighed faintly, glancing at the missive before putting it back on the table. "Is he beyond running off with a woman if he wanted her badly enough?"

Kaladin could only shake his head. "I dunna know," he said. "The man is a seducer, and women love him. I've seen it myself. Is he beyond running off with one? I canna say. But I remember that when we were being taught by the priest, he'd speak of being rich someday. A rich laird, he would say. Does running off with Emelia give him wealth?"

Lares nodded. "Wealth and a title, lad."

"Then I would say anything is possible."

"Where is Luke, Da?" Caelus asked. "Does Darien say?"

Lares shook his head. "He doesna say," he said. "But we'll know more when we get tae Blackrock and settle this matter. The three of ye will go and prepare for tomorrow's journey while I go tell yer mother. And ye'd better make sure the carriage is prepared if I canna fight her off."

Estevan looked at his brothers. "That means bring the carriage forth," he said. "If Mam wishes tae go tae Blackrock, then nothing he can say will stop her."

"Dunna be so quick tae discount me," Lares said, weakly defending himself. "I may yet be able tae convince her tae let me handle this alone."

That brought snorts from all three brothers. "Of course ye can," Caelus said. "Stand strong, Da. She'll surrender eventually."

Kaladin started laughing, but a nasty look from Lares had the young man moving away from the dais quickly. Caelus, receiving the same nasty look, fought off a grin and followed his brother out of the great hall. Only Estevan remained behind, watching his father pick up the missive one more time and look at Darien's careful writing.

It was clear that Lares was greatly troubled.

"This is going tae be a battle, isn't it?" Estevan asked softly. "Darien's battle. He'll not let Evie go without a fight."

Lares knew that. "I am aware," he said quietly. "Darien the Destroyer will make an appearance, I'm certain. And that's why I'm going tae Blackrock."

"Tae stop him?"

Lares twisted his lips ironically. "I'm fairly certain Evie wouldna like her future husband tae kill her father," he said. "That would cripple the marriage before it starts. And I canna let that happen."

Estevan couldn't disagree. They departed the great hall in silence, with Lares going into the keep to inform his wife that her son's former fiancée had finally returned home. As he'd known, Mabel was extremely unhappy with the situation. Predictably, she accompanied her husband and sons to Blackrock the very next morning.

A tense situation was about to get worse.

CHAPTER FOURTEEN

IT WAS QUIET.

So much of his life hadn't been quiet over the past day that a moment like this, of peace, was something of a shock to his system. Fergus had planned to go over a bill of sale from some sheep he'd purchased at a livestock market last month because he wanted to sell some of the sheep to a neighbor, but he found himself staring at the bill of sale without actually reading it.

His thoughts were turning to the situation at hand.

Emelia.

Perhaps in the past he would have believed her story. The tears, the completely sincere delivery—he would have believed her without question. But something had happened to him in the wake of her disappearance—too many people had spoken of Emelia and what she was really like. The true character that he'd been willing to overlook. But his eyes had been opened to his eldest daughter, finally, and he was having difficulty with what he was seeing. The truth was that it would have been better had she stayed away. He'd been happier, and Eventide had certainly been happier. His wife… Well, she was never happy to begin with, so it didn't matter much with her. But now, Emelia was back and everything was in chaos.

He knew he had to make a decision.

He wasn't looking forward to it.

"Da?"

A soft rap on the door broke him out of his train of thought, and he looked up to see Emelia entering the chamber. She smiled at him when their eyes met and shut the door behind her, coming over to his table and giving him a kiss on the forehead.

"Ye look weary, Da," she said, sitting down next to him. "Can I help?"

Fergus smiled weakly. "I'm afraid my burdens are all mine tae bear," he said. "How are ye feeling today? Did ye sleep well?"

Emelia nodded, laying her head on his shoulder. "Very well," she said. "But I'm sad."

"Why, lass?"

"Ye know why."

"If I did, I wouldna ask."

Emelia sighed heavily. "Because my world is being taken away from me," she said. "Everything I thought I was coming home tae has changed."

"Ye mean Darien?"

"Aye," Emelia said. "I love him, Da. I'm very sad about the situation."

Fergus knew she didn't love Darien. Even before she ran off, or was abducted, she'd never shown Darien a huge amount of interest. Nay, she didn't love him.

But she was laying her groundwork for the conversation to come.

"I'm sorry ye're sad," he said after a moment. "But we dinna think ye were coming back. Ye were dead for all we knew. Do ye not expect people tae get on with their lives in the face of death?"

Emelia lifted her head and looked at him. "But I'm not dead," she said. "I'm very much alive. 'Tis not fair that I should return tae a husband who is no longer mine."

Fergus shook his head. "Ye canna expect a man tae mourn ye the rest of his life," he said. "Nay, lass, Darien has moved on with Evie, and they love one another. Even if I told him not tae marry her, he'd find a way."

"Then you must *make* him marry me."

"How? He's a grown man. I cannot command him tae do anything he doesna want tae do."

Emelia frowned. "Then find Evie another husband," she snapped. "I want mine back."

"He'll not go back tae ye, Emelia."

"Of course he willna if ye dunna take Evie away from him," she said angrily, rising from her chair. "Send her away, Da. Send her tae a convent and get her away from here!"

Fergus scowled. "I'll not send yer sister away," he said. "She'll remain here and she'll marry Darien. He'll take her tae Edinburgh and then ye'll not see her again, I'd wager. Neither one of them are particularly fond of ye after the way ye've behaved."

Emelia looked as if she'd been struck. "Ye think poorly of me, too?" she said, sobbing dramatically when no tears were readily available. "How could ye do such a thing?"

Fergus sighed heavily as he leaned back in his chair. "Emelia, I've learned a lot about ye since ye've been gone," he said. "Things I suppose I knew all along, but nothing I would acknowledge. But since ye left with Luke—"

She interrupted him. "He abducted me!"

Fergus shook his head. "Nay, he dinna," he said. "I dunna believe that, and nor does anyone else. Ye ran off with him, and when ye realized life would be too difficult, ye came home and made up the excuse that he stole away with ye, and fool that I am, I blamed his father. I took his castle. All tae avenge myself on a family I blamed for yer behavior."

Emelia was genuinely horrified by what she was hearing. Her father had never gone against her when it came to her lies or wants. He simply took everything at face value.

But not today.

Today, she stood alone.

"I canna believe ye would think such things about me," she said, scrambling to gain the upper hand in the conversation. "Evie steals my husband and ye blame me for it? That's cruel, Da. Cruel and selfish."

Fergus shrugged. "Probably," he said. "If it is, then ye learned all ye know from me. I only have myself tae blame for the way ye are."

Emelia was genuinely flabbergasted. She'd never had her father deny her anything, so this was something completely alien to her. He seemed to want to go back to the tasks in front of him, rummaging through the vellum on his table, but Emelia wouldn't let him get away from her so easily.

She had to make him understand.

"Da," she said, struggling to keep calm, "ye pledged Darien tae me. Me. Ye know the church views a betrothal as very nearly a marriage. 'Tis binding. Ye canna simply break it because Evie fancies herself in love with Darien."

"Make no mistake," Fergus said, "she *is* in love with Darien. And he loves her. I'll find ye another husband, Emelia, but

Darien is spoken for. Forget about him."

"I dunna want another husband! I want Darien!"

"Ye canna have him."

He sounded final. So very final. Astonished, and enraged, Emelia stared at her father's lowered head as he went back to his business. As if she didn't matter at all. Well, she *did* matter. Her wants and dreams mattered most of all. This wasn't the end of the subject, but her father didn't seem to want to listen.

She knew who would.

The church views a betrothal as very nearly a marriage.

This wasn't over.

Chapter Fifteen

St. Mary's Church
Inverness

"I IMPLORE YE tae take action. What my sister intends tae do is against the law of God and the church!"

"She is marrying the man you are betrothed to?"

"Aye! She stole him from me!"

Emelia was convincing—oh so convincing. That was one of her many gifts. In this case, she was trying to convince the monsignor at St. Mary's in Inverness that the church needed to intervene in this situation.

So very much had happened since she returned home.

Nothing was going as she had planned it. Gone were the days of Emelia controlling everything around her, including her parents. While her mother was still very malleable, her father seemed to have hardened in some ways. He said he believed her story, yet he was unwilling to rescind his permission for Eventide to marry Darien. That, at least, kept Darien from tearing Blackrock apart with his rage, but he still wasn't a happy man because Fergus had asked him to wait for the marriage.

And the man didn't want to wait.

Emelia could see this situation slipping from her grasp, and that wasn't something she could allow. She had tried to talk to Darien, to perhaps soften the man and even seduce him, but he wouldn't talk to her, period—he wouldn't even look at her. She'd gone so far as to plant herself in front of his chamber door so that when he awoke in the morning, she would be right there waiting for him, but all he did was glance at her and walk around her. When she tried to grab his arm, he pulled her fingers off and tossed her arm away.

Somehow, her desire to marry Darien had become something more. Now, it had turned into a tug of war, a contest against her sister that she intended to win. Eventide had Darien under her spell, and that was clear, but Emelia wasn't one to give up or give in. As she had so often rejoiced over in the past, she had managed to take Luke away from her sister. She was confident she could also take Darien away, only that was going to take more time, and time was something she didn't have. Her father, uncharacteristically, refused to discuss the matter with her.

That meant she had to take drastic measures.

It all started when she heard from one of the servants that Darien had sent a missive to his father. Emelia knew that once Lares dun Tarh arrived, the situation would move markedly against her. She didn't really know Darien's father, but she did know that he believed what everyone else believed, that she had willingly run off with Luke and wasn't abducted. That meant the man was against her, and Emilia had to find somebody that was stronger than the Earl of Torridon.

She had to bring the church into the situation.

And that was where she found herself now.

The man she was in discussion with was in charge of St.

Mary's, Monsignor Carrick. He was well respected, having received the honorific title of "monsignor" from the pope himself for exemplary service to the church. He knew her entire family because her parents were generous with their donations and had attended mass there, about once a month, since Emelia was a child. Since Fergus was trying to ignore her pleas and her mother had no power, Emelia had come to a man who could not only force Fergus to her will, but also match Lares dun Tarh's power.

Monsignor Carrick had listened to her explain the situation for almost an hour. The problem was that he was a man not prone to taking sides unless it directly affected church teachings, so as the minutes passed and Emelia pleaded, she became more and more emotional. By the time she'd told him everything, she was in tears. Real tears this time.

She couldn't tell if he was sympathetic or not.

"Please, monsignor," she begged as he sat there and pondered the situation, "I am betrothed tae this man. I'm stolen by another, and when I manage tae return, my sister has taken my betrothed from me. It's not right! The church must intervene because we are talking about the sanctity of marriage. He is *my* husband!"

The man sat in his chair, hands folded at his chin, clearly thinking on what she'd said but in no hurry to make a judgment. "Was there a written contract of this?" he asked in a low, slow voice. He was from England and perhaps viewed the Scots as inferior, as was suggested in everything about him. "And who, exactly, brokered this contract?"

Emelia nodded. "There is a written contract," she said. "My father and Lares dun Tarh, Earl of Torridon, agreed on the terms. I was tae marry the earl's second son, Darien, and he would inherit my father's titles."

"So this was to be an alliance marriage."

"I suppose so," Emelia said. "What difference does it make if my sister is marrying the man in my stead?"

The monsignor shrugged. "Because there would still be an alliance should he marry your sister," he said. "But you are correct—if the contract calls for you and this man to marry, then he was your husband the moment the contract was agreed upon."

Emelia nearly collapsed in relief. "Then ye'll do something about it?"

The monsignor didn't seem too excited to intervene. He shrugged lazily and sat back in his chair, gazing off into the small chamber they were seated in as if finding everything around but the lass in front of him of interest.

"The Earl of Torridon, you say?" he finally asked.

Emelia nodded. "Lares dun Tarh."

"I have heard that name."

"He is a powerful earl," she said. "And… and I'm sure he wouldna appreciate his original intentions being thwarted by my sister. He made the decision that his son and I should wed. I canna imagine he is pleased with the changes."

The monsignor scratched his head. "I suppose this is something to investigate," he said. "As men of the cloth, we are protectors of everything the church represents, and that includes marriage. What does your father say to all of this?"

The question caused Emelia to falter, though it shouldn't have. She should have known it would come up at some point. She was so glad that the priest seemed to be seeing her side of the situation that a question like that threw her.

"My… my father has been bewitched by my sister," she

said. "He has told me that his word is above God's."

The monsignor frowned. "That does not sound like Fergus."

"I know," Emelia said. "But that is why I've come tae ye for help. My father is not himself these days. Something evil is afoot."

"Why do you say that?" he asked. "Is he possessed by a demon?"

Emelia did what she did best. She lied. "He has no regard for the church these days and will do as he pleases," she said. "Monsignor, I have been wronged. God's holy union of marriage has been wronged. Will ye not help me?"

The monsignor yawned. "What about Torridon?" he said. "Has he protested this change of brides?"

"He would if he knew."

"He does not know?"

Emelia shook her head. "I dunna believe so," she said. "Monsignor, *please*. Will ye come tae Blackrock and stop this… this travesty?"

He shrugged, a gesture that eventually turned into a nod. "You are in luck, lady," he said. "The Bishop of St. Andrews is supposed to visit this parish this week, so when he comes, I will refer the matter to him. Mayhap we will visit your father and convince him that making decisions that go against the church's teachings does not put him in our favor."

Emelia was feeling that familiar rush of relief again. "I believe he needs tae be reminded of that," she said. "But ye must hurry. I fear my sister and my betrothed are planning tae marry very soon, and it must be prevented."

"I take it that your betrothed does not wish to marry you?"

"Nay," Emelia said, embarrassed. "As I said, my sister has

bewitched him. He doesna know what he wants right now."

"Another man who must see the truth of God."

"Aye."

The monsignor nodded. Given that he'd expended all of the energy he intended to on this matter, he stood up from his chair, signifying the end of the meeting. Emelia stood up quickly, wanting to pester him with more questions on the timing of the bishop's arrival, but she wisely kept her mouth shut. She already had an agreement for the visit, but it concerned her that everything was predicated on the arrival of the bishop. Then they would have to travel to Blackrock, which wasn't particularly far away, but it would take time.

She wanted the priest to come with her now.

"I'm sorry," she said, suddenly feigning tears. "Ye know my family and I dinna want tae spill our secrets, but ye should know… I've only told ye a partial truth."

"Oh?" the monsignor said curiously. "What more is there?"

She lowered her head, pretending to be quite upset. "I love my sister," she whispered. "When I told ye that she bewitched men, I believe she has summoned the darkness tae do it. Tae give her power."

The monsignor's curiosity turned to concern. "And how would you know this?"

Emelia crouched down. Using her finger, she traced a triangle with three points and a gap at the bottom on the floor of the church. "This," she whispered. "I've seen her draw this symbol in blood. 'Tis the devil's symbol. Monsignor, I believe we're all in terrible danger. It's not simply the marriage or the broken contract. I believe my sister is bringing hell and damnation upon us. I dunna think we can wait for the bishop."

Monsignor Carrick took a few steps, standing over her as he

gazed down at the well-known symbol. It represented the cloven hoof of a goat, most often associated with Lucifer.

Evil.

"Are you sure you saw this?" he asked.

Emelia nodded as she stood up, wiping her eyes. "I am," she said. "I was afraid tae ask her because I dinna want her tae cast a spell on me."

"You think she's a witch?"

Emelia shook her head. "I dunna think so," she said. "But someone has taught her how tae bewitch a man. She must be saved. We must all be saved, monsignor. Will ye please come with me now, before it's too late?"

The man gazed at her, his brow furrowed with real concern. He hadn't shown much enthusiasm through the entire meeting, but one mention of a cloven-hoof symbol and, out of sheer obligation and attention to duty, he was showing interest. If what Emelia said was true and he failed to act, it would be very bad for him, indeed.

Catastrophic, even.

He didn't want his superiors catching wind of it.

"Very well," he finally said, with great reluctance. "Wait for me on the road in front."

Emelia did. She scampered out of the chamber and out into the sanctuary of the church with its dirt floors, soaring spires, and elaborate windows. A small palfrey waited for her just inside the gate, and beyond that was a road and the River Ness. Truly, Emelia felt better than she had since her return to Blackrock, knowing that Monsignor Carrick was going to get involved. She didn't know why she hadn't thought of it sooner.

Darien was as good as hers.

Chapter Sixteen

Seated in the kitchen yard near the pond that kept the castle with a supply of fish, Eventide was sewing a blue silk dress. It was among the finest goods she had, a color she'd seen at a merchant stall in Inverness about a year earlier, and the merchant swore the blue was the same color as her eyes. Though she had no use for silk dresses, the man had managed to talk her into buying a dress length with her hard-earned money. Athole had a fit when she saw it and tried to convince her to take it back, but Eventide wouldn't. She'd tucked it away and hoped to make a fine dress out of it someday.

Today was that day.

Things were quiet this morning, which was good. She felt as if she'd been walking on thin ice ever since Emelia had returned, so to have a day that felt somewhat peaceful was good for her state of mind. Darien was in the stable the last time she saw him, putting a poultice on his horse's right front fetlock because the animal had developed some swelling since its arrival. Her mother was still in her bed, as usual, and her father was in the hall the last time she saw him. Emelia was nowhere to be found, and Eventide found herself hoping that her sister had simply run off again and would never return.

That was the dream, anyway.

Everything was so strange now. It wasn't dreamlike, but a living nightmare. On the night Emelia had returned to Blackrock, the evening's feast had been a horror show because Emelia immediately went on the attack once the meal started. She had some scratching and bruising from the fight she had with her sister earlier in the day, and she made a point of trying to tell everyone that Eventide had beaten her. There had been no fairness in Emelia's argument, only the fact that she had been attacked and not why. She said nothing about throwing the first strike or the fact that her sister had only been defending herself, but Eventide made sure to bring it up. In the past, she would have let such things go and simply not said anything, but not this time.

She'd had enough of her sister's lies.

Therefore, the two simply avoided each other, or had tried to. Even though they shared adjoining chambers, there was a door that separated the two of them and Eventide had made sure to bolt it. She didn't trust that her sister wasn't going to try to knife her in the middle of the night, so she made sure that the bolts on the doors were secure. Strangely, Emelia hadn't tried to break the door down, but the week was still young. There was still plenty of time.

That was why Eventide was enjoying the quiet morning.

So, she continued to work on the blue dress, which she had cut out the day before and was now basting together. She probably should have done it inside, where there wasn't so much dirt, but the day was so lovely and bright that she'd wanted to work outside. Even now, the majority of the dress lay on the bench beside her, resting on a linen sheet that she'd brought with her to keep the fabric from getting dirty. Eventide was excellent with a needle, so the seams of the dress were coming together quite nicely. Perhaps there was an urgency to finish it because she hoped to be married in it.

A marriage that was still uncertain.

Pausing in her sewing, she looked around the kitchen yard, thinking of a marriage that needed to happen sooner rather than later. She didn't trust her sister not to do something drastic, and she had relayed that to Darien, who agreed with her. She hated the uncertainty of it all because with Emelia around, her father seemed reluctant to actually move forward with the wedding.

That scared Eventide the most.

With a sigh, she returned to her sewing. The stitches were very neat and tidy, and perfectly measured one after the other. She'd just finished a row on the sleeve and, after inspecting it, turned the dress over so she could work on the opposite sleeve. She was about halfway through it when a shadow fell over her.

"Ye always did have a talent for sewing," Fergus said. "Is that the fabric that the merchant said matched yer eyes?"

Eventide looked up at her father, holding the material near her eye so he could see. "Aye," she said. "Don't ye think so?"

"I do," he said. "Ye bought it and tucked it away for quite some time. I'm surprised tae see it."

Eventide put the fabric back in her lap and resumed sewing. "I wanted tae use it for a special occasion," she said. "I'd say a wedding is special enough."

"True," Fergus said. Then he indicated the empty end of the bench. "May I sit?"

"Please."

He did, lowering himself down onto the wood as Eventide

watched his face. The man seemed to be looking at everything but her, and that concerned her.

"Da?" she said quietly. "Is something amiss?"

Fergus looked over his shoulder, toward the stables and the ward. "Where's Darien?"

"With his horse."

The answer satisfied him, or seemed to, and he returned his attention to Eventide. "How soon will ye finish that garment?" he asked.

Eventide cocked her head thoughtfully. "Probably in the next day or two," she said. "Why do ye ask?"

"Because I think ye and Darien should marry immediately."

She stopped sewing and looked at him. "Why?" she said, concerned. "Has something happened?"

Fergus shook his head and started to speak, but he caught movement out of the corner of his eye and turned to see Darien entering the kitchen yard. He had dirt all over his tunic and smudged on his face, but he was smiling as he approached.

"I saw ye come in here," he said, looking at Fergus. "Did ye see the garment she's working on?"

Fergus nodded, glancing at the fine silk in his daughter's hands. "I did," he said. "But ye look like ye rolled in the mud with the pigs. Why are ye so dirty?"

Darien grinned. "Because I put a poultice on my horse's leg and he kept trying tae shake it free," he said. "Calum and Guthrie were helping me, but the horse doesna like it when I touch his legs."

Fergus grunted. "Are the Munro lads still here?"

"Still."

Fergus didn't have much to say to that. "Well," he said, "ye'll have tae be more clever than yer horse next time and avoid the mud bath."

Darien snorted, but Eventide spoke up. "Father says we must marry as soon as possible," she said. "But he's not told me why."

The smile faded from Darien's face as he looked at Fergus. "What's amiss?" he said.

Fergus took a long, deep breath, one of thought and contemplation, before answering. "I'm not entirely sure, but Emelia left this morning, very early, and rode south," he said. "I dunna know where she went and, tae be honest, I dunna know if she's going tae return, but I suspect she will. She dinna take an escort with her, nor did she tell me or her mother where she was going, which tells me she wants it kept secret. I dunna like it when she keeps secrets because nothing good can come from them."

Darien took the warning seriously. "What could she possibly do?" he said. "Run back tae Luke? Or somehow involve the Cannich clan, since I hold their castle?"

Fergus shrugged. "Who knows?" he said. "What if she promises Luke and Reelig that she'll bring ye tae them and they can use ye as leverage tae regain their castle?"

Darien frowned. "I would never go anywhere with her," he said. "She couldna betray me so."

Fergus simply shook his head. "All I'm saying is that I dunna trust her," he said. Then he paused, looking at the pair of them. "I know that when she came back, I seemed sympathetic tae her. And I was. I wanted tae believe her. I wanted tae believe that she hadn't done anything wrong, but even I could see that she was lying about the situation. But the fact that she's returned… and people know she's returned… I'm warning ye both that people around here may look down on the two of ye for marrying, especially if they know Emelia was betrothed tae Darien. She has a way of stirring up sympathy with those too stupid tae realize she's lying."

Darien's gaze lingered on the old man. "Yet ye've encouraged us tae marry right away."

"I think ye should," Fergus said. "If she's gone, and she hasna told anyone where she's going, then I'll wager she's out stirring up trouble, no matter what it is. If the two of ye want tae be married, then do it now before she does something tae stop it."

Darien looked at Eventide. "I wanted tae wait for my family, but not if it'll cost us a marriage," he said. "Are ye at peace with that?"

Eventide nodded. "I dunna need trappings or celebrations," she said. "I just need ye. I'll marry ye right now if ye wish."

He smiled at her. "Yer da says I look like I've slept with the pigs."

"I'm marrying the body, laddie, not the clothing."

Darien chuckled before returning his attention to Fergus. "Then we'll do it now," he said. "We dunna even need a priest."

Fergus shook his head. "Nay," he said. "We can gather everyone at Blackrock and ye simply say in front of everyone that ye take each other for husband and wife. A public declaration is just as binding."

A gleam came to Darien's eye as he looked at Eventide. "Shall we do this?"

A smile spread across her face. "We shall."

Fergus was already turning for the ward. "I'll tell everyone tae gather near the keep," he said. "Ye'd better go tell yer mother, Evie. She'll want tae be there!"

Eventide jumped up from the bench, gathering the blue

dress and the linen sheet it was wrapped in. "I'll go fetch her," she said. "Will ye at least wash yer face?" she asked Darien.

He rubbed his cheeks, looking at the dirt that came off on his fingers. "I'll clean up," he assured her. Then he bent over swiftly and kissed her. "I'll meet ye at the door tae the keep. And hurry."

Eventide's face was bright with joy. "Did ye think I'd drag my feet?" she said. "Who do ye think ye're talking to?"

Darien chuckled. "My future wife," he said, watching her as she quickly walked away. "But ye're not moving fast enough."

Eventide took off at a run, the blue dress billowing in her arms. Once she was out of the kitchen yard, Darien went on a run of his own, but in his case, it was for a quick bath.

He had a wedding to attend, after all.

And he'd never been happier about anything in his life.

♋

"How much longer?" Mabel demanded. "And why are we moving so slowly?"

Lares had been listening to his wife since they departed the Hydra and headed east for Blackrock. It was midday on the third day of travel, and Lares was about to spur his horse forward and keep running until he fell off into the sea. He loved his wife dearly, but sometimes she could be a…

"*Lares!*"

He was forced to acknowledge her shout. "Aye, my love?" he said patiently.

"Did you hear me?"

"All of Scotland heard ye."

As their sons, riding in various positions around their father and the carriage, began to snicker, Mabel refused to acknowledge their sense of humor. She was more interested in why it seemed to be taking so long to reach Blackrock.

"Well?" she said. "Answer me."

Lares slowed his horse so he could position himself back by the carriage and stop yelling for all to hear. "We're not far," he said. "Ye must be patient. Ye've been here before—why the rush?"

Mabel was seated next to the driver today. Zora and Lilliana hadn't come on this particular journey, but all of the dun Tarh sons had, along with Mabel. She was supposed to be inside the carriage, but she didn't want to be. Lares let her ride next to the driver, but he wasn't particularly comfortable with it. Still, she had insisted.

And when she insisted, he dared not oppose her.

"I'm not sure," she said in answer to his question. "Something feels wrong. I must get to Darien."

Lares had a healthy respect for his wife's intuition. "Nothing is wrong," he said softly. "The situation has ye overwrought."

Mabel was looking ahead, to the horizon, as if seeing a castle that had not yet come into view. "I *am* overwrought," she murmured. "I'm overwrought because that girl has returned. Lares, if you had run away with a woman, would it be planned or on impulse?"

He shrugged. "It could be a little of both, I suppose," he said. "Running away implies urgency. A lack of choices."

"Or it means making your own choice rather than one that was made for you," Mabel said. "But whatever it means, the ultimate message it conveys is a lack of concern for anyone else. It is very selfish."

Lares nodded. "I canna disagree with ye," he said. But he hesitated before continuing. "I canna help but think this is my fault. Ye know I was only trying tae do what I felt was best for Darien, but it seems I've landed him in the middle of a hornet's nest."

Mabel glanced at him. "We've had this discussion, my love," she said. "*I know you were trying to do what was right for him, and so does he, but the one thing you should never overlook is the woman's reputation.*"

"I was only looking at the title."

"A title cannot keep a man warm on a cold night," Mabel said. "It also cannot give him the joy that a good wife would give him."

Lares sighed. "I've learned my lesson."

"I hope so. Because there are six more sons that do not wish to have you make the same mistake with them."

Lares knew that. He was struggling with the guilt over the situation. Up ahead, he could see three of the six sons he'd brought with him. Estevan the natural leader, Caelus the Giant, Kaladin the Baby Bull… He was so proud of each of them. Any man would be proud of having just one of them as a son, but Lares was fortunate to have eight of them. Eight impeccable men.

Eight souls who looked up to him for guidance.

Eight hearts that trusted him.

Glancing over his shoulder, he could see the younger three. Lucan the Champion, Leandro the Strong, and Cruz the Invincible. Even at their young ages, they were flawless, with the exception of Cruz, who was still quite young and mostly reckless. The young man was hilarious and wild. But he was powerful—so very powerful. And he had a heart bigger than the Highlands.

Aye… They all deserved a father who wasn't blinded by a title over character.

He wouldn't make that mistake again.

The sun was behind them as they made their way east, and sunset was just a few hours away. They were coming up on a fork in the road, one that led south into Inverness, and they could see from a distance that there was a small party heading north on it. They would probably run into the group just about the time they got to the fork in the road. Since there was strength in numbers when traveling, Lares didn't think anything of it. If they were going in his direction, he would simply put them in the rear of the group.

"Da!" Estevan shouted from the front of the escort. "Another party!"

He was pointing to what his father already saw. "I know," Lares said, waving him off. "Go see where they're headed. If it's east, ask them if they wish tae join us."

Estevan and Caelus took off, spurring their big horses down the road. All Lares could see were fat horse butts and flying legs as they thundered away from them, heading to the fork in the road up ahead. Everyone was watching at that point as Estevan and Caelus met up with the group in the distance, now little specks amidst the green fields.

"There's not much this far north," Mabel said, shielding her eyes. "I wonder who it is?"

Lares shrugged. "There are a few villages up the coast," he said. "And the islands beyond tae the north."

Mabel looked at him. "Have you ever been that far north?"

He shook his head. "Not me," he said. "Too many Northmen, still. They rule those isles."

Mabel grunted, looking back toward the fork in the road. "Northmen, you say?" she said. "They're very handsome."

He fought off a grin. "If ye want one, ye'll have tae make it there yerself. They're welcome to ye."

She smoothed at the wisps of her hair blowing in the breeze. "Thank you," she said. "I'll be sure to send a few Valkyries down your way to take care of you."

"Big, beautiful women, ye say?" he said, rubbing his chin.

"How many do you want? Three or four?"

"How many Northmen are ye going tae have?"

"Probably a dozen."

"Then I'll take as many lasses."

"As you wish," Mabel said. "When I get up there, I'll send them back to you."

"When will that be?"

"Never, you old fool."

Lares burst out laughing and Mabel grinned. He reached over and pulled her toward him, kissing her temple as she tried to push him away.

"I love ye, lass," he said, kissing her again. "I'll take ye over a dozen Valkyries any day of the week."

She slapped at him, weakly, and he let her go. They were caught up in the gentle flirting, hardly noticing when Estevan and Caelus started heading back in their direction. But they became aware as the men came closer and Estevan left Caelus at the front as he pushed back to his parents.

"Da," he gasped, his expression tight, "I think we've got troubles."

Lares frowned. "Why?" he said. "Who are those people?"

Estevan sighed sharply. "Emelia Moriston," he said. "And she's got priests with her."

That didn't clarify things for Lares. "Why on earth does she have priests with her?"

"Tae stop Darien's wedding."

They rushed on to Blackrock in record time.

CHAPTER SEVENTEEN

"I TAKE THEE as my true and lawful wife, forsaking all others, until death separates us," Darien said softly. "*Airson a h-uile àm*, Eventide. For all time."

He'd just said his vows in front of a ward full of people, all of them witnessing what was a perfectly legal marriage. It wasn't with a blessing or a priest, as would have been preferred, but it was legal.

That was all Darien cared about.

In the blue silk dress that wasn't quite finished, with a wreath of bluebells around her head because she'd found a small patch growing near the front gates, Eventide smiled up at Darien, tears glistening in her eyes.

"And I take thee as my true and lawful husband, forsaking all others, until death separates us," she said. "*Airson a h-uile àm*. For all time, my love."

People were beginning to cheer because that was the extent of the vows. Grinning, Darien took Eventide in his arms and kissed her deeply as a roar of approval went up. Fergus, standing next to them, was probably cheering the loudest. When Darien was finished kissing her, Fergus made sure to hug his daughter tightly. This was such a precious moment in their lives. Darien took congratulations from Calum and Guthrie, who were very happy to have been present at the wedding. But it was over now, and things needed to happen. It was the Munro brothers who began pushing both Darien and Eventide toward the keep.

"Go," Calum said. "Ye must finish this so no one can ever tear ye apart. Take the lass tae bed, man!"

Darien was on the move. He took Eventide by the hand, pulling her away from her emotional father and walking very quickly toward the keep. The crowd was calling after them, shouting encouragement, giving bawdy suggestions. They knew exactly where the couple was heading, so the mood was light and vulgar at times. Some of them started to follow, until Darien got to the top of the steps leading into the keep and turned around to shake a balled fist at the crowd.

Everyone roared with laughter.

But he didn't take any chances. Leading his new wife inside, he shut the entry door and bolted it.

"Ah," Eventide said, laughing. "Ye dunna trust them."

Darien shook his head firmly. "I dunna trust any of them," he said frankly. "They'll be pounding on the door while I'm trying tae take advantage of my own wife."

Eventide paused. "Say it again."

He looked at her curiously. "Say what?"

"Wife."

That was a moment that fed the soul. *Wife.* Darien felt like he'd been waiting all his life to use that word and mean it. With a grin, he kissed her and then picked her up in his big arms, sweeping her up the stairs to the level above.

Eventide's chamber, attached to her sister's, was on this

level, along with a third chamber used for storage or guests. Darien really had no idea where he was going—in all the times he'd bedded her, it had never been in her own chamber—so she pointed to a door and he practically kicked it open, ducking under the doorway as he carried her into the room.

Inside, a comfortable chamber unfolded with a big bed, a dressing table, and a wardrobe. Eventide kept it very neat. Next to her chamber, the door was open into Emelia's, which looked as if a tempest had moved through it. Once he put Eventide on her feet, she went to the connecting door and shut it, bolting it on her side. When Darien saw what she did, he bolted the door they'd just come through. Locked in the chamber, there was no one to bother them.

They stood there, just for a moment, and looked at one another.

Darien finally grinned, a rather lascivious gesture.

"Well?" he said. "We actually have permission tae do this now. What are we waiting for?"

Eventide motioned to his clothing. "I'm waiting for ye," she said as if he were a slowpoke. "What are *ye* waiting for? I thought ye'd be stripped and intae the bed by now."

Still grinning, Darien began to yank his clothing off—tunic, boots, and finally his breeches. By the time he was finished, Eventide was already in the bed and her dress was in a heap on the floor. With a growl, he launched himself at her, and her bed, unused to such forceful weight, collapsed on one side. They both grabbed on to the mattress, laughing uproariously as they tried not to roll off. But they finally crawled off, with Eventide holding her coverlet over her nude form, as Darien tried to figure out how to fix what had broken. But he couldn't, or he didn't want to take the time to figure it out, so he pulled the bed apart completely so the mattress lay evenly on the floor.

He pointed to it.

"Get in there," he said. "No more delays."

Biting off a smile, Eventide lay down on the bed again before he grabbed the coverlet, yanking it off her body. For a moment, he simply stood there and looked at her.

"Ye're so beautiful," he murmured. "And ye belong tae me. I can hardly believe it even as I say it."

"I've always belonged tae ye," she said softly. "We just made it official."

He was still smiling when he lowered himself onto her, pushing her hair away from her face, touching her cheek as he gazed into her eyes. There was so much more he wanted to say, but he couldn't seem to find the words. Love, in the deepest of times, went beyond words, and this was one of those times. A love that encompassed everything it touched, like the air they breathed. Love filled their lungs, their hearts, their souls.

This was the moment.

Lowering his head, he kissed her gently.

The magic began.

Eventide responded instantly to him, engaging in a heated kiss as their tongues plunged deep. His arms went around her, pulling her against him, feeling every curve. It was wildly arousing. Eventide had her arms around his head, trapping him against her, and when she suckled his tongue, Darien nearly went out of his mind. That was a sensual trick he'd taught her, and she had learned it well. That same suckling had been accomplished on his manhood, but he didn't want that tonight.

He simply wanted *her*.

Eventide was no longer a maiden. She hadn't been for a while. Now, she was a woman grown, with a woman's needs that had quickly developed. Every time he touched her, he showed her a new need until there wasn't one part of her body that didn't need him desperately.

The man set her on fire.

As they touched and kissed and fondled, Eventide took on the aggressor role. She opened her thighs for him, wrapping her legs around his waist as she deeply kissed him. Darien's hands roamed over her silken flesh, seeking out her breasts because he loved them so much. They were warm and soft against his palms, more than a handful for him.

He'd never been more consumed by a woman in his life.

His wife.

Darien's mouth went to her neck, gently suckling her skin, and a hand began to knead her right breast. He could hear her grunting with pleasure, her hands on his head, her face in his hair. Eventide cried out softly as his mouth clamped over a tender nipple, and she wrapped herself around him as he suckled first one and then the other, his big arousal pushing at her. Darien was a big man and his male member was proportionate, something that had terrified Eventide the first time he bedded her, but now it was something that she craved. Her hands moved to his thick erection as she guided him into her body. When he felt her slick, wet heat, he thrust firmly into her.

Eventide bit off her cries of pleasure into his enormous bicep, and the feel of her mouth against his flesh only served to inflame him. She was deliciously tight and hot, and he thrust again and again, feeling her body draw him in deeper.

It was paradise.

Darien's mouth was on hers, kissing her deeply, as he made love to her on the collapsed bed. He felt things for her that he had never felt in his life, for anyone, feelings of love and temptation that he couldn't control. It wasn't the mere act of sex itself—it was the physical demonstration of everything he felt, every joy and every sorrow. It was a declaration of joy that they were finally man and wife.

Eventide was far gone with passion, feeling his body with the greatest of pleasure. He was so big, and thrusting himself so deeply, that the pleasure of it was quickly pulling her toward release. These moments had come frequently over the past month, but they grew better each successive time. Darien was a man in his prime that she had never seen equaled.

She never wanted this moment to end.

Darien's thrusts grew harder, faster, and he withdrew completely every time, only to plunge deep again. He toyed with her nipples as he thrust, listening to her grunts of pleasure. It was a moment of great emotion, beautiful and powerful, and after one particularly deep thrust, he felt her release around him as pants of rapture escaped her lips. Still, he continued to make love to her until he could hold back no more.

His release came so hard that he nearly blacked out as he spilled himself into her sweet body. He could feel what he put in her, loving it, relishing it, wondering if they would soon have a son to bear the dun Tarh name. A strong son to ride alongside him into battle, to make him proud in every way possible. He'd never had such thoughts until now. Now, he wanted everything.

He wanted a family with her.

That was how he knew that his feelings for her were real.

With his body still joined to hers, Darien lifted his head to look at her. Eventide's eyes were closed, one arm over her head, and he used that opportunity to nuzzle the exposed breast. Gently, he kissed the flesh before taking a nipple in his mouth again and suckling tenderly.

In his arms, he could feel Eventide shudder. When he started suckling her again, she put one hand down to where their bodies joined, gently fondling herself. She did it until she released again and he gathered her up against him, still part of her just as she was a part of him. He'd been lucky enough to marry for love, and he swore that he'd never take a day with her for granted.

Airson a h-uile àm—for all time

He meant it.

PART THREE:
EMELIA'S FATE
To be heard from Nevermore

CHAPTER EIGHTEEN

"EMELIA," FERGUS RUMBLED, "what have ye done?"

"I'll tell you what she's done," Mabel said angrily. She was within spitting distance of Emelia, and she reached over and slapped the girl on the side of the head, twice, before Lares managed to pull her away. "This spoiled, selfish girl has tried to ruin this for everyone. Monsignor, did she tell you the entire story? Or just her version of her sister stealing her betrothed?"

Monsignor Carrick could see that he'd walked into a hell of a situation. All he knew was that he had to get to the bottom of it, and Lares dun Tarh and Fergus Moriston held the key to whatever this was. Lady Torridon, Lares' fiery wife, was intent on beating Emelia, who cowered behind her father so Mabel couldn't get another shot at her.

Everyone was up in arms.

"My lords," he said in his deep, authoritative voice, "I will not waste my time with chaos, but it is clear that something has happened, and I will discover what it is. I want everyone out of the chamber except Lady Emelia, her father, and Lord Torridon. Lady Torridon, that means you. Please leave."

Mabel didn't take that well in the least. "Nay," she said calmly. "I am going to remain because this young woman has lied to you and you must know the truth. I am here to support my husband, so if you want me removed, you will have to carry me out yourself."

Clearly, Monsignor Carrick wasn't going to do that, especially with six of Lady Torridon's hulking sons nearby. Frustrated, he pointed to a chair.

"Then sit down and be silent," he said. "I have come on business for the church and you will not disrupt it. Is that clear?"

Mabel went over to the chair he'd indicated and sat down, silently looking at the man as if she had a bone to pick with him. It was an unnerving expression, but Monsignor Carrick ignored it as best he could. He indicated for everyone to sit down, but before he began to speak, Lares fixed on his wife.

"Please, my love," he said softly. "Leave us for now. I think it would be best."

Mabel wasn't happy about his request. "I would like to remain."

Lares shook his head. "I love yer passion, but we need calmer heads," he said. "Go outside. I'll send for ye if I need ye."

"But—"

"*Go.*"

He'd made the decision. Annoyed, Mabel stood up and left the chamber, much to the relief of Emelia and Monsignor Carrick. When she shut the door behind her, the priest turned to Fergus.

"Now," he said, "Lord Shandwick, I have heard your daughter's version of the story. Now I will hear yours. Was there, or was there not, a written contract of marriage between your daughter and Darien dun Tarh?"

Fergus sighed sharply, unable to look at his troublemaking daughter. "I will tell ye the entire story, with God as my witness," he said. "But let me finish it before ye interrupt me. Can ye do that, monsignor?"

"I can."

Fergus took him at his word. "About two years ago, Torridon and I discussed a marriage contract between my eldest daughter, my heiress, and his son, Darien," he said. "Aye, there was a contract. But the day Darien showed up for the wedding, Emelia was nowhere tae be found. We also discovered that the man betrothed tae my younger daughter, Evie, was missing. Given the reputation of my eldest daughter, as she is unchaste, and the reputation of my younger daughter's betrothed, as Luke probably has a bastard or two running loose in the Highlands, we came tae the conclusion that they ran away together. All the signs pointed tae it. Emelia stayed away for two months, but we thought she was gone forever. When she returned, she lied and told us that Luke had abducted her. She demanded tae marry Darien, but that was not possible."

"Why not?" Monsignor Carrick asked.

"Because he has already married her sister."

Emelia shrieked. "When?" she demanded. "They werena married when I left earlier this morning!"

Fergus wouldn't look at her. "They were married today."

Emelia flew off the stool she'd been sitting on. "Do ye see what he's done?" she said to the priest. "He is violating the contract!"

"He has not," Lares said, his gaze fixed on the young woman. "I agreed tae dissolve the contract, and so did yer father. We created it and we dissolved it. Nothing has been violated."

Emelia gasped in outrage, but the monsignor threw up his hand to stop an argument. "Wait," he said forcefully. Then he turned to Emelia. "You did not tell me that you had run away for two months."

Caught defending a part of the story she'd conveniently left out, Emelia immediately began to weep. "I dinna run," she said. "I was abducted!"

"Is that the truth?"

She nodded emphatically. "He... he took me," she said, hand over her face as she feigned sobbing. "He took me and I couldna fight him."

"Where did he take you?"

"Glasgow," she said. "He forced me tae work for him so he could take my money. All he cared about was the money!"

"Ye said that he took ye to Sterling," Fergus said, frowning. "Did ye lie about that, too?"

Realizing she hadn't kept her story straight, Emelia was forced to scramble. "We went tae Sterling first," she said. "Then it was tae Glasgow. He worked on the river while he forced me tae work in a tavern. It was a horrible place."

Fergus shook his head in disgust as he looked at the monsignor. "She told me that he'd taken her tae Sterling," he said. "The lass has lied about everything, monsignor. She's pulled ye out here tae mediate something that doesna need tae be mediated. I'm sorry she did it tae ye, but we dunna need ye here."

Monsignor Carrick was looking at both Fergus and Emelia with frustration. He didn't know whom to believe, but he knew where he stood. The church's teachings had to be defended in all things.

"Your daughter had a marriage contract," he said to Fergus.

"And she says she was abducted."

Fergus was shaking his head even as the man spoke. "She was *not* abducted."

"Do you have proof of this?"

Fergus didn't, and that was a problem. It was his word against hers. He looked at his daughter as he answered. "My daughter has a fondness for men," he said. "'Tis difficult for me tae speak of such things, but it is true."

"Father!" Emelia burst out. "Dunna say such things about me. Ye know they aren't true!"

"I wish tae God they weren't," Fergus said with some sincerity. "But yer mother, yer sister, and others I've spoken with since ye've been away have told me otherwise. I was blind tae it, Emelia. I wanted tae believe the best in ye because ye were my eldest, so I was blind tae it. Ye used that blindness. Ye took advantage of it. Ye soiled the name of Moriston, and I let ye. I'm ashamed of ye, but more than that, I'm ashamed of myself. Now, stop with the lies. Tell the monsignor what truly happened. If ye have one shred of decency, ye will."

Emelia was looking at her father with wide eyes. For someone who had been sobbing only moments earlier, her eyes were quite dry.

"Whoever ye spoke with has lied tae ye," she said, oddly calm. "Evie told lies because she's jealous. She's—"

"Ye aborted a child, Emelia," Fergus said, cutting her off. "Shall I bring the apothecary from Inverness here tae swear that he sold ye things that would kill the child growing in ye?"

"*Father!*" Emelia screamed.

"Silence!" Monsignor Carrick roared. "Everyone will be silent! I demand it!"

Fergus shook his head and turned away. "I have nothing

more tae say about this," he said. "My daughter lied tae ye, yet still, ye refuse tae accept it. I can bring ye a dozen men who swear they've bedded her. She ran away on her wedding day and she's trying tae convince ye otherwise. It's simply not true, but if ye dunna believe that now, I dunna know what more I can say tae ye."

Emelia was truly weeping at this point. Her father had revealed her darkest secret, and she was certain the priest was going to leave and her quest for Darien would be finished. She resumed her seat on the stool, refusing to look at anyone, as Monsignor Carrick mulled over the situation.

There was a good deal to consider.

After a moment, he simply shook his head.

"She has a case," he said. "Regardless of what she has done, or the life she has led, the truth is that your daughter had a marriage contract, one that you dissolved without any permission from the church. A betrothal contract is as binding as a marriage. You cannot simply dissolve it. You do not have the power to do that."

Fergus looked at Lares, who wasn't happy with what he was hearing. "My son has already married," he said. "The marriage has been consummated. Not even the church can dissolve it if it has been consummated."

Monsignor Carrick looked at him. "It is not a valid marriage if your son was already married, contractually, to Lady Emelia," he said. "I am sorry. I am coming to see that this is a difficult situation, but this is something we must bring up to the Bishop of St. Andrews. He is my superior and head of the diocese. I am afraid I must separate the married couple and take your son, along with the two of you, to St. Andrews. We must let the bishop make the ultimate decision on this."

Lares closed his eyes tightly, briefly, for a moment before opening them. It was a gesture of sheer pain. "My son is in love with his wife," he said hoarsely. "They are happy. And ye want tae separate them?"

"I am afraid that I must," Monsignor Carrick said. "I am truly sorry, my lord."

Lares' pained look remained. "When do ye want tae go tae St. Andrews?"

"I would say as soon as possible," the monsignor said. "Would you not agree?"

Lares' gaze lingered on the man before he looked at Emelia. "Nay," he said, growling, "I wouldna agree. I would have never agreed tae my son marrying this petty, vindictive, foolish woman if I'd known her true character. But her father withheld that from me because he saw a dun Tarh husband for a daughter he was afraid he'd never marry off. Lass, if you break up my son's marriage because ye are determined tae make everyone miserable, know that ye'll never be accepted by my family and I'll make sure tae turn my wife loose on ye. Ye'll live in hell every day of yer life. I hope ye know that."

Emelia was drawn with fear. Lares was quite intimidating when he wanted to be. "I'll earn yer love, I promise," she said sincerely. "I'll be a good wife tae him, I swear it."

Lares snorted ironically. "Ye'll never be anything tae him except someone he hates," he said. "And ye'll never be anything tae me, either. If ye dropped dead this moment, I wouldna mourn ye. Sorry, Fergus, but 'tis the truth."

Fergus couldn't even say anything. He simply hung his head, knowing that nothing Lares said was untrue. He couldn't even apologize.

There was no apology deep enough for this.

Without another word, Lares headed out of the solar, pausing in the entry. He looked to the stairs that led to the upper level, knowing Darien and Eventide were up there but not wanting to interrupt what might be their last time together, ever. If Monsignor Carrick thought the marriage contract with Emelia had been violated, regardless of the circumstances, then there was a good chance that the bishop would think so, too.

And that ate at Lares.

Therefore, he wasn't going to interrupt their time together.

But he would wait for them. Moving to the opposite side of the entry, with his eyes on the stairwell, he waited.

It was a long and sorrowful wait.

౮౩

"What do ye think is going tae happen?" Caelus asked. "A damn priest is here. Can he actually annul the marriage?"

No one knew.

Caelus was standing with his brothers—Kaladin, Estevan, Leandro, Lucan, and Cruz—as well as Calum and Guthrie. Monsignor Carrick had briefly explained why he was coming to Blackrock on the journey over from the fork in the road, but beyond that, no one knew the details. They only knew that Emelia, having not received the answers she wanted from her father and Lares, had complained to the church that her betrothal contract had been violated and she wanted church intervention.

She'd gotten it.

And no one was happy about it.

A cloud of mystery and uncertainty hung over everything.

"I dunna think anyone can answer that," Estevan said solemnly. "But I do know that Da is inside, fighting for Darien and for Evie. God's Bones, if that bitch had only stayed away. Why did she have tae come back? Everything was better without her."

"Then why not send her away again?"

The softly uttered words had come from Calum. Everyone looked at him, but he was staring at the ground, lost in thought. It took him a moment to look up and see the curious faces gazing at him.

"I'm serious," he muttered. "She's run off twice, once with Cannich and the second time this morning. She just ran off and dinna tell anyone where she was going. So why not run her off again so she never returns?"

Estevan's eyes narrowed. "What do ye mean?" he said. "If ye have a suggestion, lad, make it. We're listening."

Calum looked around to make sure no one was nearby, potentially listening in, before he responded. "The problem for Darien started with her," he said. "It will end with her. But not by yer hand. Darien's brothers must be above suspicion."

"Suspicion of what?" Caelus said. "As much as I dunna like the woman, I'm not sure I want tae see her drown in a loch. Though I wouldna mourn her, I dunna think my da would be very proud if we had a hand in it."

"Ye wouldna," Calum insisted. "Guth and I would take her away, mayhap north tae Thurso. The Northmen still come there tae trade. We'd sell them a wench tae take with them back tae their lands. Or mayhap we'll take her down tae Edinburgh and sell her tae a crew of one of the cogs that come upriver. Whatever we do, we'll not tell ye, so when yer da asks what ye know, ye can be honest with him."

The brothers were listening with some astonishment. "Ye would do that for Darien?" Kaladin said, awe in his voice. "But why?"

"Because he'd do it for us," Calum said simply. "We've known ye all our lives. My da speaks highly of yer grandfather, whom he knew. Some may call ye Lucifer's Legion, but we know the truth. There are many kinds of loyalty, lads. Not simply on the battlefield."

Estevan put his hand on Calum's shoulder. "Well put," he said. "But taking Emelia away from here… That's a serious offer. A serious undertaking and something we'd have tae discuss with Darien. The man would have tae know."

"Why?" Kaladin asked, catching on to Calum's way of thinking. "It would be better if we dinna. That way, he can honestly say he knows nothing about it."

Estevan shook his head. "I disagree," he said. "If someone was offering tae change yer life, wouldn't ye want tae know?"

Kaladin wouldn't back down. "Why?" he repeated. "There's no reason for him tae. If he does, then he's complicit. Do ye really want the man tae be complicit in the disappearance of the woman he was supposed tae marry simply so he could be with the woman he loved? That makes him as bad as Emelia."

That put a bit of an ethical twist on the dilemma. Estevan put his hands on his hips, deliberating the offer, but as he looked around the ward and pondered the situation, he caught sight of his mother walking in the waning afternoon sun. In her fine clothing and tight wimple, she was over near the stables, looking at the horses in the small corral. The last he saw of her, she was in the ward, trying to smack Emelia as she headed into the keep. She disliked Emelia more than anyone.

That gave him an idea.

"Just a moment, lads," he said, eyes still on his mother. "I'll be back."

The men watched him walk over to his mother and say something to her. She immediately looked over at the group, and seven different hands lifted to wave at her. She said something to Estevan, slipped her hand into the crook of his elbow, and made her way back over to the men standing around.

"Calum," he said, "tell my mother what ye told me. Tell her what ye offered. See what she thinks of it."

Calum looked stricken but did as he was told. "Lady Torridon," he said, "I… Well, 'tis only that Guth and I have been here at Blackrock for a time, and we've seen how happy Darien is with Evie. We were at his wedding earlier, and ye've never seen a more joyful man. I can honestly say the two of them are made for one another. With Emelia coming back as she did and causing trouble, we… Well, we thought—"

"We've offered tae get rid of her for ye," Guthrie cut in, saying what his brother couldn't. "The lass has disappeared before and come back. We can make her disappear for good, and all anyone will think is that she's run off again. Then Darien has no more troubles."

Mabel looked at the Munro brothers in surprise. "Are you serious?" she asked.

Calum and Guthrie nodded. "Aye, m'lady," Calum said. "Very serious."

To their surprise, Mabel wasn't enraged. She didn't berate them. What they were suggesting was underhanded in the best of circumstances, but this wasn't the best of circumstances. They were talking about righting a wrong.

That was how they saw it.

Perhaps Mabel would, too.

"What would you do with her?" she finally asked.

Calum glanced at his brother for silent support before answering. "Taking her north and selling her tae the Northmen who trade in the villages," he said. "Or take her tae Edinburgh and find a cog tae put her on so she sails away and never returns"

"Then you are not suggesting to kill her."

"Nay, m'lady. No murder."

"Simply sending her away."

"Aye, m'lady."

Mabel's gaze turned toward the keep where Monsignor Carrick was in the process of making decisions that would affect her family for the rest of her life. More specifically, decisions that would affect Darien. He was a good man and deserved to be happy, and, as his mother, that was what she wanted for her son above all. It made her ill to think that the church might decide the betrothal contract with Emelia would take precedence over an actual marriage to Eventide.

Nay, she didn't want to see Darien miserable, forever, with an unworthy woman.

And she was willing to do what was necessary.

With that on her mind, she turned her attention back to the Munro brothers.

"Do it," she spat.

With that, she walked away, heading in the direction of the keep. The men in the group watched her go before Estevan returned his attention to the Munro brothers.

"Ye heard her," he said quietly. "Make it so. And make it soon."

The mission was set.

CHAPTER NINETEEN

TWO DAYS.
Two days since Monsignor Carrick had made his decision. Two days of trying to keep Darien from living up to the moniker of Darien the Destroyer. He was bent on murder, and the only thing keeping the man in check was being shut up in his wife's chamber, being with her every moment of the day. Basking in her presence, hearing every breath she took.

It was the only way to keep him from going on a rampage.

Two long, tense days of hell.

But he tried not to bring that hell into his wife's small bower. That was a place of comfort, where the world couldn't touch them, and even now he sat in the window, watching the activity below, pondering their next move as Eventide sat near the hearth, finishing the blue dress she'd worn at their wedding.

The day was starting to cloud over, and those in the ward were moving things inside so they wouldn't get wet with the coming storm. Horses in the corral were being brushed down and herded inside the stable. Growing bored with the view, Darien turned inside, watching Eventide embroider tiny silver honeybees on the hem of the bell sleeves of the dress. She seemed quiet and peaceful, but he knew the truth. She was anything but peaceful. Her sister was trying to ruin her happiness, and the Eventide he knew wasn't going to stand for it much longer. She was biding her time, or so he thought.

But he hated the thought of her being so unhappy.

She must have sensed that he was looking at her because she glanced up, smiling at him when their eyes met. He smiled weakly in return.

"That garment will be magnificent for Robbie Stewart's table," he said.

"Oh?" she said, lifting up a sleeve. "Do ye think so?"

"I do."

She was still looking at the sleeve. "May I ask ye a question?" she said after a moment.

"Anything."

"Why can't we simply run away?"

There it was, the hell he'd been trying to keep out of the chamber. The status of their daily lives. As he knew, she'd been stewing on it, the truth behind her peaceful façade.

He could only answer her honestly.

"I've thought about it," he admitted. "But there is a problem with that."

"What problem?"

He shrugged. "Ye'd be running from yer family and the church would probably punish them for yer actions," he said. "Same with mine, only my da hates the church, so he wouldna care, but there's the matter of my running away tae avoid the church's judgment—do ye think I could go back tae Robbie's court after that? His council is full of priests. I couldna hide from them, so I'd have tae give up everything I've worked for. Everything that would give us a stable life. Evie, I dunna want tae hide in shame. I want tae live in pride—the pride of being married tae the woman I love, a great woman. Ye dunna deserve tae be hidden away."

He was flattering her and giving her an unhappy answer at the same time. "Then what do we do if they choose tae annul our marriage?"

He came away from the window. "If the bishop tries, I'll take it tae the pope," he said firmly. "I'll take ye on a lovely journey tae Rome and we'll see the pope. Evie, I'll not let sexless, frigid men make a decision for our lives. We've done nothing wrong."

She nodded. Then she burst into quiet tears. With a sigh of genuine sorrow, he went to her and knelt down, putting his arms around her.

"Dunna weep, my love," he murmured, his cheek against hers. "We will be victorious in the end, but yer sister has made this very difficult. She'll not win, Evie, I swear it."

Eventide didn't say anything, mostly because she'd heard the argument before. Many times. Darien seemed convinced that they would triumph, eventually, but she wasn't so sure. Emelia had made it difficult for them, indeed. She hadn't even spoken to the woman since she returned. Her father had visited, and so had Lares and Mabel, but no Athole and no Emelia. Mabel, in fact, was more upset than anyone about the situation, and she hugged Eventide for a very long time each time she saw her, promising that all would be well in the end.

Eventide truly wanted to believe it.

But she couldn't.

"What happens if no one in Rome listens tae us?" she said, sniffling. "What happens if they declare yer marriage contract with Emelia valid? What then?"

He grunted softly. "*Then* we'll run away," he said. "But only as a last resort. Evie, one way or the other, we'll remain married. No one is going tae take that away from us, least of all yer sister."

He couldn't bring himself to say Emelia's name. He didn't want to bring the poison she perpetuated into the very air he breathed. He, too, had a genuine fear that the church was going to side with Emelia, and if that was the case, he had no problem running. He'd run as far and fast as he could and take Eventide with him. His father had friends in France. They had kin in the House of de Wolfe, although that was too close to Scotland for his taste. Too easy for ecclesiastical guards to get to him. The diocese of St. Andrews had their own army, and he wanted to stay away from them, but when or if they fled, Castle Questing, seat of the House of de Wolfe, would be his first stop. They knew everyone in England and could send him someplace where he could be safe, serving as a warrior and making a living.

But hopefully he wouldn't have to go that route. As he pondered the future, Eventide slipped her hand into his.

"I am sorry for Emelia," she said. "She has always been selfish, but this goes beyond even what I thought she was capable of. I dunna even think it's the fact that she simply wants ye. I think it's the fact that she's being denied, and she has never accepted denial. The entire world agrees with her wants and she's satisfied, so the battle for ye… It's because I have ye. And she would consider it a victory over me."

Darien didn't want to agree with her or say anything about Emelia because he would only end up raging and insulting the woman, and he truly didn't want to waste his time on her. There was no point. Leaning over, he kissed Eventide on the temple.

"I could try tae dissuade her," he said. "Tell her tae her face what I think of her."

Eventide shook her head. "Dunna do it," she said. "She'd take it as a challenge, so ye'd be wasting yer breath."

He already knew that, but he was trying to show her how willing he was to take a stand. He knew it would probably inflame Emelia, and not in a good way, but he was willing to try. He took Eventide's hand and kissed it, trying to comfort her, feeling her anguish along with his own. Darien had always been rather empathetic when it came to the pain of others, and he felt everything that Eventide was feeling.

The sadness, the devastation, the fear.

It was heartbreaking in so many ways.

A knock on the door caught their attention. As Eventide quickly wiped her tears away, Darien stood up and went to the door. He opened the panel to find Estevan standing there.

"Brother," Estevan greeted him, seeing Eventide through the open door and nodding at her. But his focus returned to Darien. "The monsignor wants to speak with ye. Will ye come?"

Darien hadn't spoken to the priest for two days. He was hoping he wouldn't have to, maybe ever again. "Why?" he said. "What does he want?"

Estevan shook his head. "He dinna say," he said. "But Da and Fergus are with him, too. I'm sure he wants tae speak with ye about the trip tae St. Andrews."

Darien sighed heavily, turning to look at Eventide. "I'll be back," he said. "Shall I send anything up tae ye? Food? Drink?"

She shook her head. "Nay, thank ye," she said. "Estevan, where is yer mother?"

Estevan pointed to the floor above. "She was trying tae force yer mother out of her chamber earlier," he said. "But I dunna know where she is now. Shall I send her tae ye?"

Eventide nodded. "If it is not too much trouble."

"Ye know she'll fly tae yer side, lass."

Eventide smiled. She genuinely liked Estevan and was coming to know, and like, the other brothers as well. Since she didn't have any brothers herself, becoming acquainted with Darien's had been an eye-opening experience.

Wonderful, but eye-opening.

"Stop flirting with my wife," Darien said to his brother, smacking him on the sternum when he returned Eventide's smile. "I've warned ye about that."

Estevan grunted with the force of the minor blow, rubbing the spot and chuckling as he followed Darien down the stairs. Still grinning, Eventide stood up and closed the door, going back to her garment. It gave her something to focus on other than the turmoil her life had become. She didn't even want to think about why the monsignor had summoned Darien, but she could guess.

Perhaps their time together was growing even shorter than she'd hoped.

But she continued focusing on the dress, carefully stitching those little bees, as the sun reached its zenith. More clouds were rolling in, and she worked for another hour or so before finally putting the dress down, standing up to stretch her legs as she walked over to the window seat and peered at the activity in the ward. The Firth of Cromarty was spread out to the south, the sea to the east, and the hills of the Highlands to the west and north. She could see them in the distance, the grayish-green hue, darker now that the clouds were overhead. The smell of rain was in the air. She was thinking of going down to the kitchens and procuring something to eat when she heard noise in Emelia's chamber.

Someone was moving around inside.

Curious, she went over to the adjoining door, which she now kept bolted, and listened. She could hear her mother's voice and, soon enough, also heard Emelia's. Given that she'd stayed away from her sister since the woman's return, she hadn't yet had the chance to talk to her.

But that was about to change with this unexpected opportunity.

Unbolting the door, she shoved it open.

Athole and Emelia looked at her in surprise. There was a satchel on the bed, and it was clear they were going to pack it.

Perhaps for Emelia to go to St. Andrews with Darien and the priest.

That realization didn't sit well with Eventide.

"Where do ye think ye're going?" she asked.

Nervously, Emelia faced her. She'd been glad that she hadn't been in contact with her sister since her return because what she needed to do would be easier if she didn't have to see Eventide's sad face. Staying away from her sister dehumanized the toll of her efforts. But now, she found herself looking at Eventide head-on and could see that her sister did not look pleased.

Not that she'd expected her to.

"Evie," she said somewhat hesitantly, "I... I know ye're upset with me and I understand that, but ye have tae believe me when I tell ye what happened. I was abducted and then found my way back. Thoughts of Darien are the only thing that kept me alive. Tae come home and find him attached tae ye is—"

"He's not merely attached," Eventide interrupted, coming

into the room. Her gaze was riveted to her sister. "He's my husband. He loves me and I love him. He will never love ye, Emelia. He will never care for ye. And ye were never abducted, so stop telling me that lie. Ye ran away with Luke because he belonged tae me. And now that Darien belongs tae me, ye want tae take him, too. This is about taking men away from me and nothing more."

Athole tried to put herself between her daughters. "Evie," she said, "go back intae yer room. This doesna concern ye."

Eventide looked at her mother. "And ye're dead tae me," she said calmly. "For all of the times ye ignored me, for all of the times ye took Emelia's word over mine, for all of the apathy ye showed me, and for supporting Emelia in this matter over me, know that ye're dead tae me. I consider my mother Mabel dun Tarh. Not ye. So dunna talk tae me ever again."

Athole, weak in spirit and in heart, was taken aback by these words. She gasped, recoiling in horror, and quickly ran out of the chamber. That was normal behavior for their mother, an insipid woman who had no strength in any given situation. Eventide didn't give her a second thought as she returned her attention to Emelia.

There was pure venom in her eyes.

"Ye'll never have him," she said in a low, threatening voice. "Darien is my husband. He will never be yers. This is one thing ye canna take from me, so I'm telling ye tae stop this right now. Go down tae Monsignor Carrick and tell him ye withdraw yer protest."

Emelia was hardening. "Why would I do that?" she said. "Ye may have married him, Evie, but not for long."

Eventide shook her head in disgust. "Ye dunna love him," she said. "There are a thousand other men ye could have, so why Darien? He's not even an heir. He can bring nothing tae ye."

Emelia had an answer for it, but she wasn't sure she wanted to give it. So she simply shrugged. "We had a contract."

"And ye violated that when ye ran away with Luke," Eventide said. "And what ye did was not on a whim, either. How long had ye been planning it?"

"I dinna plan it."

"Then where is the satchel that Mother bought ye when we went tae Carlisle last year?" Eventide said. "Did ye think I never noticed that it was missing? When everyone was searching for ye on the day ye disappeared, I noticed it was missing from yer wardrobe. So, ye'd been planning tae run away with Luke. The missing satchel is proof ye weren't abducted."

Emelia seemed to lose some of her hardness at the realization that her sister was countering her lies—and quite ably. "It's not proof of anything," she said. "The satchel could be anywhere. I could have loaned it tae someone."

"Who?" Eventide said. "Ye havena any friends. No decent woman will be associated with the likes of ye, so who would ye loan it tae? More importantly, we've not had a visitor here at Blackrock since ye purchased it in Carlisle, so no one walked off with it. *Where* is the satchel, Emelia?"

Emelia stood her ground. "I dunna know what ye're talking about."

Eventide was used to the stubbornness, the evasiveness. She stepped closer and lowered her voice. "I dinna tell Darien or Da," she said. "No one knows but me. I dinna tell them because at the time I noticed the missing bag, it was confirmation that ye'd run away and I dinna want Da tae double his efforts tae bring ye back. If he knew ye were with Luke, then it would make him work harder at trying tae find ye. Without proof, he only assumed ye ran away. He dinna truly know. But now ye return with this tale of abduction simply tae force Darien intae marriage, and I willna let ye. The satchel is the proof that ye lied."

Emelia was losing ground quickly. "Ye're mad!" she said. "Ye canna prove anything!"

"I can and I will," she said. "Emelia, ye're the only person who can stop this action with the church. Ye started it and ye must end it. If ye dunna go tae the monsignor and tell him that ye withdraw yer protest, then I'll tell him about the satchel. I'll tell everyone and your web of lies will collapse. But I'm giving ye a chance tae make this right."

Emelia resorted to bullying, like she always did with Eventide. "Nay, ye willna tell," she said. "Ye willna risk Da's wrath because ye withheld that information. He'll be furious with ye."

Eventide shrugged. "He'll be angrier at ye," she said. "I'll also tell them that ye confessed tae running off with Luke. It'll be your word against mine, but by that time, no one will know who's telling the truth and who isn't. The chance the monsignor disbelieves ye will be great."

That was probably true. If Eventide was willing to do all that to save her marriage, then it would be a battle. A big one. Emelia had never had to battle her sister before.

But she had to now.

And Eventide was a clever opponent.

"He'll not disbelieve me," Emelia said, fighting down her fear. "I've been wronged and he knows it."

Eventide shook her head. "Do ye think the man wants tae look like a fool in front of his superiors, bringing this situation tae them when he doesna even know who is telling the truth?"

she said. "He would look daft. He willna risk it."

She was right, and they both knew it. Emelia could feel her control slipping away, stolen by her sister. Eventide had never been a factor in anything Emelia had done because *she'd* always had the power. The control. But now, Eventide had the control because of that damnable satchel. Her father knew that Emelia had such a satchel, and if she couldn't produce it, or give a reasonable explanation as to why it was missing, then doubt would be cast over her entire story.

She couldn't let her sister do that to her.

She had to reclaim control.

Emelia launched herself at Eventide, catching the woman off guard. Eventide tried to get away from her but tripped over a chair, and they both fell to the ground. Eventide hit her head on the floor, which stunned her, giving Emelia time to wrap her hands around her throat.

The fight was on.

"I'll kill ye," Emelia said, squeezing Eventide's neck. "I'll kill ye and marry Darien and fuck him every night of his life until memories of ye are wiped from his mind. I'll make it so ye never existed!"

Eventide was shorter than her sister, but she was stronger. Emelia had her in a bad position, but she managed to poke the woman in the eye with a finger. As Emelia faltered, Eventide took her fist and shoved it into her sister's face as hard as she could. Emelia screamed and sat up, taking her weight off Eventide, as a figure suddenly appeared in the adjoining doorway. Before Eventide could react, someone had Emelia by the hair and yanked her back with such force that Emelia screamed in agony.

Eventide looked up to see Mabel, like an avenging angel.

And the woman was ready for battle.

"You vile creature," Mabel spat, her right hand wrapped up in Emelia's hair. "What were you trying to do to her? Tell me this instant or I'll pull your hair from your scalp!"

"Nay, m'lady!" Emelia cried, her hands on her head where Mabel was pulling. "She… she attacked me first! I was defending myself!"

Eventide rubbed her neck as she stood up. "She lunged at me and tried tae strangle me," she said, showing Mabel the marks on her neck. "I told her that I knew her story about being abducted was a lie because her favorite satchel is missing. I noticed it from the first but dinna tell anyone. I thought if I told her that I knew, she'd withdraw her protest. But she tried tae kill me because I know the missing satchel proves she ran away and wasna abducted."

Mabel's jaw tightened as she listened to the explanation. "Is that true?" she said, yanking Emelia's head again. "Tell me the truth or I'll start pulling hair out, strand by strand. No more lies, Emelia. Tell me the truth immediately."

Emelia was struggling, unwilling to answer, so Mabel did what she said she was going to do—she took a strand of hair and yanked it out. Emelia yelped. Mabel pulled out another and another until Emelia was trying to slap her hands away.

"Stop!" she cried. "Stop at once!"

"Not until you tell me the truth, young lady."

Emelia started kicking now, trying to fight Mabel. A balled fist made contact with Mabel's left arm. Eventide intervened, slapping her sister across the face so hard that Emelia came to a halt simply because she was stunned by the force of the blow. To make sure she wouldn't try to strike Mabel again, Eventide slapped her a second time, as hard as she could, and Emelia stopped struggling altogether.

She just sat there and wept.

"Well," Mabel said, blowing errant hair out of her face after the tussle died down, "though I'm not an advocate for beating a woman, in this case, I will make an exception. Your sister needs it badly. But if she is going to tell the truth, then I want everyone to hear it. We'll take her down to the solar, where the men are gathering. Evie, I suggest you tell them about the missing satchel immediately. They must know."

Eventide nodded. Was it actually possible they were close to a confession? Thank God Mabel had come in when she had. Together, they pulled Emelia to her feet.

It was a tribulation getting her down the stairs, however. Emelia tried to dig in, to grab the walls, anything to prevent them from taking her to the solar, but in the end, they managed to get her down the stairs. They were in the entry now, making enough noise that Darien and Fergus came out of the solar to see what the fuss was about. They saw both Mabel and Eventide dragging Emelia toward them, and the girl was in hysterics.

"Da!" she cried. "Tell them tae release me! Please!"

Fergus knew better than to make that demand, especially of Lady Torridon. But he was understandably concerned.

"M'lady?" he said timidly. "What is happening?"

Eventide let her sister go, but Mabel didn't. She was furious with the lies, furious with what the woman had done to her son, so she wasn't going to ease up. She still held Emelia by the hair, forcing her to her knees as Darien and now Lares, in the solar doorway, watched in astonishment.

"Evie," Mabel said calmly, "tell them what you told me. No more secrets, please."

Eventide looked at her husband, somewhat hesitantly, before finally looking at her father. "I have something tae tell ye," she said. "When we were searching for Emelia on the day she vanished, I noticed that she had taken a satchel out of her wardrobe. The one Mother purchased for her in Carlisle. I dinna tell ye because... because I dinna want her back. I thought that if I told ye, then it would confirm she ran away with Luke and ye'd try harder tae find her. But I dinna want ye tae, so I dinna tell ye. I'm sorry, Father. And I'm sorry tae ye, Darien. I should have told ye what I saw."

Fergus was astonished. He looked at Emelia. "Then ye *did* run off with him," he said. "Ye took yer satchel and ye ran. He dinna abduct ye!"

Emelia was on her knees, but she still had fight left in her. "I dunna know about the satchel," she insisted. "Mayhap it was lost. Or mayhap I gave it tae someone. The fact that it's missing proves nothing. Now, tell Lady Torridon tae let me go or I'll break her hand!"

She reached up and began beating on the hand that Mabel had wound in her hair, but Mabel simply yanked, hard, and that stilled her quickly. The men in the doorway winced as Mabel tugged again for good measure, bringing Emelia to tears.

Monsignor Carrick had heard the commotion and stepped out of the solar. The ruthless and righteous Lady Torridon had Emelia by the hair, and the young woman was trapped. But he'd heard the confession about the missing satchel and Emelia's denial.

"Lady Torridon," he said evenly, "would you mind releasing her?"

Mabel shook her head. "Not until she confesses to her lies," she said. "Monsignor, surely you know you've been taken in by a prevaricator. Emelia Moriston makes up things to suit her purposes. She ran away with Eventide's betrothed and then, when she tired of him, returned with a story of abduction and demanded to marry my son. Understand that she violated the contract first when she ran off with Luke Cannich."

"I wanted her money and titles. And that's why we ran."

The voice came from the entry door. In all of the commotion, no one had seen a figure come up the stairs and stand in the partially open doorway. All eyes turned, with shock, to see the very man in question stepping into the foyer.

A vision back from the dead.

CHAPTER TWENTY

"MY... GOD!" FERGUS gasped. "*Luke!*"

Luke Cannich looked like hell. Pale, his hair filthy and matted with blood, he staggered into the entry with a bandaged right arm and shoulder. His gaze was fixed on Emelia, who screamed when she saw him.

"Luke!" she cried. "God in heaven! Ye... ye're *alive!*"

Luke looked at her, displeasure evident on his face. "Aye," he said. "No thanks tae ye."

Darien, who had been watching the scene with astonishment like everyone else, found his tongue. "What do ye mean by that?" he asked. "Why did she believe ye tae be dead?"

Luke glanced at him, but nothing more. His focus, and his ire, was strictly on Emelia at this point. He'd spent the past several days making his way to Blackrock, injured and sick, beaten and sore, but he had made it.

And he'd never been more furious about anything in his life.

"Because she tried tae kill me," he rumbled. "She pushed me out of a window."

"Nay!" Emelia shrieked. "I dinna push ye! Ye fell!"

Luke shook his head with disgust. "Lass, yer life is one built on lies, but I'll not believe that one as long as I live," he said with some irony. Finally, he turned to Darien, to Fergus. "Aye, we ran away when she was supposed tae marry Darien. I wanted the wealth and the titles. No offense tae ye, Darien. This wasna personal. But ye have so much—a big family, people who love ye, a good home and food on yer table. What do I have? Nothing. No money, no title. A castle that belongs tae my da. I wanted what ye were going tae get, and I will admit it tae ye. But it came at a price. A very high price."

Darien was listening closely, putting the pieces of the puzzle together. "Then yer running away was planned."

"It was."

"Did ye marry her, then?"

Luke nodded. "Absolutely," he said, looking at a sobbing Emelia, still on her knees. "She's my wife. Consider yerself lucky. She's not worth the price I had tae pay."

"Ye seduced me, ye bastard," Emelia wept, grasping at the last vestiges of her lies in an attempt to defend herself. "Ye seduced me and ye forced me tae run away with ye. Ye promised me a good life and we had nothing. *Nothing!* I was forced tae work because ye couldna support yer own wife. 'Tis yer fault we were so miserable!"

So much of the situation was starting to make sense. Darien looked at his father for the man's reaction, only to see that Lares had a deeply contemplative expression on his face. When he saw that Darien was looking at him, he turned to Monsignor Carrick.

"Now that ye've heard the truth of the situation, my son has a good case against young Cannick for thievery," he said. "He can be charged with stealing my son's bride—and along with her, the titles and property she brings with her. Is that not true?"

Monsignor Carrick was regretting the day he'd ever agreed to speak with Emelia Moriston. "It is true," he said with a sigh. "If you produce the betrothal contracts that prove this, I can arrest him."

"Nay," Darien said, holding out a hand to stop that particular conversation. "No one is being arrested. Luke, ye look terrible, man. What, exactly, happened tae ye?"

Luke sighed wearily. "Exactly what I told ye," he said. "We were having an argument because I discovered that my wife, whilst working in a tavern, was allowing men tae suck her toes for money. And God only knows what else she let them suck for money. So, she attacked me and pushed me out of a window. I fell tae the street below and lay unconscious for most of the night, I suppose. I dunna really know. All I know is that no one came tae my aid, and when I awoke, I went back tae the rooms we occupied only tae find her gone. And I knew exactly where she'd gone—back tae Blackrock. There was no doubt in my mind."

That explained why Luke appeared so beaten. "But how did *ye* make it back tae Blackrock?" Darien asked.

Luke glanced at Emelia. "Probably the same way she did," he said. "I left as soon as I could find someone tae travel with. I rode in the back of a farmer's wagon for quite some time before he found me other transportation north. A physic in Perth wrapped my arm and shoulder. He doesna think I'll be able tae use it properly again, given the break, but it should heal. I couldna have been more than a day or two behind her. When did she arrive?"

"About three days ago."

Luke sighed, returning his attention to Emelia. "And lying about everything that happened, I'm guessing," he said. "Did she even tell ye we were married?"

Darien shook his head. "She told us ye abducted her," he said. "She told us she had fought tae get back tae Blackrock and expected tae marry me as if nothing had happened."

Luke snorted. "I assumed she'd lie about it," he said. "We were married in Perth on the flight south, at St. John the Baptist church. Ye can ask the priests there. They have a record of it."

Emelia hung her head and wept. Her house of lies had collapsed and everything was naked for all to see. A man she thought dead had returned to ruin her life, and there was nothing left for her. Monsignor Carrick was already packing up his things to leave.

Everything was in ruin.

"This isna fair," she sobbed. "I dinna want tae go. I dinna want tae leave Darien and hurt Evie!"

Luke wasn't in a sympathetic mood. No one was. Fergus, who usually had pity for his eldest, couldn't seem to muster any for her either. She'd done this to herself. He could see that clearly.

After a moment, he simply shook his head.

"This is my fault," he said, his gaze lingering on his weeping daughter. "I indulged her too much. I let her believe that she could have anything she wanted, and even when she needed punishment, I never gave it tae her. Usually, she would talk me out of it. But the result is what ye see—a failure. She's a failure as a woman, as a person, and the people she has failed the most are Luke and Darien and Evie. I had a viper in my very own house and I couldna see it."

Darien and Luke were looking at him as he apologized for

his shortcomings. "Everyone has choices, Fergus," Darien said. "Emelia had choices. She could have chosen not tae behave as she did. Ye're not tae blame for that."

Fergus sighed heavily and looked at Luke. "What will ye do with her now?" he asked. "She's yer wife. If ye want tae have her arrested for trying tae kill ye, we can have her brought tae the local magistrate."

Luke shook his head. "Nay," he said. "I'll not do that. But she's going tae learn how tae be a good wife when I take her back tae Moy. She's going tae learn tae obey her husband in every way, or I'll lock her up and throw the key intae the sea."

At the mention of Moy, Darien looked at his father and Fergus, realizing that Luke didn't know about the siege of his home. Since the decision to attack Moy had come from Fergus and Lares, Darien silently encouraged someone to say something about it.

The truth finally came from Lares.

"There's something ye should know, Luke," he said. "When we realized what had happened with ye and Emelia, we made the decision tae punish yer father."

Luke looked at him with concern. "My da had nothing tae do with my decision," he said. "He dinna know anything. Oh, God... What did ye do?"

Lares held up a hand to ease him. "Yer father is alive as far as I know," he said. "We never touched him. But we confiscated Moy Castle. It's a dun Tarh property now, and I have given it tae Darien, since ye ran off with his bride."

Wide-eyed with shock, Luke looked at Darien. "It's yers?"

Darien nodded. "It is."

Luke looked like he wanted to say something more, but he thought better of it. As if he could protest what they'd done. He couldn't, of course, and he knew it. Taking a deep breath, he raked the fingers of his good hand through his dirty, matted hair.

"I suppose if there's any justice in the situation, ye settled it," he said. "Where's my da?"

Darien shook his head. "We dunna know," he said. "The castle was mostly vacant when we arrived, so we assume he fled. We've not heard from him."

Luke pondered that for a moment. "My mother is a MacKay," he said. "We spent the days of my youth in my grandfather's village in Durness, far tae the north. My guess is that he went there."

Darien watched the man struggle with the way his world had been upended as a result of his actions. There was genuine regret there. Empathetic as always, Darien could sense it. Everyone made a bad decision at least once in their life, and Luke's decision had cost him everything, including his family home. The only reward was a wife who had no loyalty to him and, in fact, had tried to kill him.

It was an extremely difficult lesson for Luke to learn.

"Luke," Darien said, "I dunna like what ye did. Ye stole something that belongs tae me in the Shandwick title, not tae mention Blackrock, but I dunna think ye did it maliciously. As ye said, it was nothing personal, and I suspect ye sorely regret doing what ye did."

Luke could hardly look him in the eye. "I do."

"I know," Darien said. "But I'll tell ye what I said when we discovered what had happened. I said I'd buy ye a drink if I ever saw ye again because yer selfishness saved my life. Ye saved me from marrying Emelia and, in fact, made it so I married a woman I love with all my heart. Evie is everything tae me. My happiness couldna have happened were it not for ye, so I owe ye a great deal."

Luke's expression rippled in confusion. "Ye think so, do ye?"

"I do," Darien said. "And because I'm grateful, I'm going tae return Moy tae ye. Ye can have it back. And when Fergus passes on, Blackrock will become yer property, too, so I'd say ye're going tae have a great deal in life through your marriage tae Emelia. Just try not tae let her kill ye before ye can enjoy it all."

Luke stared at him in amazement. "Ye… ye'd truly do that, Darien?"

Darien nodded, smiling when Eventide came over to him and put her arms around his torso, giving him a squeeze. He put his arm around her shoulders, kissing her on the forehead.

"Aye, I'd truly do that," he said quietly. "I have so much already. Ye pointed it out. I have a loving family, a beautiful wife, and my mother has given me her father's former courtesy title, Lord Lowmoor, and the property associated with it. I dunna need Moy or even Blackrock. But ye do. For what ye have tae go through being married tae Emelia, I think ye deserve it."

Luke had no idea what to say. He put an astonished hand to his mouth, realizing that the man he'd so terribly wronged was actually going to reward him for it. He'd never seen such forgiveness in his life, and it was directed at him, which made him feel very humble. It also made him feel some joy—joy that, perhaps, he might have something to look forward to in this life after all.

All thanks to Darien dun Tarh.

"I'm speechless, Darien," he finally said. "I dunna know how tae thank ye."

Darien smiled at him. "Thank me by keeping Emelia away from me, her sister, and our family," he said, his smile fading. "I never want tae see, or hear, that woman again. Do this and there will be peace. Forget yerself and there won't. Do I make myself clear?"

Luke nodded. "All too well," he said, his gaze moving over to his wife, with Mabel's hand still in the woman's hair. "She's done a great deal of damage tae a great many people and deserves tae be punished. Because of that, may I ask something of yer mother?"

Darien extended his arm in his mother's direction, silently indicating for Luke to ask her directly. Luke limped over to his wife, and to Lady Torridon, his gaze lingering on Emelia for a moment before he looked at Mabel.

"M'lady," he said, "forgive me that we've met under such disheartening circumstances. But yer reputation for fairness, boldness, and righteousness is well known. I am wondering if I might ask a favor."

Mabel didn't have any real animosity toward the man because, as Darien explained it, he had really saved her son's life and happiness. That being the case, she was feeling a bit generous.

"You may ask," she said.

Luke pointed to Emelia. "As ye can see, I'm without an arm," he said. "I was going tae punish Emelia myself, but it seems I canna do it. May I ask ye tae help me?"

"How?"

Luke leaned over and whispered in her ear. Mabel's lips twitched with a smile before she nodded. Then she pulled Emelia to her feet.

"Get up, lass," she said. "Come with me."

Emelia was sniffling and groaning, but Lady Torridon at least removed the hand from her hair. However, she didn't let go of Emelia entirely. She grasped the woman by the arm and dragged her over to a bench that was next to the entry door. Sitting down, she threw Emelia over her lap.

Arse up.

Witnessing Mabel dun Tarh spank Emelia within an inch of her life was the most satisfying thing anyone had ever seen. As Emelia screamed and Mabel told her what a rotten creature she was, Darien laughed all the way to the entry door, which was still only partially open. He threw it open wide so the whole of Blackrock could hear what was going on, and hear they did. Darien happened to notice his brothers and the Munro siblings at the base of the stairs, gazing up at him with concern and curiosity.

He crooked a finger at them.

"Come and see," he told them as they hurriedly mounted the steps. "Come and see my mother punish Emelia for her dastardly deeds. A little public humiliation does wonders for the soul, lads."

Caelus, Estevan, Kaladin, Lucan, Leandro, and Cruz entered the foyer to witness Emelia's great embarrassment, but more than that, they were simply glad it wasn't them being spanked. They'd all felt Mabel's hand during the course of their lives, and her aim was true. As Darien watched his siblings enjoy someone else's well-deserved pain, he caught a glimpse of the Munro brothers still standing just outside the door.

"Come in," he said. "Ye can tell yer father what ye saw today. True dun Tarh justice delivered."

Calum and Guthrie could only partially see what was going on, but they refused to come in. In fact, they drew Darien out onto the landing.

"What's happening, Darien?" Calum asked. "Why is yer mother beating Emelia?"

Darien was smiling. "Because Luke Cannich returned," he said. "Did ye not see him come in?"

Both Calum and Guthrie shook their heads. "Nay," Calum said. "I've never met Luke Cannich. I dunna know him on sight."

Darien frowned. "No one told ye he had come?"

"I hadn't heard."

That didn't make sense to Darien. "Surely someone at the gate noticed him when he walked in," he muttered, almost to himself, but his focus returned to the brothers. "Your homes are only about a day's ride from one another. How can ye not know him?"

"Because my mother always said the Cannich clan was rubbish," Calum said. "My father had a quarrel with Reelig, so we never really knew the family. So Luke returned, did he?"

"He did," Darien said. "He simply walked intae the keep and told us that he ran off with Emelia but that she tried tae kill him. Evidently, she thought he was dead, but the man has returned. And Emelia's lies are exposed."

That was excellent, but surprising, news. "No more priests?" Calum asked. "No more annulment threat?"

Darien shook his head. "Nothing," he said. "It is finished. Thank God, it is finished."

The brothers seemed to show some relief. "Thank God, indeed," Guthrie muttered. "That means we dunna have tae send Emelia tae the Northmen."

Darien turned to him curiously. "What does that mean?"

Guthrie snorted. "It means that Calum and me were planning on making Emelia disappear so the way would be clear for ye tae remain married tae Evie," he said. "But now we dunna have tae. The way is already clear, thanks tae Luke's appearance."

Darien was shocked. "Ye were going tae make Emelia disappear?" he asked. "Lads... would ye truly make such a sacrifice for a fight that wasna yer own?"

The mood was turning serious. Guthrie nodded. "We discussed it with yer brothers," he said. "We wanted them tae know, but we wanted tae keep them clean. It wouldna be good for a family tae have brothers involved in a secret like that. Making yer legal wife disappear, I mean. So Calum and I were going tae spirit Emelia away and make it so she never returned. Yer mother gave us her blessing."

The last six words astonished Darien. He found himself looking back into the entry where Mabel had just finished spanking Emelia, who was now crumpled on the ground in shameful tears.

"My *mother* knew about this plot?" he asked. "You told her?"

Both Guthrie and Calum nodded. "Darien, ye have tae know that we all knew what Emelia was doing tae ye," Calum said quietly. "Do ye truly think we'd all stand around and watch that happen? Ye had enough tae deal with by taking care of yer wife and yerself and wondering what was going tae happen if the monsignor took ye tae the bishop. That's the time when true friends and family come together tae do what they can tae help. It wasna a plot as much as it was a path tae justice."

Darien was in awe to realize all of this had been going on behind his back. He'd had his own plan to save his marriage, but his friends, and evidently family, had had plans of their own. So many people working to save him and Eventide.

He was overcome.

"I have no words," he said after a moment. "That ye'd do such a thing seems unfathomable. Ye've humbled me, lads."

Calum grinned. "And we'd do it again if needed," he said. "But remember this if *I* ever need tae make a wife disappear."

"I'll be the first one tae take her out tae sea."

"Good," Calum said. "Now, if we're no longer needed, we'll be heading home."

"Give yer da our love. We'll pray for him."

Guthrie slapped Darien on the shoulder, smiling, as the Munro brothers headed back down the steps, moving for the stables to return home now that a major crisis had been avoided. Darien and Eventide were safe and there was no reason for the Munros to remain. Darien watched them go, deeply touched that he had such good friends. A "path to justice" was what Calum had called it.

Justice, indeed.

But no one delivered justice better than Mabel. As Fergus and Luke led Emelia away, taking her to a chamber where she would be closely watched, Lares went to speak to Monsignor Carrick, promising the man a generous donation for his trouble and time. Eventide went with him, hopefully to soothe any ruffled feathers, because she was good at that kind of thing. The monsignor had been badly abused by Emelia, and even though the man had the power to ruin her life, Eventide wanted to make it right because he'd been sucked into her sister's lies.

As people began to move now that the drama was concluded, Darien came into the entry in time to be mobbed by his brothers, demanding to know what had happened. Mabel called them off, however, sending them back outside to await her while spoke to Darien alone.

It was a private moment between them, just mother and son.

"And?" Mabel said, gazing up into his face and putting a gentle hand on his cheek. "Do you feel hopeful again, my darling?"

He smiled at her, kissing the palm of her hand. "Everything has happened so quickly," he said. "Not an hour ago I thought my life was about tae take a terrible turn. Da and I were in the solar with the monsignor and he was resolute that we were going tae St. Andrews. He wanted tae leave tomorrow, but I refused."

"I'm certain that did not make him happy."

"Nay," Darien said, shaking his head, "it did *not*. I thought we were at a stalemate. I could see my life flashing before my eyes, terrified it was not going tae be as I wanted it tae be. Terrified I was going tae lose so much."

"And now?"

Darien was close to a loss for words again. "And now, here we are," he said, looking around the entry. "The man who saved my life once has saved it again. I never knew Luke Cannich very well, but he has given me my life."

"By not marrying Evie?"

"Aye," Darien said. "And by coming tae Blackrock, as beaten and injured as he is, tae save me once again."

Mabel smiled, patting his cheek because he seemed completely stunned by the whole thing. "I heard you return Moy Castle to him," she said. "That was extremely generous of you, Darien. You did not have to do that."

"I know," he said. "But he has earned it. The man has set himself up for a difficult life with Emelia. Thank God it isna me."

"Agreed," she said. "I wonder what he'll do now."

Darien shrugged. "I'm sure he'll take her back tae Moy," he said. "It's his home, after all."

"Blackrock will be his when Fergus passes. Does that not trouble you?"

Darien shook his head. "Not in the least," he said. "As I told him, I have Wigton. I have my home in Edinburgh. And I have Evie and ye and Da and the rest of our bunch. I have people who love me and are loved in return. Honestly, Mam, there is no man on this earth richer than I am."

Mabel put her hand on his arm, squeezing it. "I agree," she said. "You are a fortunate man, indeed."

"But it was worth everything tae see you spank Emelia."

Mabel snorted softly. "I do not normally condone spanking or lifting a hand to a grown woman, but she had it coming," she said. "Neither Fergus nor Athole disciplined her as a child, which means it must be done as an adult. I hope she learns from this. I truly do."

"Me too."

Fergus suddenly appeared, returning to the foyer. He caught sight of Darien and Mabel and made his way over to them with all of the enthusiasm of a lad heading to his father for a beating.

He could hardly meet their eyes.

"Darien," he said, "I suppose ye know how terribly I feel about this. I'm so very sorry Emelia did what she did."

"I know," Darien said. "But she made her own choices. As I said, it was not yer fault."

Fergus nodded, contrite even in the face of Darien's forgiveness. "I wanted tae let ye know that I told Luke he'll only receive half of Emelia's dowry," he said. "Yer da and I discussed it long ago. He suggested I split Emelia's dowry between ye and Luke, and I'm going tae do that. I've told Luke already, so he's aware. The money will help ye and Evie as ye start yer life together."

"That's very generous, Fergus," Mabel said. "I am appreciative that you took Lares' suggestion."

"As am I," Darien said. "My da mentioned the same thing tae me, too, before I was even betrothed tae Evie, and I'm glad ye took his advice. But ye should know that I dinna expect the money. I married Evie because I love her, not because of what she brings me."

Fergus put up a hand to quiet him. "I know," he said. "But ye've earned it."

Darien opened his mouth to reply, but Mabel caught his attention and shook her head. She knew that Darien was going to perhaps protest the dowry just a little more, just to make sure Fergus knew he wasn't in it for the money, but it really wasn't necessary. Fergus felt bad for what had happened and this was his way of making up for it.

Darien would have to accept it.

"What happens tae Luke and Emelia now?" he asked. "Truthfully, I'm not sure I'd trust her if I were Luke. She tried tae kill him once."

Fergus smiled without humor. "And they're in a chamber back there discussing that very thing," he said. "Tae be truthful, I dunna know what will happen with them. But I know what will happen with Evie, and that does my heart good. May yer lives together be much more peaceful now that this storm has passed."

Just as he said that, thunder crashed overhead as the storm

that had been rolling in all day let loose. The entry door was open and they could see the rain as it began to pound. Lares and Eventide chose that moment to emerge from the solar, where the monsignor had decided to stay until the storm cleared up. As Fergus went into the solar to entertain the man, Lares and Eventide met up with their respective spouses.

"Monsignor Carrick is a good-natured man," Lares said. "He doesna harbor any ill will about this situation. He simply wants tae return tae his parish and forget about all of us."

Mabel and Darien chuckled. "No doubt he'll tell stories about the madness at Blackrock he had tae endure," he said before looking at her. "And that is why I intend tae take my wife and return tae Edinburgh as soon as the weather clears. I've got a great many things waiting for me, and Evie has a house tae take charge of."

Eventide grinned at him as he put his arm around her. "A house of our own," she said dreamily. "A life of our own. I can hardly believe it."

"Believe it, lass," Darien said, gazing down at her. "I hope ye're ready for it, because it will be a different world. But a wonderful one."

Eventide squeezed him tightly, her head on his chest as he wrapped her up in his big arms. "Any world where ye are is a wonderful world," she said. "I'm looking forward tae it. And ye. *Airson a h-uile àm.*"

Smiling, Darien kissed her on the top of the head. "For all time, indeed," he whispered.

Lares and Mabel watched the pair walk away, heading back up the stairs to the chamber they shared. When they were finally alone in the entry, so still and quiet after the madness it had so recently witnessed, Lares looked at his wife of many years.

To say he loved her was an understatement.

"And another son will live happily ever after," he said. "Aurelius found love. Now Darien has. I couldna ask for a better ending."

Mabel looked at him. "And I only had to nearly beat a girl to death in order to achieve it," she said with some sarcasm. "Truly, Lares, you are forbidden from brokering any more marriage contracts without me. I am *not* going through this havoc again."

Lares fought off a grin as he put his arm around her. "Ye'll go through what I say ye go through," he said. "Ye'll go through it and ye'll like it."

She cocked an eyebrow at him. "Is that so?" she said. "Broker a contract without me and see what happens."

"Yer wrath shall be swift?"

"My wrath shall be swift."

He started leading her toward the solar, where there was a fire and wine waiting. "Will ye spank me if I dunna obey?"

"I'll beat you within an inch of your life."

"The last time ye did that, we had Zora."

Mabel started to clap back but ended up breaking down into snorts of laughter. Leave it to Lares to lighten a mood. And lighten her life. If Darien and Eventide were only half as happy as she and Lares had been all of these years, then their life would have been worth living.

For certain, she knew hers was.

Every day was worth a lifetime.

EPILOGUE

Wigton House
Cumbria
Year of Our Lord 1362

CHILDREN WERE RUNNING everywhere.

Darien could hear them overhead, running down the stairs, screaming at each other, calling for their mother, and any number of noises, bumps, and bangs. He could also hear Eventide's calm voice, answering questions, encouraging the children to get a move on.

It was pandemonium in Lord Lowmoor's household.

Wigton House was an enormous, gray-stoned building that had been part of Mabel's family for more than two hundred years. It had survived Scots attacks and, being so close to the Solway Firth, even pirate attacks. It wasn't a castle but a fortified manse, with thirty rooms, three levels, all of it enclosed within a massive curtain wall. When Darien inherited Wigton, it had come with the remnants of the de Waverton army, so he had about three hundred Englishmen under his command.

That had taken some getting used to.

But today was a special day for the inhabitants of Wigton.

Darien's brother, Lucan, was marrying a lass from Berwick and the entire dun Tarh family, including everyone from the Hydra and Aurelius' family from Lydgate Castle in Yorkshire, would be in attendance. There were about fifty family members converging on Berwick, where Lucan was marrying a Pembury daughter. An English bride.

But that was a story in and of itself.

"Evie?" Darien shouted as he stood in the open door of the manse, looking at the escort beyond. "Evie, my love? If we dunna leave now, then we're going tae be late and ye know what my mother will do tae us if we are. Evie?"

He heard a muffled reply from an upper floor and, very quickly, his two eldest sons appeared. Aristeo dun Tarh, or Téo as he was called by the family, was the eldest at eleven years of age. But he was going through a growth spurt and had already surpassed his mother in height. He had his father's dark hair without the white streak, his mother's bright blue eyes, and was an intelligent and lively lad. He was also following the dun Tarh tradition that the eldest son in the family foster in England and learn English ways, so he had spent the past two years at Carlisle Castle and was home for a brief time before he moved to Northwood Castle, which sat on the Scots border with England.

Beside Aristeo was his younger brother by two years, Cortez, who couldn't have looked more like Lares if he tried. Dark haired and dark eyed, Cortez was as tall as Aristeo and possessed a big build. While Aristeo was more of an introverted intellectual, Cortez was the natural leader. The lad knew how to get things done. He was heading to Northwood, too, because Darien wanted his boys well educated but also wanted to keep them together.

Even if keeping them together meant keeping them in England.

"Mother has the girls, Da," Cortez said. "I've told Mateo if he's not down tae the escort in the next minute that I'm going tae carry him outside myself."

Darien grinned because he knew Cortez would most certainly do that. "Give Matty a little more than a minute, lad," he said. "He's younger than ye are and ye know that he doesna move as fast. But where are your mother and sisters?"

"Here," Eventide said as she came down the stairs with three red-haired daughters and bags in her hands. "Help me, please."

Darien, Aristeo, and Cortez rushed to help her, but little Sofia, the youngest dun Tarh child, thought her father was reaching for her, so she whined for him and held up her arms. Darien took a satchel in one hand and his toddler in the other, carrying them both outside to the waiting carriage. Six-year-old Adelina and four-year-old Juliana, very much mirror images of their beauteous mother, were escorted outside by their bag-carrying brothers. That left Mateo.

Eventide, realizing she'd left a child behind, went back up the stairs and down a corridor that led to the children's nursery. This was where they slept and played and learned from a tutor who lived in a small house on the grounds. She found Mateo, her eight-year-old, sitting at a small table. The boy was just staring at the tabletop, unmoving.

"Matty?" she said curiously. "What are ye doing, my love?"

Mateo dun Tarh looked at his mother reluctantly. Also dark haired and dark eyed, he had been born prematurely and was small for his age. His eyesight was also poor as a result of his early birth, and Mateo had a challenging time keeping up with his siblings sometimes. But Darien and Eventide had never treated him any differently because of his shortcomings. They had the same expectations with him that they had with all of their children, only Mateo sometimes just needed a little more patience.

Deep down, Eventide had a soft spot for her sweet little boy.

"Well?" she said. "Everyone is waiting for ye downstairs. Why are ye sitting here?"

He frowned and looked away. "Cortez said I was boil-brained," he said glumly. "He told me tae put my shoes on, and I broke a strap. Now I cannot tie them."

Eventide, who was clad in a magnificent yellow brocade as befitting her position as Lady Lowmoor, knelt down beside her son in all of her finery.

"Let me see it," she said, and the lad held up the shoe. She took it, inspecting it. "Is this all? 'Tis not a terrible thing. We can fix it, but we must get going. Do ye not want tae see Avia and Papa?"

She was referring to Mabel and Lares by what the grandchildren called them. But Mateo was sad and didn't seem too eager to move.

"Am I boil-brained, Mama?" he asked. "I did not mean tae break the strap."

Before Eventide could answer, Darien appeared in the doorway, a look of exasperation on his face.

"What is taking so long?" he asked. "Matty, we must go, lad. Come with yer mother now."

Eventide stood up, holding up Mateo's broken shoe. "Cortez told Matty that he was boil-brained," she said with a hint of hazard in her tone. "Matty broke a strap putting on his shoe and now he's upset about it. He thinks that he's… Well, Cortez calling him boil-brained dinna help."

Darien cocked an eyebrow. Coming into the chamber, he took the shoe from his wife. "I willna stand in yer way if ye want tae tell Cortez just what ye think of his name calling," he said in a quiet voice. "I'll fix the shoe and bring Matty."

Eventide's eyes narrowed. Cortez was in for a verbal beating. She blew a kiss to Mateo before leaving the chamber as Darien inspected the shoe.

"Well, now," he said, kneeling down in front of the small boy in all of his mail and protection. With the traveling they would be doing, it was required that he be prepared to protect his family. "Let me see yer foot. Let's see if we can make the shoe fit for now."

Mateo was seated, but he turned to face his father. He had skinny legs and was knock-kneed, which didn't help him walk very well. Usually, Aristeo and Cortez were extremely protective of him and had been known to throw punches if anyone dared insult Mateo. But sometimes, Cortez forgot himself. He was impatient and bossy and, at times, cruel. Aristeo and Cortez had been known to get into scuffles over the way Cortez spoke to Mateo sometimes because Aristeo wouldn't even let Cortez speak unkindly to the boy. But it happened.

Like now.

Darien picked up a little foot, covered with hose, and slid the shoe on. "Matty," he said as he fussed with the broken strap, "I'm going tae tell ye something and ye must swear tae me that ye'll keep it a secret. Can ye do that?"

Mateo nodded solemnly. "Aye, Papa."

Darien didn't look up from the shoe as he spoke. "Every family has someone special, someone that will go on tae do the very greatest things," he said. "In my family, it was me. In

Papa's family, it was him. Yer grandfather is the Earl of Torridon, a very great man, and me… ye know I serve the people of Scotland."

"As the Lord Keeper of the Council."

"Aye," Darien said, giving his boy a smile. "That means I am the great one out of all of my brothers. Or, at least, I've done well. Every family has that one great brother."

"Who is our great brother, Papa?"

"Ye are."

Mateo's eyes widened. "Me?"

Darien nodded. "*Ye,*" he confirmed. "Téo and Cortez know it, so if Cortez seems unkind sometimes, ye're not tae pay him any mind, because he knows ye're going tae be the greatest brother someday. But ye mustn't let him know that ye know. He thinks ye dunna, so sometimes, he's going tae say unkind things. But he doesna mean them."

"He doesn't?"

"Nay."

"Then why does he say them?"

"Tae prepare ye for what is tae come," Darien said. He managed to secure the shoe in spite of the broken strap. "Matty, not everyone is going tae be kind tae ye as ye grow up. They may think ye small or even weak, but we know ye're not. Cortez is helping ye prepare for those who are unkind, so ye'll not take their insults tae heart. We know ye're going tae grow up tae do great and noble things someday. Ye just need that chance tae grow. Do ye understand me, lad?"

Mateo nodded. "Aye, Papa."

"What do ye understand, then?"

He thought a moment, looking very much like his father. "That I'll be better than everyone someday."

Darien grinned. "Exactly," he said. "But remember what I told ye—ye're never tae tell anyone. They wouldna believe ye anyway. But we know the truth."

"How *do* you know?"

"Because God told me," Darien said. "The moment ye were born, we knew ye were special. Someday, everyone else will know, too."

That explanation seemed to satisfy an eight-year-old. Mateo's father always had a way of making him feel better. With his shoe fixed for the moment, he stood up and took his father's hand, walking with his usual limp. They headed down to the entry of Wigton, where a servant who usually tended the children was waiting with Mateo's little cloak. There had been a chill in the air this spring, so the servant made sure that all of the dun Tarh children were warmly dressed. Darien turned his son over to the servant, who took the boy down to the waiting carriage just as Eventide was heading in his direction. She smiled at Mateo as he walked by, meeting up with her husband just as he closed the entry door.

"Well?" Darien said. "Did ye tell Cortez we dinna appreciate his insults?"

Eventide turned to look at the carriage with the children in it. "I did," she said. "I told him if he did it again, not only would he feel the sting of my hand tae his backside, but I'd tell Mabel and she'd give him a spanking he'd not soon forget. That seems tae have made an impression on him."

Darien fought off a grin as he took Eventide's hand and tucked it into the crook of his elbow. "I canna decide if it is hilarious or sad that my mother is known for her spankings," he said as he and Eventide headed toward the carriage. "I'm sure that is not the legacy she hoped for."

Eventide held on to her husband's elbow proudly. "Dunna fool yerself," she said. "Yer mother is quite proud of that reputation. I seem tae remember my sister learning that the hard way."

Darien couldn't help but grin as he remembered the spanking Emelia Cannich had taken those years ago in front of everyone. "I wonder if she ever recovered from that?" he muttered.

"I dunna know," Eventide said. "My da never mentioned her again tae the day he died, and I dunna speak with my mother or my sister, so who knows how they have fared."

"Ye never think of Emelia?"

"Nay. Should I?"

"Probably not," he said "But I could tell ye what I heard last month when I was in Edinburgh—from someone who knows Reelig Cannich."

"Is he still alive?"

"Evidently," Darien said. "Do ye want tae know what I was told?"

Eventide didn't say anything for a moment. They were on a touchy subject, if not a downright forbidden one. She hadn't spoken to her mother or sister in twelve years, ever since leaving Blackrock, and Darien rarely brought it up. It wasn't that she was bitter about her family—it was simply that she'd chosen to eliminate them from all thought. They were nearly to the carriage when she came to a halt and faced him.

"Nay," she finally said. "I dunna think I want tae hear about her. I dunna want mention of her entering our world. We have such a wonderful world, Darien. She's not part of it and she never will be. Why would I care anything about her?"

He smiled, touching her face gently. "I just thought I'd ask," he said. "I know how ye feel about her, but there may be a time when ye change yer mind. That's why I asked."

She smiled in return. "I willna change my mind," she said. "When my da died, my last connection tae that life died with him. I'll not go back, not even tae hear about my sister twelve years later."

"As ye wish, Lady Lowmoor."

"Will ye just tell me one thing?"

"Of course."

"Is she dead?"

"Nay."

"Then that's all I want tae know," she said. "The rest… it matters not."

With that, she gently patted his cheek and went on to the carriage, where she could hear raised voices. The children were starting to get restless. Aristeo and Cortez, however, were permitted to ride with their father and were already astride their big, sturdy ponies, waiting patiently. Darien helped his wife into the carriage, watching her pull the toddler onto her lap as Mateo snuggled up beside her.

His Evie.

He couldn't imagine his life without her.

As Darien made his way to the front of the escort, where a groom held his big, dappled steed, he couldn't help but be grateful for this moment. His life could have been so different. Instead of being married to a woman he loved more than life itself, he could have been married to a liar and a cheat. He could have had children that might have possibly not been his own. There wasn't a day that went by that he wasn't grateful for what he had, because he knew how differently life could have been for him.

But he'd been saved by a man who had wronged him.

A man, he'd heard, who was living the life that might have been Darien's. A man who had evidently pissed away his portion of the dowry he'd been given, and Moy was so rundown that Emelia had to find work as a servant at nearby Brodie Castle because the family had no money. Four children, he'd been told, and rumor had it that only one belonged to Luke, which was exactly what Darien had feared those years ago.

As it turned out, his instincts had been correct.

But Eventide didn't want to know about her sister's life, and he wouldn't tell her. That was a little secret he would keep, unsympathetic to Luke and Emelia's situation. At least Luke had done the right thing at the end, but Emelia never learned right from wrong. The woman's moral compass wasn't merely broken—it had never worked correctly to begin with. Still, Darien had a small amount of compassion for her husband because, as he'd told the man once, Luke had literally saved his life—twice.

Darien would never forget that.

But he'd more than repaid that debt.

Repaid it in the form of a castle he hadn't kept and a dowry he'd shared. The truth was that Emelia's dowry had belonged to him, and he could have easily put up a fight when Fergus wanted to split it, but he hadn't. He'd been generous because he knew that Luke was going to need that generosity. A bad decision, an impulse he should have ignored, had cost Luke everything, and Darien had done what he could to at least give the man some compensation.

But he still thanked God, every day, that Luke's bad decision had given him a perfect life.

Perfect for him, anyway. As Darien mounted his steed and began to move the escort out of Wigton's bailey under the black bull standards of Lord Lowmoor, they passed by the entry and its great stone facing. At the very top was a big corbel in the shape of a rose, and at the top of the rose he'd had stonemasons carve out what had come to mean a great deal to both him and Eventide.

Airson a h-uile àm.

For all time.

For all time, he would love her and she would love him. For all time, their love story would be as legendary as the one his parents had. For all time, their names would be written for generations to see on the doorway of Wigton.

L and E

Airson a h-uile àm.

Because their love, and their legacy, were the stuff dreams were made of.

ଓଃ THE END ଃଠ

Darien and Evie's children
Aristeo
Cortez
Mateo
Adelina
Juliana
Sofia
Madelina
Irene
Cristofer

Kathryn Le Veque Novels

Medieval Romance:

De Wolfe Pack Series:
Warwolfe
The Wolfe
Nighthawk
ShadowWolfe
DarkWolfe
A Joyous de Wolfe Christmas
BlackWolfe
Serpent
A Wolfe Among Dragons
Scorpion
StormWolfe
Dark Destroyer
The Lion of the North
Walls of Babylon
The Best Is Yet To Be
BattleWolfe
Castle of Bones

De Wolfe Pack Generations:
WolfeHeart
WolfeStrike
WolfeSword
WolfeBlade
WolfeLord
WolfeShield
Nevermore
WolfeAx
WolfeBorn
WolfeBite

The Executioner Knights:
By the Unholy Hand
The Mountain Dark
Starless
A Time of End
Winter of Solace
Lord of the Sky
The Splendid Hour
The Whispering Night
Netherworld
Lord of the Shadows
Of Mortal Fury
'Twas the Executioner Knight Before Christmas
Crimson Shield
The Black Dragon

The de Russe Legacy:
The Falls of Erith
Lord of War: Black Angel
The Iron Knight
Beast
The Dark One: Dark Knight
The White Lord of Wellesbourne
Dark Moon
Dark Steel
A de Russe Christmas Miracle
Dark Warrior

The de Lohr Dynasty:
While Angels Slept
Rise of the Defender
Steelheart

Shadowmoor
Silversword
Spectre of the Sword
Unending Love
Archangel
A Blessed de Lohr Christmas
Lion of Twilight
Lion of War
Lion of Hearts
Lion of Steel

The Brothers de Lohr:
The Earl in Winter

Lords of East Anglia:
While Angels Slept
Godspeed
Age of Gods and Mortals

Great Lords of le Bec:
Great Protector

House of de Royans:
Lord of Winter
To the Lady Born
The Centurion

Lords of Eire:
Echoes of Ancient Dreams
Lord of Black Castle
The Darkland

Ancient Kings of Anglecynn:
The Whispering Night
Netherworld

Battle Lords of de Velt:
The Dark Lord
Devil's Dominion
Bay of Fear
The Dark Lord's First Christmas

The Dark Spawn
The Dark Conqueror
The Dark Angel

Reign of the House of de Winter:
Lespada
Swords and Shields

De Reyne Domination:
Guardian of Darkness
The Black Storm
A Cold Wynter's Knight
With Dreams
Master of the Dawn
One Wylde Knight

House of d'Vant:
Tender is the Knight (House of d'Vant)
The Red Fury (House of d'Vant)

The Dragonblade Series:
Fragments of Grace
Dragonblade
Island of Glass
The Savage Curtain
The Fallen One
The Phantom Bride

Great Marcher Lords of de Lara
Lord of the Shadows
Dragonblade

House of St. Hever
Fragments of Grace
Island of Glass
Queen of Lost Stars

Lords of Pembury:
The Savage Curtain

Lords of Thunder: The de Shera Brotherhood Trilogy
The Thunder Lord
The Thunder Warrior
The Thunder Knight

The Great Knights of de Moray:
Shield of Kronos
The Gorgon

The House of De Nerra:
The Promise
The Falls of Erith
Vestiges of Valor
Realm of Angels

Highland Legion:
Highland Born
Highland Destroyer

Highland Warriors of Munro:
The Red Lion
Deep Into Darkness

The House of de Garr:
Lord of Light
Realm of Angels

Saxon Lords of Hage:
The Crusader
Kingdom Come

High Warriors of Rohan:
High Warrior
High King

The House of Ashbourne:
Upon a Midnight Dream

The House of D'Aurilliac:
Valiant Chaos

The House of De Dere:
Of Love and Legend

St. John and de Gare Clans:
The Warrior Poet

The House of de Bretagne:
The Questing

The House of Summerlin:
The Legend

The Kingdom of Hendocia:
Kingdom by the Sea

The BlackChurch Guild: Shadow Knights:
The Leviathan
The Protector
The Swordsman

Guard of Six:
Absolution

Regency Historical Romance:
Sin Like Flynn: A Regency Historical Romance Duet
The Sin Commandments
Georgina and the Red Charger

Gothic Regency Romance:
Emma

Historical Fiction:
The Girl Made Of Stars

Contemporary Romance:

Kathlyn Trent/Marcus Burton Series:
Valley of the Shadow
The Eden Factor

Canyon of the Sphinx

The Eagle Brotherhood (under the pen name Kat Le Veque):
The Sunset Hour
The Killing Hour
The Secret Hour
The Unholy Hour
The Burning Hour
The Ancient Hour
The Devil's Hour

Sons of Poseidon:
The Immortal Sea

Pirates of Britannia Series (with Eliza Knight):
Savage of the Sea by Eliza Knight
Leader of Titans by Kathryn Le Veque
The Sea Devil by Eliza Knight
Sea Wolfe by Kathryn Le Veque

Note: All Kathryn's novels are designed to be read as stand-alones, although many have cross-over characters or cross-over family groups. Novels that are grouped together have related characters or family groups. You will notice that some series have the same books; that is because they are cross-overs. A hero in one book may be the secondary character in another.

There is NO reading order except by chronology, but even in that case, you can still read the books as stand-alones. No novel is connected to another by a cliff hanger, and every book has an HEA.

Series are clearly marked. All series contain the same characters or family groups except the American Heroes Series, which is an anthology with unrelated characters.

For more information, find it in **A Reader's Guide to the Medieval World of Le Veque**.

About Kathryn Le Veque

Bringing the Medieval to Romance

KATHRYN LE VEQUE is a critically acclaimed, multiple USA TODAY Bestselling author, an Indie Reader bestseller, a charter Amazon All-Star author, and a #1 bestselling, award-winning, multi-published author in Medieval Historical Romance with over 100 published novels.

Kathryn is a multiple award nominee and winner, including the winner of Uncaged Book Reviews Magazine 2017 and 2018 "Raven Award" for Favorite Medieval Romance. Kathryn is also a multiple RONE nominee (InD'Tale Magazine), holding a record for the number of nominations. In 2018, her novel WARWOLFE was the winner in the Romance category of the Book Excellence Award and in 2019, her novel A WOLFE AMONG DRAGONS won the prestigious RONE award for best pre-16th century romance.

Kathryn is considered one of the top Indie authors in the world with over 2M copies in circulation, and her novels have been translated into several languages. Kathryn recently signed with Sourcebooks Casablanca for a Medieval Fight Club series, first published in 2020.

In addition to her own published works, Kathryn is also the President/CEO of Dragonblade Publishing, a boutique publishing house specializing in Historical Romance. Dragonblade's success has seen it rise in the ranks to become Amazon's #1 e-book publisher of Historical Romance (K-Lytics report July 2020).

Kathryn loves to hear from her readers. Please find Kathryn on Facebook at Kathryn Le Veque, Author, or join her on Twitter @kathrynleveque. Sign up for Kathryn's blog at www.kathrynleveque.com for the latest news and sales.